When Michael Sattler was shoved into his cell and heard the gate locked behind him, it seemed that the very demons of hell gathered to torment him. The dungeon was damp and stank from the offal of other prisoners who had been there before.

As Michael sat on the stone bench, slumped over under the weight of his doom, the stark horror of death suddenly gripped him. From down the corridor and outside the prison came sounds of soldiers, jesting and laughing about the affairs of the day, mocking the foolish Anabaptists.

Something in Michael's spirit stirred in indignation. "What do they know of the meaning of life, of its value and purpose? Yet they can live and we must die."

His thoughts were of Margareta in the cell with the women on the opposite side of the prison. To think of her being drowned, he shuddered and broke into tears. Their life together had been wonderful and full, but oh so short! Never again would they be free to share life together, to enjoy the embrace of love, to sit in conversation, or to walk the forests trails together.

Life was closing here for both of them. His heart beat heavily. But they had thought of this; it was not unexpected. They had agreed to pay the price!

PILGRIM AFLAME

Myron S. Augsburger

Introduction by Simon Schrock

Illustrated by Allan Eitzen

HERALD PRESS
Scottdale, Pennsylvania
Kitchener, Ontario

PILGRIM AFLAME

Copyright © 1967, 1977 by Herald Press, Scottdale, Pa. 15683
 Published simultaneously in Canada by Herald Press,
 Kitchener, Ont. N2G 4M5
Library of Congress Catalog Card Number: 67-15993
International Standard Book Number: 0-8361-1840-5
Printed in the United States of America

10 9 8 7 6 5 4 3

Introduction

Who are these people called Mennonites, who hold to a radical biblicism, who believe the true church does not condone the use of the "sword" or weapons of warfare? Who are these people who refuse to bear arms, who refrain from taking the oath, who live in this world as members of another kingdom? They are a people committed to carry out Christ's doctrine in a "believers' church."

Pilgrim Aflame is a window into the past, skillfully recreating some of their early experiences. It's the true story of Michael Sattler, an intense man acclaimed even by his enemies as "a friend of God." In graphic terms, it tells of a young leader who was tortured and executed for his faith.

What makes a man willing to suffer pain and imprisonment himself and from his cell encourage his brothers and sisters in Christ to remain steadfast? Sattler's faith made him the victor at his own execution. He sang with joy as he was tortured and burned for the beliefs by which he had lived.

Why did Sattler choose death in the face of a promising future? Why did he give up dreams of a family for himself and his lovely young wife? Why was he willing to accept death at thirty-two in the bloom of life? *Pilgrim Aflame* tells of a cause so important that a young man and his wife voluntarily paid the ultimate price.

Did execution crush and end the movement? No! It fanned a fire that has not gone out. It's still aflame, spreading into many parts of the world today. Adherents of the movement in North America express their faith in various forms. Mennonites range from the simple lifestyle of the "plain people" to more modern Christians similar to mainline Protestants. A related group, the Amish, drive horse-drawn buggies in their local communities, attracting the attention of tourists.

Although the pressures of "this world" are pressing many Mennonites into its mold, others are expressing their faith through sacrificial service to their neighbors around the world. Young people share their lives with persons in the inner city through the church's Voluntary Service programs. Members of the group are active in many underdeveloped countries of the world giving aid, easing hunger, and teaching skills. Persons of all ages and of various groups work together at the scene of catastrophes, helping the victims restore their losses and property through a program called Mennonite Disaster Service.

Pilgrim Aflame will help you understand the origins and the deeply held beliefs of these people. It will give you a glimpse of who they are and why they choose to give their lives, if necessary, for their faith in Christ and their commitment to His kingdom. It's a moving story, a story that is still unfolding in the lives of Christians today.

Simon Schrock

Fairfax, Virginia
September 15, 1977

Preface

This is a historical novel of the life of the Anabaptist leader, Michael Sattler, who joined the Swiss Brethren movement in March 1525 and who gave his ultimate witness in martyrdom in May 1527 at Rottenburg. Much of the conversation of the book is created by the author, as well as the plot of the first several chapters. The name of Mrs. Sattler is unknown, and the name Margareta was chosen arbitrarily. However, the historical details of Sattler's life and role in the "third wing" of the Reformation are the results of research and, according to the source material available, are as accurate as possible.

For those interested in examining sources, the *Mennonite Encyclopedia* is the most accessible for articles on Michael Sattler, his life, his teachings, his trial and death. Related articles on other Swiss Brethren leaders contribute to the whole, as well as articles on "Zollikon," "Zurich," "Grüningen," "St. Gall," "Horb," "Strasbourg," "Capito," "Bucer," and "Rottenburg." A copy of Sattler's letter from prison is found in the *Martyrs Mirror* by van Braght, as well as an account of his trial. Translated sermons from Sattler are to be found in *The Mennonite*

Quarterly Review. The account of the Synod at Schleitheim with the Seven Articles can be found in the same source, and in J. C. Wenger's *Glimpses of Mennonite History and Doctrine.* Hymns of Sattler are to be found in the German songbook first called *Ausbund* in 1583. The account of Sattler's trial appears in Fosdick's *Great Voices of the Reformation,* and in Volume XXV of the *Library of Christian Classics.* In 1973 a new volume, *The Legacy of Michael Sattler,* translated by John H. Yoder, was published by Herald Press, Scottdale, Pennsylvania. For a depth study on Sattler as a theologian, see the doctoral dissertation on the same by the author of this work, at Union Theological Seminary, Richmond, Virginia, 1964.

It is the prayer of the author that the reader may be stimulated as much by the witness of Michael Sattler as the author has been in writing. A satisfying faith is the best security for the stress of days like ours, and faith in Christ is our security for the ages to come.

Myron S. Augsburger

Harrisonburg, Virginia
September 20, 1977

Chapter I

The muffled sound of his sandaled feet fell on the quiet evening as he traveled on his way. The atmosphere seemed almost sullen in the heavy stillness of the encroaching hour. At the edge of the forest he looked off toward the west. A faint wisp of cloud added color to the evening glow. All about, the earth was parched and thirsty. The dust felt warm and soft, oozing in powdery puffs through the webbing of his sandals.

He was a young man, this weary traveler, and a religious man—a Benedictine monk. He wore the white habit of the Cistercian order. Standing straight and thin, he with his fine facial features expressed good breeding and character. His eyes, as they surveyed the landscape, seemed to express a wistfulness which may have accounted for the furrows creasing his brow. The expression was not of fear or anxiety, but of question, as if reaching for an answer. For some time he stood gazing toward the sunset, his face turned slightly upward, as though hesitant to move on.

It was the month of August 1523 and South Germany was caught in the grip of two great forces struggling for men's souls. For twelve centuries Europe had lived under the influence of a state church. From the days of Constantine, Christian parents dutifully had their infants baptized into the church. Few questions were asked about the individual's own responsibility for his faith. As long as the populace supported the church, attended mass, and covered their sins with proper penance, their spiritual welfare was guaranteed by the vicar of Christ in Rome.

But now this was being challenged. A new quest for freedom had begun to stir. An Augustinian. monk at Wittenberg had provided the challenge. On October 31, 1517, Martin Luther had nailed ninety-five thesis on the Wittenberg cathedral door. Later he defied the pope by burning the papal bull. Hundreds of persons now aligned themselves with Luther's cause, ready for any leader who would restore their selfhood.

The lone monk was pondering this movement in his thoughts. Had Luther come on the scene a few years earlier, it was certain he would have been burned in the same ruthless manner as John Huss. The times were quite different! Men were emerging as individuals! This was the beginning of a new era. A modern world was coming into existence. Luther was challenging their faith about God, His Word, and the church: Copernicus, the sharp Polish astronomer, was beginning to change their views of the world and the universe.

Men were thinking for themselves. The printing press had been invented, and Luther's doctrine quickly covered all of Germany. The new privilege of reading printed pages prompted people to reach eagerly for his tracts. For the first time in history a little-known leader could develop a reading public. It was a new day politically, for German people were tired of being taxed by the church to build greater cathedrals in Rome. Even at this level they were asserting their new individualism. This independence represented an awakened force of great portent. The new form of granular gunpowder developed by Schwarz had placed a means of power in the hands of princes for more autonomy. Germany was in transition.

Every man is in some degree a child of his age, and these matters had an effect upon the traveler at the forest edge near Freiburg. But what troubled him most was the challenge of Luther's thought to his own faith, the faith of Rome. Returning from the city, he had just heard the fluent and intelligent Dean Peter Spengler of Schlatt present the doctrine of the Wittenberg reformer. The clarity of his argument had not been missed by the Benedictine monk. Michael Sattler was a man of keen intellect, a trained theologian. As prior of St. Peter's Monastery, he was a defender of the faith. But he was also honest enough to examine his own thought and open enough to give ear to the thinking of another.

Luther's attack upon the Roman church was sharp, and Spengler had been most pointed. "The church has no right to sell forgiveness, for forgiveness is a free gift of God's grace. The selling of indulgences is not only a farce; it is blasphemy! Sin is not covered so cheaply. Repentance is an attitude expressed through the whole of one's life. The Bible is to be obeyed above the pope!" Michael was amazed at the man's boldness. The man had conviction, all right; was it possible that he also had the truth?

Michael pondered Luther's theses on indulgences and forgiveness. He could see them now in his mind, as

11

though the page were before him. "When our Lord and Master Jesus Christ says 'Repent,' He means that the whole life of His followers on earth should be a constant and continual repentance. . . . This word cannot be understood of the sacrament of penance as it is administered by the priest . . . internal repentance is null, if it produces not externally every kind of mortification of the flesh. . . . The commissioners of indulgences are in error when they say that by the pope's indulgences man is delivered from all punishment and saved. . . . Every Christian who truly repents of his sins enjoys an entire remission both of the penalty and of the guilt, without any need for indulgences. . . . We should exhort Christians to diligence in following Christ, their Head, through crosses, death, and hell. . . ."

Michael was troubled. Others, secure in their position and satisfied with their lot, might shrug their shoulders and pass off the preaching as fanaticism. He took this whole matter seriously. For a movement to have continued for six years and multiplied its adherents suggested there was something to it. Men did not leave the Roman church with the security it offered unless they were convinced of a greater faith.

Troubling him was the sudden awareness that in listening to the message in Freiburg his own mind and conscience were assenting to what he heard. The message corresponded to what he had read in the Scriptures. That it was being expressed in a totally different context and system did not erase the fact that the message of the reformer was one from Scripture. His own monastic order had risen in an attempt to reform the church. Was it possible that Spengler was right? Had the Roman church

y

12

elevated Augustine's doctrine of the church until it obscured the doctrine of grace? Was Paul's message of grace the sole basis of salvation?

Michael Sattler turned abruptly and stepped into the protective covering of the forest. The dusk was heavier here, but he followed the path with the familiarity of one who had gone this way often. He quickened his pace, for night would soon overtake him. The forest was cooler, its freshness exhilarating. He drew in deeply the air-laden fragrance of the odor of firs. In his white mantle he appeared almost phantomlike as he glided along.

Suddenly as the forest opened, he stepped into a clearing. Before him on a knoll stood the bleak, barren walls of St. Peter's Monastery. For over ten years this had been his home. He was acquainted with every nook and corner. From his term as a novitiate until reaching his present position, he had worked and walked these grounds. He scanned the cleared fields before him, small fields that hemmed the monastery. He noted their cultivated appearance. The crops were greener here than on the farms around Freiburg, for more rain fell in the hills. For this reason, coupled with the quiet seclusion of the tumbled terrain, the monastery was situated here. Michael smiled to himself. "St. Benedict would be pleased with this site," he thought. "No better place could be found for study and prayer—and for work." He chuckled to himself as he started across the field where he had bent his own back many a day under the warm sun.

Passing through the gate into the monastery court, the cold facts of his responsibility struck him again. Somehow, in his trip to Freiburg he had been able to shake it off, to be just himself, Michael Sattler, and to think for himself as a free man. But here—he was prior, responsible to counsel and administer, to discuss and to discipline, and always according to the authority of Rome. Today he saw it in a new light. Where was the freedom of Christ he read about, the freedom to be a real person?

Walking down the passageway of the silent cloister, his figure cast a dark shadow against the cold stone wall. Through the opposite arches, he saw the movement of several novices who were completing their duties. As he entered the common hall, his nose twitched at the ever-present musty odor. This place was indeed otherworldly; they had closed the world out, denying its gaiety with its sin.

Brother Tanny, master of the novices, was sitting on a bench, reading the scroll on the table. Inquisitive, he was a dependable soul, ever punctual with his monotonous duties. Michael knew he was there in the hope of some word concerning the day's experience. Michael greeted him shortly but left without discussion.

He was not fully at ease. Suppose he shared some of his more honest thoughts. What would the brothers think if they knew the questions that were churning in his mind? He could not be strictly true to Rome in paying attention to the challenge of Luther. On the other hand, he could not be true to himself if he did not search for truth. Was not this a part of the order of St. Benedict? Was not the quest for truth and piety to be first for every monk?

But how well he knew that this privilege was perverted. Many monks were satisfied merely with the security of their monastic life. Some used their position to extract favors from the populace about them. Numerous chests were filled with accumulated values for the monastery. Michael had often been troubled by moral failure on the part of his fellows who instead of being examples of piety found ways of using their calls to gain sensual pleasure.

While the brothels in Freiburg were not as elaborate as the tales of such in Rome, it was evident that the courtesans were well provided for. Attending mass twice a day, they paid their fee for indulgence and often remunerated the monks in turn. Their clientele was not the riffraff, but men of good family, bishops, and notable artists. Their profession did not prevent them from being pious churchgoers and of cultivated intelligence. The hypocrisy of such behavior smote Michael with new force. What a farce to seek a pardon with no sense of deep guilt nor plans for changing the life! This could not be repentance.

For some time he sat on the cot in his room, looking out through the opening in the wall opposite him. The darkness closed in, and the moonlight cast eerie shadows about him. He cupped his face in his hands and sat in silent meditation. The message of Spengler passed through his mind again. . . .

"All of life is a repentance . . . it is by faith alone that man is justified . . . only by trust in Christ can we receive forgiveness . . . it is by God's grace that we are called . . . the true church is known only to Him . . . church is not an ecclesiastical structure, but happens wherever the Word is rightly preached and the sacraments rightly administered. . . ."

To each of these statements his own mind added thoughts.

Much later he reached for his woolen shirt. Carefully he stretched his body upon the narrow, hard pallet that served as his bed. The hours until midnight dragged by slowly. His wakefulness was not due alone to the irritating shirt or the narrow bunk which scarcely permitted a change of position. Sleep had fled, for his mind was active and troubled.

The scenes of his life moved across his mind, the carelessness of his earlier life, the quest for peace of soul which led him to the monastery, and the questions that now disturbed the degree of peace he had obtained. Finally in the exhaustion of unanswered questions he dropped into a fitful sleep. Perhaps tomorrow would hold the answer—or some tomorrow. At least, if it could be found, he wanted it, and he would be restless until the thirst of his soul was satisfied with the certainty of God.

Chapter II

The candle in the little room flickered and sputtered in the early morning breeze. The wind whistled as it blew through the opening in the monastery wall. Reaching out like cool hands, it clutched at the lone figure sitting by the small table. The prior drew his white mantle closer about his shoulders and buried himself even more deeply in thought. His intense face expressed deep inner hunger as he pored over the verses on the vellum before him. Early prayers had been conducted at two o'clock in the morning, and now, until matins at five o'clock, the monk could study the Scriptures.

Outside in the black forests of southern Germany, dawn broke. Inside, within the mind of Michael Sattler, a new dawn was breaking. The light of truth was dispersing the shadows in his mind. It would be some time until full daylight, but long night ends with the dawn.

Michael Sattler's life had been an inner longing for peace. From a pious home in Staufen he had gone to the University of Freiburg and then to St. Peter's Monastery. His becoming a Benedictine monk had not been just for the privilege of being known as a learned man.

He had known the turbulence of passion in his own experience and the emptiness of selfish living. Beyond the desire to be a scholar was a new longing to be a saint. Following the Christ in a life of crossbearing had now become his obsession. In sacrificial living he fully expected to gain God's grace.

As a novitiate he had not been careless, but rigorously disciplined himself in fortitude, anticipating the peace he so desperately sought. This would come, he believed, with acceptance, when he was a full brother in the monastery! Yet each achievement brought only greater frustration.

There were days when he thought of the yesteryear of the lad who knew every street and alley in little Staufen, whose laughter rang out in the morning air as his feet padded on the cobblestones. Days passed, and from the times of sitting in his father's shop listening to the prattle of men who came and went he moved to a job of his own. He loved the out-of-doors, the smell of freshly turned earth, of hay drying in the sun, or the sound of milk against the side of the pail. There was something down-to-earth about this kind of life, free from artificiality. And there had been friends, rollicking laughter, competition, and companionship—but also guilt. And this had brought a change in his life, a new quest for meaning and for peace.

The years followed his initiation and he fulfilled his duties as a monk with conscientious care. Gaining a name for himself as a respected and eloquent preacher, he was a frequent visitor at the University of Freiburg. He was known as a capable guest-lecturer and a scholarly exponent of his faith. His achievement of integrity and purity of life earned the respect of many.

His disciplined life and diligent scholarship did not go unnoticed. The request of the abbot won him the appointment as prior of St. Peter's. He was exacting and demanding, determined to become what he desired to be. Success brought satisfaction. Position offered respect and prestige. He was pleased with the security and power of his position. He was now a lord among men. But Michael Sattler, yet in his early thirties, was haunted by the knowledge that he needed a Lord in his own heart. Becoming a monk had not removed the guilt of his troubled conscience nor had it corrected his inner problem with evil.

On this morning in late summer of 1523, Michael was studying Paul's letter to the Romans. He was now in chapter eight. Since first hearing evangelistic preaching in the district of Breisgau and discovering the nature of Luther's movement, he was restless. The frequent trips to his home area of Staufen were not merely for sentimental reasons. He had listened to the messages of Otter and Brunfels and told himself they were challenges he must answer. The more recent hearing of Dean Spengler, with his warm spirit and logical treatise, had irked Michael. In fact, they had shaken his faith in the Roman system. He was now searching the Scriptures to see whether this new declaration of faith was valid.

He was beginning to recognize honestly the hunger in his soul for assurance of salvation. Well he knew the futility of the long prayer vigils, the hours from two o'clock each morning until nine spent in meditation, the emptiness of religious ritual, and the failure of afflictions placed upon his own body to bring peace. He was humbled by the awareness of hypocrisy in his own group.

The perversions he sought to escape were here as well. In some, it was immorality under the cloak of celibacy. In others, it was pride in scholarship and in the prestige of their position. Sin haunted the lives of monks irrespective of their religious forms.

As prior of the monastery Michael experienced the loneliness of such a position. Leadership meant fewer persons with whom he could share freely. He always anticipated discussions with men at Freiburg where he shared in theological dialogue. At the monastery he did have a close friend in Fritz Kennan. Fritz was a young monk with an active, inquiring mind. Of late their discussions turned almost exclusively to Luther and his revolutionary doctrines. The question of salvation, of the nature of repentance and faith, was uppermost in their minds.

Only day before yesterday Fritz had opened his heart to him. "Michael, I cannot escape the conviction that Luther is right. Salvation is by grace, and you well know Augustine said as much in the fifth century!"

He recalled his answer to Fritz, "True, but how does one receive grace—through some vague action of God in one's life or through the sacraments administered by the church?"

Even now Michael knew that he had not been as honest as Fritz, for his answer had defended rather than examined his faith.

This morning the words of the Apostle Paul spoke to him from the vellum spread on the little table: "As many as are led by the Spirit of God, they are the sons of God." This was not a statement promoting sacramental benefits. This appeared to correspond to the early part of the question he had answered in response to Fritz.

The words spoke pointedly to Michael's soul as he read on. This freedom and power were neither experienced in his life nor demonstrated in the lives of the brother monks. The words burning through the shadows kindled within the prior of St. Peter's a new interest, and a new hope. He mused, ". . . led by the Spirit . . . a new control . . . a dying to oneself. . . ." For long years he lived with the conviction that Christ asks His disciples to bear a cross. Now he was suddenly confronted with a cross that was to be laid not upon his shoulders, but upon his heart.

The call to matins echoed through the monastery. Michael stepped from his room and moved quickly across the court. The monks emerging from their various quarters walked in silence, shrouded with an air of piety. The novitiates behaved nervously, anxious to prove themselves worthy. The older men moved perfunctorily, following the prescribed routine.

Following prayers the monks went about their duties. Then came the midmorning call to worship. Michael entered the chapel, robed for the mass. Taking his place as prior, he led the choir in the chant and liturgy. The brothers had filed in quietly behind the crucifix. The great golden cross with its drooping figure of Christ caught the faint light rays from the narrow windows, stabbing the gloom with flecks of light. He prostrated himself before it, and the choir joined in the Gloria. He chanted the first prayer in Latin and listened to the chorus of "Amens." This morning he was particularly conscious of the "Our Father." He was suddenly struck by the empty way it was parroted by the brothers. His comments at the close of the period reflected the new awareness of divine grace that was beginning to permeate his own soul.

"The duties to which the order calls us are not merely the affairs of our temporal lives. We do well in the disciplines of our toils, but this is not the whole of life. Coupled with work must be the discipline of our souls. Ours is not only the mission of doing, but of being. Let us, my brothers, seek to know God's presence," he paused and looked over the group and then continued, "to share His cross, to live by His Spirit today. It is in His presence that we have grace to excel."

It was not strange to hear a prior speak of the inner discipline of man's spirit before God. But this was different. The prior was speaking of the work of God's Spirit as a communication of grace. This was even beyond the sacrament and the Word, a communication by divine presence—this was new! Some of the older monks raised their eyebrows in surprise. They had covetously watched Michael's rise to the office of prior. Others looked at the prior questioningly. A few, who used their office to exploit people, or who indulged in practices less than moral, only responded with a scowl. On the face of Fritz Kennan was a look of interest, as though he would hear more. It was quite evident that the community of common life did not have identical thoughts.

Michael was not surprised that his remarks caused some hostility. Several monks had taunted him with suggestive remarks regarding his trips to the university or to hear the evangelical preachers in the Breisgau area. Either they suspected him of being at least tolerant of the evangelicals, or used this as one occasion to speak back even while they obeyed his every order. He covered his actions by reference to the Benedictine emphasis on stability in the order and broad-mindedness in studying schools of theology.

In Michael's mind a change was taking place. During the last few days the "heresy" of Luther and the conversations with Brother Kennan had led him to crystallize his thinking. If Rome was wrong in its structure of faith, in its system of merit in a treasury of grace, in its demands of celibacy and its self-afflicting penance, then his entire system of life was crumbling!

This was happening to others. Numerous monks were deserting the monasteries under the impact of the Reformation which Luther had inaugurated. This raised further questions of his own place in the kingdom which until now the church of Rome personified. It was common news that many of the renegade monks were marrying. They were declaring openly that marriage is sacred and for the servants of God as well as the laity. He admitted to himself that marriage would be far better than the immorality of many priests committed to celibacy. This conviction, that marriage was an honorable life, caused him to give tolerant attention to this news. Word had come from Zurich that several pastors, Zwingli, Reublin, and Stumpf, were challenging Rome on this as well. Monks and nuns were finding in Zurich a city where they could solemnize their vows and establish homes of their own. Fritz Kennan had raised the subject and asked what the prior had to say about marriage. Michael was at first amazed that Fritz would suggest it. At least his friend was willing to confide in him.

At the close of prayers Father Bossinger, abbot of St. Peter's, called Michael to his room. Bossinger was a

24

large man with a congenial personality. There was a firmness about him that expressed the conviction that his was a position of importance and responsibility. His sharp eye never missed a thing, and his keen mind was both discerning and analytical. After looking at Michael in prolonged silence, he said, "Prior, what do you think of the preaching you've been hearing in the district of Breisgau?"

For a moment the question hung between them. Guardedly Michael answered, "A further challenge, Father Abbot, in the task of clarifying the truth."

The abbot leaned back in his chair, folded his hands across his rotund stomach, and smiled. "Well said, Michael, but aren't you more than a little interested in this movement? Is Luther a challenge to clarify the truth or a temptation to a new way of life?"

Michael's brow puckered as he replied, "Father Bossinger, would you call a longing for assurance, for peace in the depth of one's soul, for a full sense of reconciliation with God a temptation? You've known me these many years. My reputation is hardly that of one who jumps quickly to some new position."

The abbot waved his hand impatiently and said, "Michael, crossbearing is not easy. It is a path of sacrifice and service, a lonely life of labor and longing, but it has merit. Your treasury is growing. What more can a monk want than the assurance of obtained grace by serving God?" He looked at Michael with a hint of mockery on his face. "Don't take it too seriously, my son, this matter of adding merit and gaining assurance. A little indulgence occasionally is not so serious. Your treasury of grace can't be depleted overnight. You might even find there is a little pleasure to be had in this world along the way. Not so?"

Michael lifted his chin and looked the abbot in the face. "I should leave the monastery before I'd sacrifice its purpose, and leave the order before I would surrender its principles."

Bossinger replied testily, "Very well, very well, prior. Have it your way. I've feared you may be absorbing more of Luther than you are refuting. Remember, you may challenge the behavior of the Roman church, but don't challenge her beliefs!"

He nodded his head in dismissal and Michael turned to leave. The abbot's voice rasped a parting warning. "Don't forget, prior, that I called you to your office, and I can dismiss you. Don't throw your honors away! And the Zurich movement is just as treacherous as Luther's. Those who play with fire are likely to get burned! Don't overlook what we did to Savonarola, the Italian fanatic reformer!"

Michael strode swiftly down the hall and across the court. He was thinking of the abbot's last words. Such a sharp warning meant that Bossinger sensed his changing thought. The monks were about their work, the busy hum of activity turning the monastery into a little city. His stop by the bakery assured him that the day's tasks were well under way. He crossed the court to the dwelling of Brother Tanny, director of the novitiates. The general progress of the younger brothers was good. They had already left for the fields and their toils. Michael recalled his own year when, with his associates, he endured those months that tried their spirits to see if they be of God. Those were days of scrubbing floors, of emptying

26

chamber pots, of long hours in the fields—days of being taunted by the less Christian of the brothers. Walking back to his own quarters, he recalled also the experiences that filled the interval between his novitiate and his calling to the office of prior. He had made his mistakes. Bossinger had overlooked his blemishes in calling him to be his assistant.

As he stepped into the prior's chapel, designated primarily as his place of prayer, he was seized again with the emptiness and the inner longing that had been plaguing his life. Was there no greater victory than holding one's self in check? Was there no escape from one's carnality, no new life, no satisfying fellowship with God? Is prayer talking God into something, overcoming His reluctance, or is it communion with God? Is Christianity seeking to earn forgiveness, to somehow win one's peace? What is faith? Is it ideas that one can express as formulations of his beliefs, confidence in his church that its system of religion will achieve for him what his own prayers have not? Or is faith the reformer's concept of personal trust in Christ? Is this concept of personal trust the truth he had been praying God to reveal to him?

Michael crossed the room to his desk and knelt to pray. Making the sign of the cross, he began to repeat the "Our Father." As the "Amen" echoed in the empty room, he suddenly began to pray of himself. He laid bare his empty heart before God. He asked for some answer to the questions that kept haunting his mind; for the hunger that continued to gnaw at his soul. His whole being was reaching out after something. He was being led forth on a path not clear. Some unseen force urged him on and a distant glow seemed to beckon like a fire in a dark night.

He rose from his knees completely shaken. In honesty, he had admitted to God the inner longing of his heart. This was different from begging God to accept his works as merit toward salvation. Not once had he thought of how time in prayer added to his merit. Rather, he had been gripped by the sense of his emptiness and longing. He had reached out to God for mercy instead of merit.

He picked up the scroll and unrolled it across his desk. Paul's letter to the Romans, chapter eight. Many times he had sought to understand it in the past few days, and he knew it well. "There is therefore now no condemnation to them which are in Christ Jesus, who walk not after the flesh, but after the Spirit. . . . "

This must be it. This must be God's answer. Was there a difference between following Christ and being "in Christ"?

Chapter III

As Michael sat at his desk that evening, his whole future was in question. This new turmoil drained the meaning from his office as prior. To be a leader, a lord among men, what satisfaction was this if one wasn't convinced of the cause? He had entered the order to serve God, to find peace of heart and assurance of salvation. His vows of fidelity and service were made with this presupposition. Now that his faith in the power of this order was being shaken, the binding nature of his vows was also under question.

His thoughts were interrupted by a rap on his door. Opening it, he was greeted with the warm smile of Fritz Kennan.

"Welcome to my quarters, Fritz." The two clasped hands with the warmth of brothers.

"Prior, your prayers the last few mornings have given you a bit of popularity. I thought perhaps I should check up on their significance."

His eyes twinkled as he looked into Michael's blue ones, and he folded his arms, awaiting an answer.

Michael smiled. "Fritz, you're either sharp or suspicious. I'm not a follower of Luther yet. Be seated." He motioned to the lone stool in the room and seated himself on the narrow cot.

"But some say you are, and not only from envy of your position. And your emphasis on purity is like a bur under the blanket to Goeters and his clan. Have you made any progress with Bossinger in cleaning up that mess?"

Michael shook his head slowly.

"No, Bossinger is less troubled about immorality than about confessions. There can be perversions right under his nose and he pays little attention as long as those fellows are regular at matins."

"All Rome appears to be sold out to sensuality. Prior, is there no voice for holiness in the church?"

"Every brute seems to find a mate, whether he's in the orders or not. From what I hear, Bishop Ruffini keeps a mistress himself. Little chance we have of getting anything done to correct an abbot!"

"That's quite obvious." And Fritz snorted with contempt. "In fact, he likes an occasional visitor to his own quarters!"

"What's that you're saying?" Michael's voice was sharp, incredulous. "You're sure of that?"

"As sure as I'm sitting here, and what's more, it's no secret among the novitiates that he consorts with that young fellow Schlogel."

"Strange, isn't it, that men take vows of celibacy and don't mean chastity? We claim to follow the Christ and we have not even learned the lessons of Socrates, 'Know thyself.' "

"Michael, not all men have the inner discipline to

live as you, to be scholar and saint; and you cannot carry their guilt for them. It is enough for each of us to learn the way of Providence for our own lives."

Michael shook his head, "I'm not half the saint you hold me to be."

Fritz's face had grown serious. "Michael, as a friend and brother, what would you say if I left the order?"

Michael drew a deep breath. For some moments he sat in contemplative silence before he spoke. His words came slowly. "Brother Kennan, as prior I must warn you against such a step. You risk the anathema of the church and your whole future!"

Fritz smiled and waved his hand in negation. "What future? I tell you, this movement will change the church. Don't make it hard for me, prior."

Michael started to speak, then paused again as if to weigh his thoughts. "As a friend, a brother who faces the questions of truth with you, I cannot tell you what to do. Tell me, Fritz, what do you have in mind?"

With a resoluteness and assurance that surprised Michael, Fritz responded, "I would like to go to Wittenberg to hear Luther, and, I think, to join his movement. I'm convinced he has something to offer—more than I've found here. I shouldn't say this to you, Prior Sattler, but to me you are Michael, a friend. Please don't interfere with my going."

Michael was moved by his conviction and his request. He rose and extended his hand.

"Farewell, my friend. I won't stand in your way. I hope you find the answer. I too face similar questions. In the struggles of the past weeks I'm at least able to say I want God's answers."

"Do you mean you may leave, too? Would you give up the office of prior?"

"I can only say I want peace and divine approval more than anything else."

They clasped hands in farewell, and Michael watched Fritz slip out the door, listening to the scuff of his sandaled feet receding down the hall.

Another friend had crossed his path and gone on. What was the meaning of his conversations with Brother Kennan? Had he led Fritz to this point by sharing his own questions? Was he unwilling to follow the direction to which his own quest pointed while this man walked boldly on? Was this an issue that could long go unanswered in his own mind? He walked back and forth before his cot, his hands clasped behind his back, his brow knit in thought. Resolutely he squared his shoulders—to be a good prior this question must be answered, and if in answering it the truth led him from the order, this was the price he would have to pay.

Tomorrow, Thursday, he would leave for Staufen. Father Bossinger's presence meant that several days' absence from the monastery would be possible. The trip would be good for him, a change, and the service he might render to some troubled soul along the way could justify the trip. Hearing again the preaching of the evangelicals might either serve to expose their folly or help to answer his questions.

Then, too, he could stop at the Beguinage. His heart quickened with the thought. Perhaps this was a stronger motivation than he was ready to admit to himself. His frequent stops at the edge of Staufen offered the delightful possibility of sharing a few moments with the lovely Margareta. Never in his life had he found one with whom he could so freely open his heart. Her exquisite beauty and the charm of her personality entered his mind with increasing and disturbing regularity.

Michael refused to admit the possibility that he was in love with her. His commitment as a monk, and his position as prior, made love and marriage impossible. Having a clandestine affair with Margareta was utterly unthinkable. Until the last few days he had told himself that he was satisfied to pursue his "calling." Surrender of the desire for marriage and a home was the cross he was called to bear.

Michael was hesitant to admit that their friendship offered any real temptation to the prior of St. Peter's. For him, leaving the monastery would not be merely the defection of another monk, but of a leader, a lord among men. What he could not deny was that the thought of this possibility was affecting his feelings toward Margareta. Even the thought of her caused a quickening of his heart. But as a scholar and a committed man, he could regard this as only one part of the great issue of truth. The real crux of the matter was between the doctrine of the reformers and the doctrine of the Roman church. The dividing line was the issue of authority—the Bible or the pope.

Perhaps Margareta's keen mind and hungry heart had led her beyond him in the quest for peace. Her nearness to this South German Breisgau area of evangelical activity subjected her constantly to its influence. It had become a topic of conversation whenever they met.

During the past months there had come about a mutual agreement between them. Both were searching for full peace of heart and a satisfying assurance of salvation. Michael sensed that she was almost ready to leave the Beguinage and commit herself to the cause of the Reformation. This would not be such a difficult step for her. A Beguine had no binding vows as did a nun. Should her dedication to serve God call her to such a change, she would doubtless make it.

The dilemma was that both movements claimed to be serving God. The difference was not as clear to Michael as his earlier decision to enter the monastery. That decision had meant a break with the world to serve the church. The question of authority made this decision one of principle, a break within the church. The implications meant this break would be more momentous than the journey to the monastery.

Chapter IV

Early morning found Michael on his way to Staufen. The shadows in the forest began to disappear as the sun's rays shone obliquely through the dense foliage. The stillness was broken only by his footsteps on the path. Moving through the dark wood, he was deep in thought. He paused where the density gave way to the fields which spread like an apron around Freiburg.

Here a fallen log occasionally served as a resting place on his trips to the university and as an open-air chapel for meditation and prayer. Looking back over the trail, the beauty of the Black Forest filled him with a sense of awe. The deep hush was relieved by an occasional bird call, the constant hum of insects, and the rustlings of small, furtive rodents. The tall firs thrust themselves skyward like great cathedral spires.

Sitting there in the morning stillness, Michael pondered the inner struggle which had raged in his soul for weeks. The tension seemed to be increased by the experiences of the past several days. Most men lived for position and power, and as prior of St. Peter's he had both. There was the satisfaction of a well-defined course in life, as clearly known to him as the trail over which he had just come. As a Benedictine monk, his calling was clear; it was a life of scholarship and service. The Benedictine rules supplied the standards for a well-disciplined life, and the very patterns were an attempt to copy the example of Christ.

Only recently had he admitted that the standards of his order did not supply the strength to obey them. Observing rules did not make one a saint. The evangelical preaching which he had gone to investigate challenged all his presuppositions. Justification by faith had now taken on a very personal meaning. The matter was not just a conflict between Luther and the pope; it was an issue of faith. Knowledge of the law served to increase his sin rather than to procure merit. He was constantly humiliated by his own inner problems. Many who had taken up the doctrine of Luther were testifying to an assurance of peace which, instead of being frightening, was forceful. Michael's analysis recognized that such men risked all for a satisfying faith.

His recent conversation with Brother Kennan came back to him now. Discussing Luther's movement, Michael had said, "Actually, it is not that these evangelical preachers have a new theology that is revolutionary; it's just the prominence they give to aspects of the faith that are hidden in the forms of our religious system."

Fritz had responded. "Perhaps so, but it seems to me that the forms have perverted the message."

As Michael pondered this now, he recognized what the reformers were doing. They were putting Christ above the church, rather than saying He is personified in it. They were elevating the Bible above tradition, rather

than equal with it. They held faith above works as a power to produce the latter. The real issue focused on the authority in a man's life. Was it the direct authority of a heavenly Lord through His Word, or was it the authority of earthly lords? Was unqualified obedience to the abbot the way by which one should prove that he bears a cross? This absolute obedience—was it meritorious or simply a discipline parallel to that of any soldier? The obedience that he asked and received as prior—was it developing the life of Christ in the monks? Was it perhaps a counterfeit obedience, an external surrender to the order while the heart stood afar off?

Michael's own inner hunger pointed to something more meaningful than a servile obedience; there must be an obedience of love. But how can one share love with a God with whom he is trying to win favor? True love is to enjoy that favor. Paul's statement troubled him: "For to me to live is Christ." This didn't sound like straining toward something one hoped to gain in a distant tomorrow. Paul was speaking of a present reality.

His mind moved to the great heart-cry of Augustine, "For Thy glory we were and are created, and our hearts are restless until they find their rest in Thee." Had not Augustine found that rest? Was he not asserting that there is a rest in God and we are restless until we enter it? Perhaps this is what Luther meant; instead of our winning God, we are won by God. Is faith simply coming to God in Christ, trusting Him to accept one?

Michael lifted his eyes and gazed back along the trail for a long time; then he traced the tall fir before him reaching up toward the heavens. From his soul there came the prayer he recalled from Anselm, "Let me seek

Thee in longing and long for Thee in seeking; let me find Thee in loving and love Thee in finding.''

Rising from the log, he turned his back on the forest trail and started across the open fields surrounding Freiburg. The towers of the great cathedral loomed up before him like sentinels in the early morning. Somehow today they failed to inspire him with a sense of assurance, but seemed only to point mutely toward heaven.

As Michael neared the city, the road became increasingly busy. There were students and peasants, tradesmen and visitors, going to and from Freiburg. He noted their faces with interest—sensing some of their lot in life from what he read there. At the fork where the road came in from the west an elderly man on a mule approached the juncture. Something about his regal bearing caused Michael to look him over with more than casual attention. A baggage mule and driver followed closely behind. Seeing his biretta-like cap, Michael surmised that he was a scholar. His face was somewhat gaunt, rather square with a long straight nose. His bearing was dignified, almost regal.

Suddenly Michael's heart skipped a beat—could it be, hardly, but it must be—Erasmus of Rotterdam! The master spirit of the age! In the privacy of his own quarter he had laughed over Erasmus' *Colloquies* and *The Defense of Folly*, in spite of the dragon's teeth they concealed. He increased his pace that he might be at the junction at the proper moment.

"My lord, what great fortune that I meet you here! May I accompany you into the city?"

"Ah, my good Benedictine, you are without doubt a scholar yourself. Tell me, sir, whom do I address?"

"I'm Michael Sattler, prior of St. Peter's, en route

39

to Freiburg to visit the university library."

"Then we shall journey together and converse of the great things of our times," and with a chuckle he mounted the mule with the help of his stick and they were off.

As they made their way along, Erasmus turned the conversation to the issues of the Reformation, falling readily into the Latin, the international language of scholars.

Observing that Luther had much in his favor, Erasmus added, "But his concerns for the church could be expedited from within without playing the devil."

Michael exclaimed, "*Dicebas, Erasme, eruditissime!*" (What you say, Erasmus, is most outstanding.)

And for half an hour he explained to Michael his own mission to reform the church from within. Upon reaching the university, he bade Michael farewell and left him to his meditations in the library.

But the impact of the conversation did not soon leave Michael. He was now even more troubled. He had given some credence to Luther's concerns, and now to couple this with the fine arguments of which Erasmus was capable, he was inescapably confronted with perversion in the church. How long could he ignore it? And if he admitted its faults, what course was he to take?"

He recalled the parting words of Erasmus: "The ferment of our day is necessary, my friend, and may result in man's finding himself again. Even the church, great as it is, must not rob man of his right to freedom. Augustine saw this as our privilege in divine grace."

"Freedom," Michael thought, "can it be truly known, and how?" He recalled the words of Augustine, "I will this power of mine that I may approach unto Thee."

"This," he thought, "is my quest."

Chapter V

The little village of Staufen was bustling with midmorning activity. Dawn had seen the farmers travel with their oxcarts from the village to the small plots of land they worked in the surrounding area. Now loaded carts pulled by teams of oxen were moving toward town with the first loads of produce from the day's harvest. There was an atmosphere of cheer in the midst of work, as young men and maidens called to each other, more interested in conversation than in production. Now and again a muscular peasant woman would pause, straighten her back, and call, "Hans, Wilhelm, to work! No work, no dinner." The boys, though yet young lads, would smile and call back a ready response.

Suddenly a familiar feminine voice called, "Madam Getz, at work as ever, cheery as ever, I trust."

The old peasant woman looked up into the smiling face of a young woman dressed in the gray habit of the Beguinage.

"Ah, Sister Margareta," she smiled, "you lighten the day's burden just with your pleasant voice." Her own tone of voice was friendly and respectful, as her eyes shone with pleasure.

The boys stopped working, leaned on their shovels, and regarded the young woman standing at the edge of the plot with more than casual interest.

She was not especially tall, but her stately bearing gave the impression of height. The gray habit she wore did not completely disguise her form. The hood was pushed back, revealing her face, framed by her blond hair, slightly flushed from her morning walk. Her hazel eyes twinkled under lightly arched brows. Her lips curved softly and her smile, winsome and radiant, took in all three.

"That's part of my calling, Mother Getz, to lighten the burden of others, to remind them all that life is more than a contest in grasping!"

"She means we shouldn't work so hard, Mother," Hans cut in slyly.

"Quiet, young man, you know well what she means; no person yet helped bear the burden of others who has not learned to bear his own."

Turning back to Margareta she added, "Don't pay a' mind to him, he has more life than wisdom at this point. But if it weren't for Hans and Wilhelm here, I myself would no doubt be a burden to others."

"For sure, Mother," smiled Margareta, "you've two of the finest young men in Staufen," at which remark their faces glowed. "I was just stopping to ask whether the boys might come to the Beguinage this evening to help me carry some things to Widow Jantz. I'm on my way there now to help her a bit about the house; she's little better, you know."

Mrs. Getz shook her head, and wiped the sweat from

42

her face with the large kerchief about her neck. "It is too bad that she must suffer so, and I don't know what she would do if it weren't for you."

Margareta shook her head as though her role was unimportant. "Only part of my duty to the church, you know; and besides, I like to get out with the people."

The old peasant smiled broadly, "Seems to me I've seen you among the people at the evangelical preaching in Staufen. Is this a part of your duty to the church?"

Margareta's face grew sober and her voice more serious. "Mother Getz, it is my duty to know the truth. This preaching has made quite a stir in the Beguinage. The talk is all of Luther and Wittenberg, and the new ideas on repentance and faith."

Mrs. Getz leaned forward, as though sharing a secret. "I'm not a learned woman, but there is something in this new preaching that appeals to me. The behavior of those monks doesn't take much to cause one to look for something better."

"But they are not all that way, Mother Getz." Margareta was speaking defensively now.

"No doubt, no doubt of that, sister. It is your life, though, and that of others like you, which has kept many of us from losing faith in the church completely."

"You shouldn't talk so, Mother. We only serve to enlarge that faith."

The old peasant nodded. "Enlarge it, or create it; it makes little difference to me. But what if you lose faith in that church yourself? That evangelical preaching isn't going to help you any in that regard."

There was silence for a few moments; then Margareta looked up with a gesture of farewell. "I must go now.

Peace be with you."

"And with you," smiled the old peasant, "and you'll see these stout lads this evening."

As Margareta started down the bare road, its surface packed hard from the traffic of many carts, her three friends watched her fondly. Little could they know the thoughts surging deep within her.

Nearly thirty years before she had been born in this region, not many miles from Staufen in the Black Forest. She loved this country, the rolling land, the fertile fields, and the smell of the firs in the forest. As a young girl she had walked many a day in the forest, enjoying the privacy and solace it afforded. Those were carefree, happy years with the joys of home and friends—until the day of tragedy that changed her course in life.

It was her father first, who came down with the plague. She remembered him as a strong, stalwart man, always confident and assured. Gentle and kind to her, he could be fearless when opposed by strong men. But the days of his suffering had reduced him to a shrunken shadow of his former self. She watched sorrowfully as he tried feebly to form the sign of the cross, and heard his faltering voice trail into silence as he repeated the prayers he knew by rote.

And then—her mother. She bent over her father like an angel, answering his every wish, giving him comfort and encouragement, trying to smile bravely through it all. But Margareta saw her tears, and heard her desperate sobbing when she found her one day alone in the woodhouse. She had crept near and placed her hand in her mother's, wordlessly. But one morning Margareta knew with dreadful certainty—Mother had the plague too.

44

The days that followed were a blurred nightmare. She cared for them both, although they begged her to leave lest she be stricken. Death came for both in the same night—a night of storm, with wild wind and weeping skies. Mr. Himes made the coffins of boards from the woodhouse. He dug two graves on the hill beyond the house, facing the sunrise. A very small circle of friends attended the funeral. Many others would have attended, but were either too ill themselves or did not choose to risk the danger of contracting the disease.

For several months Margareta lived with the Himes family, who loved her as their own. But the shadow of her grief haunted her. It gave birth to a deep longing to find the real meaning in life. Friends tried to help by inviting her to parties and dances, but these times of enforced gaiety and frivolity failed to restore the happiness she had known. They only deepened her sense of futility.

It was the Beguinage at Staufen that seemed to beckon. Here one could belong, could serve society without the hypocrisy of forced gaiety. After consulting her relatives in Staufen, she made an appointment with the superior of the Beguinage. The welcome was genuine and warm. They listened to her story and her desire to become one of them. She soon enjoyed the companionship as well as the confidence of the sisters.

In this role Margareta discovered that the answer to the enigma of grief is not forgetting but interpreting. She could draw from memories of her parents and their suffering lessons which now aided her in ministering to others. Her discovery of purpose led to a new openness and vivaciousness. Everyone loved her. Until now she had taken for granted the role of the church in her life. It had been the center of faith for her parents. A balm for her own troubled spirit. Now it was the channel through which she found a new sense of purpose in the service of others.

But the past months brought a new challenge. She had listened many times to the preaching of the evangelicals as they were called—followers of Luther, who were spreading new doctrine. Their assertions that repentance was an attitude of the heart, that penance alone could not free one from guilt, and that faith was the only true avenue of saving relation with God, all served to challenge her simple presuppositions. She came to believe that her association with the church was far too impersonal, that, in fact, her faith was quite naïve or, at the best, second-hand.

And then, there was Michael Sattler, the prior of St. Peter's Monastery. He too was in search for spiritual reality beyond what he knew as a monk. He had seen her at one of the meetings in Staufen. This led him to open the question with her on a stop at the Beguinage. Each succeeding time he called they found opportunity to converse. Thinking of him now she felt a warm glow within. She could not deny that this handsome monk stirred her more deeply than the interest in conversational exchange. This was new—and quite disconcerting. Deeply interested in the service of the church, she had counted love to be outside her calling in life. Marriage was for others—not for her.

At this, she smiled. How ridiculous—to think of being in love with the prior of St. Peter's. She felt her cheeks flame—such would never be, though it was known to happen. She would never give herself to any man except within the bonds of love and matrimony. She had heard of monks who had their mistresses, but something about Michael's whole spirit told her this was different. Between them there was an openness and candor which enabled them to be friends and associates in the work of the church.

She was in the city now, tripping lightly over the cobblestones as she hurried along. Admiring glances were turned her way, and friends to whom she nodded spoke with evident respect. She stopped at the bakery to order some fresh bread sent to a family where the mother was ill. Conversation led to the issues of the Reformation, and to her own amazement she found herself defending the preaching of the evangelicals.

"You haven't joined this movement, have you?" the baker asked with a mischievous grin.

"When I do, you'll hear about it," she retorted. "I only try to respect truth for its own sake, no matter from whom it comes."

The baker smiled at this and nodded as though understanding, as Margareta left the shop. But he watched with puckered brow the small figure walking purposefully along the sun-flecked street.

Chapter VI

A few days later Michael and Margareta sat on a bench in the shaded court. The spot was surrounded by the loosely arranged buildings which formed the Beguinage. It was a warm day in early autumn. Margareta had just returned from another mission to the poor widow and her children on the near edge of the city. Her eyes sparkled when she saw Michael. She had something to share that would be a surprise for him.

She sensed the turmoil in his soul. She too had experienced this sense of hunger for peace. At the Beguinage she had given herself to prayer and good works in an effort to gain assurance of merit before God. This gave her a degree of satisfaction, for in this exercise she drew near to God.

But she was deeply impressed with the new note in the preaching of the reformers. The fresh insights came like water to a thirsty soul. The conviction that God is a person of love who comes to man in forgiveness was having a transforming effect.

"If forgiveness is not earned," she thought, "but is the gift of God, then works can have no saving merit."

A new faith was being born in her heart. "If salvation is by grace, then justification by faith is the only conclusion."

Only a few evenings earlier this truth had settled decisively upon her soul. After a long inner battle she had opened her heart in a new way to God. The peace and assurance that filled her life was evidence enough of the power of faith. She thrilled with a new realization of peace with God. Her life had hardly changed externally, except for the joy and sense of purpose that filled her now. But today her prayers, and even her service to the poor widow, were enriched by this inner joy. She had a new freedom, freedom from the perpetual ambition of attaining grace. As Luther expressed it, so she was finding already: "Just as it is natural for a tree to bear fruit, so it is natural for faith to have works." The study of Scripture was now a real pleasure. She shared her testimony with others in the Beguinage to find a few who joined her in this experience of faith.

As she looked into Michael's eyes, the radiance of her face struck him in a new way. It was not only her beauty, the twinkling eyes and long lashes, her slightly parted lips, which quickened his pulse. This indefinable radiance and calm assurance evidenced an inner glow.

"Michael," she began, "I've found the answer! It is not an 'it' or a new idea, but a person—the living Christ! Before this, I had been trying to come to God when He had already come to me. All my religion has been the effort of the flesh, as though I might be able to rise above my own sins and win His approval. Michael —this is the answer. 'As many as received him, to them gave he power to become the sons of God. . . .' This is true! I've received Him, and the emptiness of my life is gone. Instead of all the forms that hid Him, I've come to know the peace of forgiveness and the joy of fellowship."

She spoke with eloquent intensity. The words themselves seemed to glow with the fire of certainty. And then she blushed with embarrassment at her own boldness. There was silence as Margareta bowed her head, awaiting Michael's next words. What would be his response to her confession of faith?

Michael sat quietly, looking at her for a long moment. Then he asked, "If this is true, Margareta, where do you go from here? Where does this path lead?"

Obviously, the question was not new. Glancing up quickly as though relieved by his question, she spoke confidently. "In a few weeks I'm leaving for Schaffhausen. Others here have accepted this truth also. We feel there will be more freedom for conversation and spiritual growth outside, rather than here under the authority of Rome. We have actually forsaken it, you see, for the authority of the Scripture." She feared inwardly that this assertion might have wounded the prior of St. Peter's.

Margareta had indeed found her answer. As a Beguine she had long been free for any mystical experience of fellowship with Christ. St. Bernard left a heritage of mysticism that led many a soul to find satisfaction of heart by a mystical indentification with Christ. But Margareta's confession was not only of a mystical experience. It was a confession of an entirely different religion, a religion of reconciliation, of fellowship, of assurance.

Doubtless she was right. The question did focus on

the issue of authority. Which should be followed—the system of the Roman church or this dangerous faith in the authority of the Scripture?

"Margareta," he said quietly, "many a man has asked, 'What is truth?' but few live with the assurance that they have found it. If you are sure that the path you are following is the way of God, you cannot turn back. God grant you the boldness to follow your convictions, and may He satisfy your life with His love."

Rising to leave, he looked down at Margareta sitting on the bench. This small person, so satisfied, so resolute, and so settled in her convictions, challenged his own indecision. She looked at him as though disappointed that he could say what he did—but no more. Suddenly the hunger of his heart, the loss of faith in the religious system which he represented, and the questions which he had been analyzing demanded his answer. He too must make a decision—to have earthly security or to be a stranger, to be a prior or a pilgrim, to follow the system of Rome or know the satisfaction of responsible decision. He looked toward the Black Forest that sheltered St. Peter's far beyond, then across the fields to the city. In the one was a life of security and prestige; in the other a life of service and perhaps peace.

Margareta rose and waited quietly for his farewell.

"There is little value in my talking of truth if I'm unwilling to follow it when I'm convinced. Go to Schaffhausen, Margareta. I'll meet you there. I too must follow my convictions if I'm to find peace."

His voice was husky with deep feeling. There were tears in his eyes as he turned to leave, hesitated, then returned to take her hand for a moment. "Father Bos-

51

Chapter VII

It was October 1523 and Michael Sattler sat in his barren room looking out across the landscape. The trees of the Black Forest were diffused with the color of changing leaves. Against the deep green of the firs the beauty was breathtaking. The hush of autumn on the land suggested that another chapter was about to close. But today this beauty did not awaken the response it normally stirred in Michael's soul. Instead, his mind was filled with the gravity of his own decisions. For him, another chapter was closing. He had studied both Erasmus and Luther—the one common conviction was man's personal responsibility to seek the will of God for one's self.

Within the monastery the activity was routine. The little city of monks, rose early for prayers, gave themselves to the discipline of work, spent their designated hours in study, performed their evening rituals, and stretched themselves fully clothed upon their hard cots to sleep. Tomorrow would be a repetition of today. Tomorrow, tomorrow, and tomorrow, an unbroken repetition of prayers, work, study, and more prayers. While some broke the monotony by occasional indulgences, Michael maintained his disciplined integrity. His motivation was deeper than a desire for a few fleshly satisfactions; he longed for the inner satisfaction and assurance of peace with God.

Since his momentous decision and his conversation with Margareta, the weeks had been filled with study and planning. His several trips to Staufen had enabled him to spend short times with her. They spoke more freely of the meaning of their decision, and planned their meeting in Schaffhausen. He was sure of his love for her, and reasonably sure that she shared this love, although to this point he had only dared hint at it.

At their last meeting, a week before she planned to leave the Beguinage, he told her that whatever the new life held beyond the assurance of walking in truth, it held room for her. The quick intake of her breath gave him some assurance of her love. Yet, as prior of St. Peter's Monastery he could not speak to her of marriage. That must wait until later. He must be true to his office until he left it. Decisions which involved his life beyond must be made subsequent to the major decision of the authority of the Scripture over the authority of Rome.

His services as prior became routine. The devotion to life in the cloister gave way to skepticism. The defection of Brother Kennan had caused some stir. It was evident that Bossinger held him largely responsible. In the past months life settled back to normal. Many of the order were simply not concerned about genuine spirituality or the major issues of life. Immorality, drunkenness, or theft —all were covered by the issuing of indulgences, and the call to spiritual discipline went unheeded. Somehow the old glow had faded for him, and during those weeks his prayers to Mary had a hypocritical ring. It became increasingly difficult for him to lead the brothers in worship. He was sure the meaning of the incarnation was not understood. Jesus' words, "God so loved the world, that he gave his only begotten Son," lost their meaning if one sought Mary's intercession to get to God rather than Christ's.

For the next weeks, well into the month of November, he studied the Book of Hebrews, finding new light on the work of Christ. A letter from Fritz Kennan told of his arrival in Wittenberg and his satisfaction. He was struck by the evident assurance and peace in his words. His enthusiasm over Luther's thought added to Michael's own insights and interpretation.

Michael was now convinced that the mass perverted the meaning of the death of Christ and that indulgences made a travesty of it. He saw the system of penance as substitute for real contrition, for there was little godly sorrow that rejected sin.

The necessity of his decision was clear. He had now made definite plans for leaving the monastery. He would travel to Schaffhausen, an area of Reformation activity on the border of Switzerland. In fact, two more days and he meant to leave! Abbot Bossinger was returning from Freiburg on Wednesday. His departure the same morning would leave the monastery without a prior for only a brief period.

Wednesday morning following prayers Michael Sattler slipped out of the monastery and began his journey into another life. The rest of the day he walked with scarcely a pause, and by evening he was well on his way to the border of Schaffhausen. He was a free man in one sense, but in another he was guilty of defection, of leaving the order.

His departure from the monastery that morning was not unusual and caused no undue attention. What was unusual was the letter he left on his desk addressed to the abbot. The letter made the break clear and definite. He told Father Bossinger of the deep hunger in his life for assurance, of his studies in the letter to the Romans, and his conviction that the Scripture alone must now be his authority. He informed the abbot that he was not going with Luther, but would seek his answers in the Scripture. The letter was concluded with a few of Bossinger's own words—if this was playing with fire, he was willing to be burned. But that first day's journey was not without much thought—he could still go back, destroy his letter, and forget it. But evening found him asleep by a farmer's haystack, satisfied in mind that he had chosen correctly.

Today he felt no less convinced, and the miles slipped by without any great weariness. He felt the inner surge of a new freedom. Not the freedom from St. Peter's, but the freedom of a man who follows conviction, who is committed to a cause greater than himself.

When evening fell Friday, he secured a room at an inn near the border of Schaffhausen, and dropped off to sleep at once. It was the sleep of a man weary in body but satisfied in mind.

Michael entered the village Saturday afternoon. His immediate task was to find lodging. He was eager to meet Margareta, but did not know where she was staying. His best chance for an early meeting was to watch for her the next morning in the special services at the cathedral. He learned that Dr. Hofmeister was bringing a series of messages from the Book of Acts. Walking into the heart of the village, he noted that his white coat called little attention to himself as a Benedictine monk.

He walked through the village to observe the inns available. As he came out on the southern side, he could hear the water of the Rhine which bordered the Schaffhausen district. From the mountains to the east the waters flowed into Lake Constance, to spill down the Rhine and cascade over the rocks at the very edge of Schaffhausen. Since it was early evening, he walked on to see the falls, to watch the water spill over, splashing seventy feet below, rushing on its way. The evening sun reflected in shimmering waves off the blue-green columns that continually fell from the brink. The sunlight touched a faint rainbow on the mist at the bottom. Michael sat enthralled and watched. Like time, he mused, rushing on, but never back—and like decisions, once made the course is set!

He returned to a small inn on the east side of the street near the heart of town. Here Herr and Frau Meyers offered rooms by the day or week, and he made arrangements for the night. Herr Meyers, a gray-haired gentleman beyond middle age, had an outspoken but pleasant manner. His wife was a matronly lady, jolly and neat, who immediately made Michael feel at home. He took his dinner with them and after the meal, while Frau Meyers cleared the dishes, he sat to visit with Herr Meyers. The main topic was news of Zurich.

"Zwingli's reformation has taken hold in Zurich," Herr

Meyers said. "Already there is evidence of a break with Rome. The city of Zurich is backing Zwingli all the way. He is in cooperation with the council of two hundred, and is forming a new state church.

"What do you think of Zwingli's move?" Herr Meyers asked, but he did not wait for an answer.

"Now we hear reports," he continued, "that some of Zwingli's assistants feel the council is moving too slowly. There's a Conrad Grebel—he's the son of Jacob Grebel of the aristocracy. And Felix Manz, who is the son of a Zurich priest." He looked at Michael with the corners of his mouth drawn down. "Some of these priests have families, you know." With Michael's silence he continued, "Both of these fellows are scholars in their own right. Oh, yes, and other priests, too. Simon Stumpf and Wilhelm Reublin. These men want a complete break with the religious forms of Rome. They want to abolish the mass, remove all of the images, and serve the Lord's Supper to the entire congregation! Why, Reublin even carried the Scriptures rather than a cross in a parish parade—he raised quite a ruckus." Herr Meyers chuckled as though this was quite a joke.

Michael's deep interest was evident as he asked, "What is Zwingli's attitude on all this?"

"Zwingli had favored this, but the council of two hundred feels it is too radical a break. They say the total populace would not approve. They called a meeting and Zwingli agreed not to make this radical break with the worship patterns of the Roman church so abruptly."

Michael thought a moment and then commented, "Only the Scripture can answer the basic issues involved in such struggles."

Meyers nodded in agreement, but asked, "Who is to interpret the Scriptures? Now the city is plagued with disputations and tension. Recently, the issue of baptism was discussed. These radicals want a church of believers, a voluntary brotherhood, they call it, and they are asking for adult baptism. They charge the Roman church with giving a false hope by infant baptism and insist that the New Testament calls for personal faith to be followed by baptism. Zwingli seems to have agreed with them in a measure, adding to the force of their argument."

Michael leaned forward intently. "This is something of which I must learn more. The church of believers appeals to me. I would like to know more about what this radical group is teaching. Perhaps they have as much to offer as Zwingli."

After further discussion Michael retired to his room, pondering the significance of what he had just heard. What were these radicals doing now? What did they really mean by their rejection of infant baptism? Spent from the day's exhaustion, he soon dropped off to sleep.

Michael awoke early next morning for a quiet time of meditation and prayer, preparing his heart for the coming day and its promise of fulfillment. Today he would find Margareta—he was sure of it.

The sunny breakfast room of the small inn was empty. The other guests still slept. Michael enjoyed the quiet surroundings, the quaint homelike furnishings. This was a welcome change from the bareness of the monastery. A maid entered, inquiring if he had slept well, and brought him a simple breakfast. Somewhere in the distance a clock was chiming . . . there was no need to hurry. A feeling of peace and contentment filled him in spite of the memory of last night's talk with Herr Meyers. His host must be sleeping late, which was just as well. They could continue their discussion later. Michael wanted firsthand information today.

A brisk walk in the crisp winter morning was refreshing, and then he turned his steps to the cathedral. He took his place among the assembling congregation. Margareta was nowhere in sight. Endeavoring to keep his mind on the message, he soon discerned that the preaching carried the same evangelical tone he had heard in Breisgau.

The faces of the worshipers were serene and attentive. Michael tried to sense their thoughts. Were these people accepting what they were told? Were they able to discern the true from the false? Had they heard the reports of unrest among Zwingli's associates? At any rate, there was none of the mechanical lethargy that he sensed in morning prayers at the monastery.

After the meeting was dismissed he followed the crowd toward the entrance. Suddenly he caught sight of a familiar figure in a shaft of sunlight in the doorway. She was leaving the cathedral. He pressed his way through the crowd, reaching her at last in the sunlit street. She was alone.

"Margareta!"

Recognizing his voice, she turned quickly. "Michael!"

He reached out and caught her hand, smiling into her eyes.

"Oh, Michael, I thought you'd never come!"

Aware of the interested gaze of those leaving the

cathedral, they continued down the street. Michael told of his uneventful departure from the monastery and his arrival in Schaffhausen the night before. They had reached the edge of town and the forest seemed to welcome them into its quiet sanctuary. The tall fir trees stood like sentinels, towering above them, providing privacy from curious eyes. It was absolutely still —even as it must have been in the beginning when two people stood alone in all the vast universe.

"Margareta?" His voice was husky with deep feeling. She looked up quickly and met his warm searching gaze. Her heart missed a beat, then began racing wildly. She was sure he would hear its wild throbbing, and she knew what he was about to say, and waited for his words.

"Margareta, I've waited long to tell you this . . . I love you . . . more than I can find words to express. I love you . . . in a way that is . . . holy . . . and pure. Now that I am no longer monk nor prior, I can ask—Will you marry me?"

Her lips trembled and her voice, low but clear, thrilled him as she said, "Michael, I've loved you from Breisgau but hardly dared hope for this. I love you, and I'm . . . I'm yours."

In his arms, responding to his kiss, Margareta never felt so secure. It was a haven . . . it was home.

Michael whispered into her ear, "*Liebchen*, my own *Liebchen*." He smiled with pleasure as she nestled against him.

A new dimension of life was opening before him. Michael had resolutely put aside the thought of such blessing during all his long years in the monastery.

Now it was as though he stood in the splendor of a blazing sunrise, with its promise of a glorious new day . . . a surging, singing joy. He knew with absolute certainty that this was the will of God for him—to share life with this one who promised to be his bride. United in love, in conviction, and in purpose, they were ready for whatever might lie ahead. "Thou wilt shew me the path of life. . . ."

They returned to the village and he introduced Margareta to the Meyers'. The two lunched in a little alcove of the inn, and far into the afternoon they talked of their love. They discussed mutual convictions and their common plight in having left their posts. Yet there was little apprehension. They well knew that others were leaving the monasteries. Luther himself had been responsible for "marrying off" a score of nuns who left the order. Their major adjustment would be finding a community where they could identify themselves freely and be among friends.

It was Margareta who began seriously to plan their wedding. "It would be wonderful to be married in the cathedral, Michael, with music, flowers, friends. . . . I've envied girls many times as I've stood at the edge of a crowd and watched them march to the altar!" Her eyes sparkled and her cheeks blushed as she confessed it.

"There would be nothing too good for you, my dear. The cathedral it will be—if we can arrange it."

The last was said after a slight pause, as though he were uncertain that such was possible. It might be done in Wittenberg or Zurich, but elsewhere? It was doubtful.

Margareta looked at him, suddenly serious. "I'm sorry, Michael; I didn't think. I was so carried away that I forgot for a moment that the former prior of St. Peter's might have a bit of difficulty getting married to a Beguine in one of Rome's cathedrals." With this they both broke into quiet laughter, thinking of the change in their circumstances.

"I wish it would be possible, my little *Liebchen*," Michael began.

But she placed a finger on his lips—"Don't think any more about it. It doesn't matter where we're married, just so I'm married to you." He took her into his arms again and whispered his love into her hair that came just to his chin.

They agreed on a ceremony that could be conducted by a parish priest, and immediately began to carry through their plans.

Their days were so filled with preparations and plans that there was little time to wonder about happenings across the border in Zurich. But in the evenings as they talked, Margareta shared her impressions of the Zurich Reformation. She was deeply involved in the Reformation by her own commitments and very much concerned by the reports from Zurich.

She told him of a recent disputation that revealed the tension within Zwingli's group. Zwingli had referred the matter of breaking with the Roman observance of the mass to the city council for decision. Along with this was the matter of abolishing image worship.

"Simon Stumpf, a pastor at Hoengg, is very outspoken against this. He is an ardent supporter of Master Zwingli. Recently he asked that 'idols in the church' should be done away with. He openly challenged Rome on the matter of celibacy, and after signing a petition for its annulment, he was married himself."

"Then we're not the only ones who have challenged the church, are we?" Michael smiled. After a pause he added, "I wonder what this man Stumpf is doing now."

"I'm not sure. At the disputation he took issue with Zwingli on the matter of referring the decision to the Zurich Council. Someone told me that at one point Stumpf leaped to his feet crying, 'Master Ulrich, you have no right to leave the decision of this question to the council. The matter is already decided. The Spirit of God decides it!'"

"Margareta, that's my own conviction. The Scripture is the authority."

Eager to meet some of these men and to hear from them their answers to questions of faith, Michael said, "Margareta, we must go to Zurich."

He shared the convictions of Stumpf, having also seen hypocrisy and corruption of morals among those who claimed celibacy. It was not unusual for priests to have families even though they had never entered into matrimony. Such disobedience to rules had troubled Michael and was one of the reasons contributing to his leaving the monastery. It was with a sense of inner satisfaction that he anticipated marriage with Margareta and the honorable relationship this offered.

Having arranged lodging at the Meyers', they shared with them freely their plans for marriage. The Meyers' were quite enthused and offered to accompany them as witnesses of the ceremony. They were eager to help in the arrangements. Frau Meyers became as responsible as though Margareta were her own daughter.

The following morning Michael met Margareta at her door and together they went to a local priest to whom Herr Meyers had spoken.

It was a quiet ceremony in which they exchanged their vows with only two witnesses present, as the law required. At the final words, "I now pronounce you husband and wife," it seemed that completeness had come to them. Michael looked deep into Margareta's eyes as the ceremony closed and said, "Until death do us part."

Marriage was a tremendous step. It was an expression of faith in each other in a commitment for life. It was also a break from the Roman church and their former roles in it. The wonder of their love was a constant thrill for each of them. The peace of mind in following their convictions made their life together one of complete sharing. Their first days of marriage were spent in the country around Schaffhausen. They made several visits to the neighboring towns of Schleitheim and Hallau, but the Rheinfall was their rendezvous with love. Here they forgot other things and planned their life together. With the joys of their new relationship were the privileges and responsibilities of building their home. Both knew how to work and how to manage, and soon a rented chalet spread the warmth of their friendship among neighbors who crossed their threshold.

Chapter VIII

It was nearing Christmas, December 1523, and the cold of winter had already arrived. The ground was blanketed with snow, and an icy wind whistled past the corners of the houses and howled through the narrow streets of the city. The Rhine alone seemed to overcome the cold weather as it tumbled over the rocks and splashed its way westward. But the gaiety of the season was evident, if not somewhat accelerated, as though a new freedom stimulated a festive spirit.

Schaffhausen seethed with Reformation teaching. For the past year the preaching of Sebastian Hofmeister had stimulated the populace to freedom of thought and to the acceptance of the new doctrine of Luther. The Zurich Reformation and Hofmeister's association with Zwingli added fuel to the fire. The whole district burned with enthusiasm for a new church movement. Their break from Rome seemed not only inevitable but near.

Though enrapt in the thrill of their married love, the Sattlers were not indifferent to the Reformation nor unconscious of the tensions about them. One of the subjects which came up most frequently in these early days of their marriage was whether to go to Wittenberg or to Zurich. Michael was interested in hearing the reformers for himself. At Wittenberg he could perhaps find his old friend, Fritz Kennan. But Margareta's reports on the movement in Zurich had aroused an interest to know more about it. They agreed that for the present they would stay in Schaffhausen and try to observe the character of the movements from a distance. Delighting in their love, they were in no immediate hurry to move to a new region.

In Schleitheim, Chaplain Spohrlin was promoting the new teaching. Michael felt that he was not primarily concerned about the spiritual meaning of the new life. Spohrlin gave the impression of being more interested in promoting the freedom of new thought than in calling individuals to personal faith. His interpretation of justification by faith seemed to lack a positive message of absolute trust in Christ. Most evident was his announcement that people need not follow the Roman Catholic system to be Christian. His teaching was freedom from Rome rather than freedom in Christ.

Michael held that unless people were led to see faith in Christ as a new level of life, the movement would degenerate into careless living. He hoped Dr. Hofmeister would spearhead a genuine reformation in this area. After the holiday season he meant to have a talk with him.

The little chalet was often filled with guests and laughter. This was a new world for Michael and Margareta. The adjustment to marriage and social life had held its problems for them. It was a change that meant reorienting their whole order of life. But they were enjoying their new role to the full. His training made it easy to find work as a teacher, and the first months of their married life sped by on wings. Michael delighted in Margareta's company and understanding heart. To wake in the morning and see her golden head and peaceful face on the pillow was a perpetual wonder. At times he would slip out of bed quietly and go alone for a morning meditation. On other occasions he would draw her to himself and wake her with his expressions of love. In turn she enjoyed making their love the fulfillment that gave strength to each. Marriage was a bliss of sharing for the two of them. Their differences of opinion at times caused them to face their personal problems, but day by day they learned to work them out together. Love added a new maturity to each.

During the winter various Bible study groups met in homes in the area including their own. Michael's knowledge of the Scriptures made him a prominent figure in this movement. He conversed at length with Dr. Hofmeister as to whether the break with Rome was being carried far enough. He was disappointed with Hofmeister's plan to maintain many of the former state church practices. The new movement was failing to provide individuals with a personal faith. Michael, with Luther, wanted to see the Bible placed in the hands of all the people. He was convinced that life in Christ meant life on a superior level to the religion so prevalent in the land. "The New Testament," he taught in his classes, "expresses life in Christ as a life of relationship by faith, a life in the Spirit!"

One evening in early January, Michael was late coming

home. Margareta had the evening meal prepared and was growing anxious. When he arrived, he was accompanied by a guest. She met them at the door, welcoming the stranger into their cottage. Michael introduced him with the simple words, "Margareta, this is Simon Stumpf, recently from Zurich."

"Welcome, Master Stumpf. We are pleased to have you with us. Come in and share our table."

"Ah, it is my pleasure, Frau Sattler, and a real joy to be here," His manner was very gracious, manifesting a good degree of social grace. His face was clean-cut with a noble expression. He reminded her of someone with deliberate purpose, but, perhaps—a bit incisive.

Margareta quickly placed an extra bowl on the table and retired to the small kitchen to finish preparations for the meal. She had a feeling that the coming of this visitor was a momentous occasion in their pursuit of faith. She was sure this was the same Simon Stumpf she had earlier heard about. She recalled the story of his bold stand at the Zurich disputation, challenging Zwingli. Stumpf wanted to move according to the Scriptures alone, rather than place decisions in the hands of the council.

They had evidently been discussing this very thing on the way home. She listened as Stumpf related the happenings that followed.

"Michael," his resonant voice rang clear in the room. "I told the council that day that if they demanded further observance of the mass, I would not obey them."

"That was a bold stand, Simon. What did they say to that?"

"A week later they held another disputation and order-

69

ed that we continue the mass. Zwingli let us down and went along with the council. He said it was better to compromise and move slowly in order to carry the people."

"And then . . . ?"

"I felt led to resign my charge as a priest. I told my congregation at Hoengg that I would serve henceforth only as a minister of the gospel." He paused, looking down at his clasped hands, remembering those momentous days and the weight of his decision.

Michael sat silent, waiting. After a brief interval Stumpf raised his head and went on.

"On the third of November the council ordered me to leave the village. My congregation drew up a petition for my continued service, but it did not help. On the twentieth, I was exiled from the canton and territory of Zurich."

"And how do you feel about it now?"

Simon Stumpf's eyes flashed as he answered, "Sattler, I cannot go back on my convictions. The council is wrong. Zwingli overplayed his hand! The Scripture alone is the authority. The Reformation is only begun. It must go on!"

There was absolute stillness in the room. Margareta was about to call them to supper, but Stumpf's words caused her to hesitate.

"There are others," he said, "who feel as I do. Wilhelm Reublin, for example. Before coming to Zurich, he was a priest in Basel. He was banished from Basel for carrying a Bible in a public procession over a year ago. He refused to carry the relics. He's a pastor at Wytikon now, and he married this past August. He's a great preacher. The crowds flock to hear him!"

Michael's interest was obvious as he asked, "A married priest! How long will they let him lead a church?"

Margareta called them to supper. As they ate, Stumpf continued to tell them of happenings in Zurich.

"One of the most promising men in Zwingli's group is Conrad Grebel. He was converted over a year ago, and what a changed man he is. He speaks of that conversion as his new birth. His family are of the aristocracy and are quite embarrassed. He'll make his mark—he will; he's quite a scholar. He urges Zwingli to establish a free church."

"Free church?"

"Yes, free from the state, from the council of two hundred."

"What of the talk we've heard about infant baptism?" asked Margareta.

"Oh, they have been speaking out against it too, along with rejection of the mass, and of images."

"And what does Master Zwingli say to that?"

"Last summer I spoke with him about gathering a church of believers only. He told me he would have nothing of a Donatist church. He quoted the parable of the tares to justify a mixed church."

"But what of the mass?" asked Michael.

"He promises to serve bread and wine to all who desire it on Christmas Day coming. We shall see." Stumpf ended skeptically.

"And if he doesn't?" Margareta wanted to know.

"Grebel continues to speak against the mass, images, and infant baptism. If Zwingli does not stick to his promise, a break is inevitable. There are more people ready to follow the Scripture than Zwingli knows!"

Early in the morning Simon Stumpf bade them farewell. Looking first at one, then the other, he said, "May God grant you grace to follow His Spirit. Seek only the true church of Christ."

After he had gone, Michael took Margareta's hand and said, "My dear, the way is not yet clear, but the calling is before us. There is something about Stumpf's vision that corresponds with mine." He paused, looking thoughtfully out the window, and then added, "I wish I had the boldness to be as decisive."

Margareta touched his chin softly, turning his face to look into hers. "Michael, your caution is good. We must be certain from the Word and we must be prepared to defend our decisions. This is another major step and we must be sure of God's leading."

Chapter IX

It was spring of 1524. A radical group in Zurich was stirring up the populace, and Zwingli was hard pressed to answer them. Wilhelm Reublin was attracting as great audiences in Wytikon as Zwingli was at the Great Minster (church) in Zurich. Reublin was speaking pointedly against image worship, condemning the practice as idolatry. "The mass," he said, "is a perversion of the gospel of Christ. Infant baptism itself gives only a false hope. It is a perversion by the popish system."

Michael knew that trouble was sure to follow. Zwingli was continuing the mass according to the Roman pattern. Reublin's teaching would not go unchallenged. He could suffer the same fate as Stumpf and also lose his position. Tolerance was not a general characteristic of the church.

Almost a year had passed since the visit of Simon Stumpf. Michael wondered what had happened to Stumpf in his quest. When winter closed in, they had had little news. But for the Sattlers the winter months had flown rapidly. The joy of their love gave them a security amidst the tensions of the times. Michael found many occasions to discuss the issues of faith in the freedom of this border area. He was being recognized as a voice in the progress of the Reformation in Schaffhausen. Michael made several trips to his old home territories of Staufen and Freiburg. To his surprise he found friends at the university who admired him for following his convictions. Some were sympathetic to his marriage. Sharing the lecture hour of a former professor, he was surrounded by students obsessed with the questions of the day. Luther's thought was receiving high respect on the university campus. But it was quite clear that Catholic opposition was even more intense. Step by step the lines of battle were becoming well defined.

In early November 1524, when Michael was returning from an engagement in Hallau, he met a stranger at a fork in the road about a mile outside the city. They fell into step together, and the stranger, observing Michael's white robe, said, "A Benedictine brother, and from where?"

Michael smiled. "From Schaffhausen, my friend. I was a Benedictine, from the monastery of St. Peter's in Breisgau, but I left and entered some new vows. Michael Sattler is my name."

The stranger smiled broadly and extended his hand. "I'm Wilhelm Reublin, lately from Wytikon. I've heard of you from my friend Simon Stumpf."

"And I've heard of Wilhelm Reublin from him! And you'll spend the night in our home, of course."

Reublin chuckled, "I may as well confess that one of my reasons for passing through Schaffhausen was to see you."

As they walked the remaining distance to the Sattler home, Reublin shared with Michael some of the recent happenings in Zurich. He told of Stumpf's continued difficulties and plans to leave for the north. Reublin himself had been speaking publicly against infant baptism, and he was not alone in his convictions. As early as 1523 Zwingli had also spoken in criticism of the current practice of baptizing infants, but it appeared that Zwingli feared the consequences of trying to have a believers' church instead of a people's church. At least, he had submitted to the council in support of the practice.

Reublin told Michael of his arrest and brief imprisonment in August. He had been given a trial by the council in Zürich and told that he was to cease preaching this doctrine. Now he was in exile, supposedly avoiding unnecessary agitation.

"Michael, I cannot give up my conviction. I am sure many people are given a false hope through this practice. They have never experienced personal faith. They leave the matter of their salvation to the church, trusting in a rite that happened to them apart from their own response to Christ."

Michael was deeply interested in this man. He had already heard much about him through the earlier visit of Stumpf. Arriving at the small chalet, Reublin was welcomed by Margareta. After the evening meal the three of them sat talking into the late hours of the night.

Reublin was emphatic: "The New Testament pattern is a believers' church. This means a fellowship of persons who give evidence of repentance and faith, and confirm this by baptism."

Michael was reserved on this. Although he felt deeply

about a voluntary church of believers, the teaching against infant baptism was not clear to him. "Why must one reject infant baptism to preach voluntary commitment? Does not an adult's faith point back to his baptism?"

"A colleague of mine, Professor Hugwald of the University of Basel, wrote a booklet against infant baptism several years ago. You should get acquainted with it. He emphasizes the importance and priority of personal faith.

"Other voices are being raised now," he added. "Oecolampadius, a priest of St. Martin's Church in Basel, has written both Zwingli and Dr. Hubmaier of Moravia, expressing himself that infant baptism is an open question. Conrad Grebel's group feels very strongly that the New Testament pattern is to wait for baptism until individuals are old enough to make their own decision."

"If this is the case, why were you arrested and others not molested?" Michael asked.

"Many parents around Wytikon are following my teaching. They have not had their babies baptized. This challenges the authority of the Zurich Council and has brought me under their censure."

It was late when they retired for the night, but not to sleep. Michael tossed fitfully as if to shake off a hand that had grasped him. A believers' church, members by free choice—this was going beyond Luther, beyond anything he had conceived of.

When Reublin prepared to leave next morning, he held Michael's hand for a moment. "Michael, the Lord needs you to help in carrying this movement forward. The day is coming when you will need to declare your-

76

self on these issues. Zwingli's break with Rome is only the beginning. The Spirit of God will not desist until He has created a free church. We will see a church of voluntary believers, a church of born-again persons who live in the Spirit. Don't stop short of the full work of God."

As they watched his tall figure move swiftly down the road, it seemed to Michael and Margareta that he blazed a trail for them. A chill wind swirled the dry leaves on the doorstep. Margareta shivered, not only from the cold. She placed her hand on his arm.

"Michael, things like this don't just happen; God may have sent him here. But how can we be sure? His straightforward manner and convictions bother me. You will be careful, won't you?"

He looked at his wife's trusting face in silence for a few moments. "Yes, but—something seems to urge me on even though the way looks rough. Of one thing I am convinced—the authority of the Scripture is greater than the authority of Rome. I am more certain than ever that this is His road. This is a daring undertaking, I know, but we may be on the threshold of a new world. Even if we are not able to complete the work, we are not free to desist from it."

His voice carried a resolute ring as he spoke.

Margareta's eyes glowed in response. Her voice trembled ever so slightly as she sensed intuitively what lay ahead.

"We may be playing with fire—but it is one that we didn't kindle." After a brief pause she added, "And in this we are not alone."

Chapter X

It had been months since Wilhelm Reublin had visited the Sattlers. The little chalet had been exchanged for a rustic house in Breisgau. At first its straight lines and drab walls had seemed quite forbidding to Margareta, but with a deft touch here and there she had turned it into a cheery home. All summer long the flower boxes on the windowsills were bright with blossoms. Her skill with the needle had added curtains, and her industrious gardening had kept the larder supplied.

Michael was increasingly active as teacher to a sizable class which gathered at their home. The students paid their fees well, and the Sattlers were regarded as stable members of the community.

In the last months, however, the opposition and pressure of the state church made life much more difficult. The pope had issued orders for more severe persecution against those who left the cloisters, married, and joined the Protestant cause. The Sattlers were forced to leave, and early March of 1525 saw them en route to Zürich.

Study of the Bible stimulated Michael and Margareta

to examine the teaching which called for a believers'
church. Was this the New Testament pattern? Such a
church would break completely with the Roman liturgy.
They had read the works of Dr. Hubmaier, and heard
him speak. His movement, with tremendous prestige in
Moravia, was a regular topic of conversation around
Staufen and Freiburg.

On one occasion they had heard Thomas Muntzer,
a dissenter from Luther. He was doing considerable
preaching in South Germany, calling for a more radical
reformation with a militant tone. They did not appreciate Muntzer's spirit or his emphasis. There was a
sharp difference between his approach and the gracious
spirit Michael recalled in Wilhelm Reublin.

Michael now saw that to confess the authority of the
Scripture over the authority of Rome had not solved
all the problems. There must be a satisfying and proper
way to interpret the Scripture. Instead of clarity there
was confusion, and with it growing hostility toward reformers. Confronted by the danger of arrest, and much
concerned with questions of the full meaning of faith,
Michael felt it wise to leave the Breisgau area. Both
he and Margareta felt that it was important for them
to go to Zurich and there if possible consult further
with Wilhelm Reublin, Simon Stumpf, and perhaps Conrad Grebel.

A few evenings later they arrived at the inn of Herr
and Frau Meyers, and were given a joyous welcome.
Frau Meyers was bustling about with her usual gaiety
and Herr Meyers was ready to talk. He reported less
tension in Schaffhausen than in the region of Breisgau.
No doubt the Zwinglian movement in Zurich had caused

the local authorities to be more neutral at this time.

"Michael, you will not find things at peace in Zurich," Herr Meyers said. "Your friends Stumpf and Reublin each suffered exile. The leaders the radical group have kept up their teaching. They have moved deliberately to establish a free church! Zwingli still hasn't completely broken from Rome on the mass and other practices, and this group wouldn't wait for him any longer. The tension is now greater between Zwingli and the Anabaptists than between Zwingli and Rome!"

"Anabaptists?" Michael asked. "You mean because of their views on adult baptism?"

"Yes," Herr Meyers replied. "They have become very bold in baptizing those they call believers. They have a little congregation started in Zollikon. Johannes Brötli, a former Catholic priest, was seen baptizing a man by the name of Schumacher at the well of Hirsland. Since then, Brötli has been sent into exile, and the Zollikon congregation has been partly broken up by the Zurich authorities. Two of their leaders, Felix Manz and George Blaurock, were arrested and imprisoned in the Wellenberg Tower. Twenty-five others were jailed in the Augustinian Monastery. Think of it, a monastery turned into a prison!"

Herr Meyers laughed and slapped his knee. "Or did you think of the monastery as a prison when you were prior?"

Michael smiled, but answered, "No, I was happy there until I faced greater truth."

Herr Meyers sobered and continued, "A little over a week later Zwingli talked with the larger group and they were released. Conrad Grebel came here to Schaffhausen and spent much time talking with Hofmeister about his views. He was very open in gathering groups for Bible study. There's a report that a number were baptized and have joined the Anabaptist cause. One is Wolfgang Uolimann, a monk from St. Lucius in Chur. He met Grebel here and accepted his teachings. Grebel baptized him in the Rhine, by immersion!"

"Herr Meyers, you know a lot about this! Tell me, are you in this group?"

"Michael, I don't know what to think. At first I was very skeptical, but I've been to some of your Bible classes. Ever since learning to know you, I've been hoping to learn more of the new life you spoke about. Perhaps this group has found it."

"Where is Conrad Grebel now, Herr Meyers—is he still here?"

"No, he spent almost a month here but left again for Zurich. You may see him when you get there."

"I must talk with him. I hope to find Wilhelm Reublin there and get better acquainted with the group. What else has been happening lately? Where is Felix Manz?" Michael paused a moment, then added, "Do you think it's safe for both of us to go to Zurich?"

Margareta glanced quickly at her husband but said nothing.

Herr Meyers read his thoughts, and answered, "That is hard to say. There is a report that Manz was kept in prison but Blaurock was set free. He was at Zollikon at least on Sunday of February 26, and baptized some persons there. He left quickly and I haven't heard where he is now, perhaps at St. Gall or Appenzell. Manz was released several weeks later with stern warnings, but I'm told he is preaching and baptizing again."

Later, in their room, Michael said, "Margareta, shouldn't you stay here while I go to Zurich? If this tension is so great, you can't tell when they will arrest men again."

"Michael, we're walking this road together, and I want to share the truth with you. I want to go along."

Michael slept little that night, thinking of the news he had just heard. The path was becoming more difficult. There was no turning back from the beckoning hand of truth. The conviction was clear that the true church found its pattern in the Acts of the Apostles, and his calling was to help develop such a church again. There was so much evidence in the Roman church of idolatry and of unchanged lives. Rome could not be the true church. Surely life in Christ offered more than this. Perhaps their answer was to be found in Zurich.

Michael and Margareta entered the city in midforenoon several days later. They arranged for lodging at an inn near the north gate of Zurich. An ominous undercurrent flowed beneath the enthusiasm over the Reformation. They could feel it in the crowds that surged along the street on their way to hear Master Zwingli speak at the Lenten service.

On their right the Limmat River lay shimmering in the sunlight. Margareta caught her breath. . . . The river seemed naked and cold. Ahead of them rose the imposing Zurich City Hall. Across the street to the left was the Great Minster, its twin towers piercing the sky. Built in A.D. 1000, it had for centuries been the center of Zurich life. Even its great doors proclaimed the gospel, for divided into sections each one contained carvings depicting the life of Christ. Today it was the center of activity.

The Sattlers joined the crowd entering the doors of the Great Minster, glad to be in time for the service. Zwingli was bringing a series of Lenten messages from the Gospel of Matthew. An imposing figure in the pulpit, he was a man around forty years of age, with dignity and enthusiasm. Michael was impressed with his preaching of the gospel, an evangelical presentation similar to what he had heard in Breisgau. Zwingli's discussion that morning was on the theme, "True Religion."

The tone of the message seemed to be defensive, perhaps against the radical elements in Zurich. Zwingli was calling for more understanding and patience in carrying through a reformation that would be satisfactory to all the people. Repeatedly, Michael noted the appeal for patience and confidence in the city council. His keen mind quickly sensed that the state church system was the determining factor in the program at the Great Minster.

They left the service and crossed the narrow street to stand beside the flowing waters of the Limmat. The willows across the river were in the bright green of early spring. A pair of swan swam majestically upstream. It was beautiful here, and so quiet. Almost deathly quiet now. Margareta sensed a chill of apprehension and was about to speak of it to Michael, when they heard footsteps on the cobblestones. Turning around quickly, Michael recognized Wilhelm Reublin.

"Michael Sattler! I thought as much from your white coat and brown locks. And Frau Sattler! Welcome to

Zurich! And what brings you here, my friends, to this city of tension and persecution?"

Michael shook Reublin's hand with warm enthusiasm. "We have come, Reublin, in obedience to our inner convictions. I want to know what I may find in Zurich that will answer the questions which haunt me these last months."

"Such as?" prompted Reublin, with a smile.

"Well, how do we interpret the Scripture that we profess is sole authority, and what kind of church are we called to build?"

Reublin's eyes narrowed and he replied, "Michael, I've been expecting this. We can't talk here; it's too dangerous. A number of our leaders are imprisoned now in the Witch Tower. For over a week we've been expecting word as to their release, or at least a trial. Let me meet you tonight, and I'll tell you about it."

Michael nodded his consent, adding, "We've arranged for lodging at the inn by the north gate of the city. You will find us there this evening."

With this agreement they parted. Michael had an increasing awareness that the search was nearing its end. But news of further arrests heightened his apprehension.

In late evening Reublin called. They spoke of Michael's work as a prior, his scholarship, and the weight of the decisions that led to where he was now. Then the conversation turned to Margareta's experience as a Beguine, and how both were prepared for a larger service. Doubt as to the necessity of following conviction was completely removed as they testified to a sense of being led by God to this point. This assurance seemed to lead Reublin to relate more to them.

He shared some of the past events of the Reformation in Zurich, especially the disputations, and then turned to the more recent news.

"Following the disputation at the end of January, when the city council rejected our position against infant baptism, we felt led of God to make the further step of founding a free church!"

"That was a very bold move, Wilhelm, and surely a dangerous one."

"Yes, Michael, a state church might stand against Rome by the protection Luther had received in Germany. A free church that challenges the state church pattern and makes membership voluntary has no security." He paused and then added firmly, "Except in God."

Margareta broke in, "No wonder you are being persecuted and imprisoned. You are defying every security the world has to offer."

"We know that." Reublin's voice was level, the voice of a man taking a calculated risk. "After the city council condemned us as radicals—that was on January 21—we went to the home of Felix Manz's mother. We discussed the Word together—Grebel, Manz, and the monk George Cajacob, known more freely as Blaurock. We agreed that one must learn from the divine Word and preach a true faith that manifests itself in love. We were agreed that this faith should be symbolized by a true Christian baptism. This to be on the basis of a recognized and confessed faith of union with God and a good conscience, with the full intent of faithfulness to God unto death."

Reublin paused, the import of his words vibrating in

the silence. Michael did not speak, and Reublin went on.

"A deep sense of the fear of God was upon us then. We knelt to pray and we asked God for grace to follow our convictions. We well knew what the price might be."

He paused again, recalling the vivid experience, then continued. "After the prayer, George Cajacob arose and asked Conrad Grebel to baptize him for the sake of God and with the true Christian baptism upon his faith and knowledge. With these words George knelt again. Grebel took a dipper of water from the pail and baptized him. Following this, the others of us received baptism by the hand of George."

Reublin looked at Michael and Margareta with quiet certainty. "This marked the beginning of the free church, the brotherhood of believers, born in a prayer meeting by the regenerating power of the Spirit, born under fire."

The room was still except for the solemn ticking of the old clock by the fireplace. Reublin waited, giving his friends time to weigh carefully the decision they were making. They sat with bowed heads and clasped hands. Then as Michael raised his eyes and his steady gaze met Reublin's, Wilhelm said, "He that believeth and is baptized shall be saved."

It was a bold thrust. Without a word Michael rose to his feet and crossed the room to the window. Across the courtyard a small candle burned in the window of the house next door, its steady flame made brighter by the darkness around it. Michael's thoughts were miles and years away, remembering a baptism of fire on that momentous day when the Spirit came to those at prayer in an upper room in Jerusalem. "The People of the Flame," they were known afterward.

The candle flame across the court was a kind of symbol. Michael knew that he believed Luther's doctrine of justification by faith. But to receive this sign of baptism was to repudiate even his faith in the sacrament he had received. This was to accept a baptism that was purely a testimony of his confession of faith.

Margareta sat watching her husband. She sensed the weight of this decision. For herself, she had made it already. Reublin sensed it too.

Michael turned from the window, first to Margareta, and her serene face assured him of her decision. Then to Reublin he said, "I do believe and all my life is committed to the conviction that God's Word alone is the authority. If what I feel is actually the witness of the Spirit to the truth of your words, I should be making a grave mistake to say no. I know Christ as my Savior, and I'm ready to confess my faith in Him by receiving the sign of baptism."

Reublin turned to Margareta who was smiling through tear-filled eyes. "I stand by my husband in Christ and am ready to join him in this testimony," she paused, taking a deep breath, "at any cost."

Reublin arose and lifted the dipper of water from the pail. As they knelt before him, he exhorted them to be true disciples of Jesus Christ, to trust only His blood for the remission of their sins, and to open their hearts now for the gift of the Holy Spirit. As he poured water on their heads to symbolize the baptism with the Holy Spirit, he repeated the words, "I baptize you with water in the name of the Father, and of the Son, and of the Holy Ghost."

After the sign had been given, all was silent for a few minutes. Then Michael began to pray, thanking God for His grace and promising to be a true disciple unto death. Margareta followed, a deep spirit of devotion evident in her prayer. Reublin closed the sacred moment with his own prayer that God confirm this testimony in their lives by the full witness of the Spirit and make them strong in the kingdom of Christ.

As they rose from their knees with misty eyes, Reublin said, "There is much more to tell you of this movement, but it will wait until tomorrow. I'll leave you now with your faith."

When the door had closed behind him, Michael took his wife in his arms. "My dear," he said, "we've found peace at last. It may be a lonely road, but it is His road. If we're playing with fire, I know now that it is the fire of the Spirit."

Chapter XI

Reublin returned early the next morning and it was clear that something unusual had happened. He slipped through the doorway, looked at Michael and Margareta, and said, "You are happy in your decision?"

Margareta's face sparkled with an enthusiastic smile and Michael answered quickly, "We are, Wilhelm. To have confessed that we will follow Christ alone is a satisfaction. We've found peace at last!"

Taking the chair Michael offered, Reublin said, "I have more to tell. Yesterday I told you that Manz and Blaurock have been in prison, in the dungeon of the Witch Tower. With them were fourteen other men and seven women. Each of the leaders was called in turn before Zwingli, but no ground was given. Zwingli is as determined as ever to have a state church. He means to crush out the free church movement. The case had seemed hopeless, but a few days ago all but the leaders were released. Then Blaurock was set free. Now just this morning I learned that Felix Manz has escaped!"

Michael leaned forward. "Where is he now?"

"In Zollikon. We're meeting there tonight at the home

of Hans Kienast. Manz baptized him some weeks ago. There is quite a group of believers in Zollikon. At least eighty have been baptized in the past weeks. Some of them had been in prison earlier. Mark you, an Augustinian monastery a prison for Anabaptists! That's freedom from Rome, isn't it? It looks as though what started out to be a reformation has become simply a transfer of power."

Reublin's eyes flashed. "How can a man preach the gospel and at the same time bind it?"

Then resuming his former thought, he continued, "Some of that group will be with us tonight. We're planning our program from here on. Will you join us?"

Michael looked at Reublin, sharing and yet weighing this conviction. Because of such conviction, Luther had scarcely escaped. Huss had been burned. What faced this little group, led by men who had just escaped from prison, no one knew.

But Michael believed in the supreme authority of the Scripture, had been baptized as a believer, and shared the call of God to establish a holy church, a believers' church. With only a brief moment of reflection, he answered, "We'll be there, Wilhelm. We're ready to bear His cross as well."

After a few directions to the home of Kienast on the edge of Zollikon, Reublin was gone. Michael could not shake off the impression made by Reublin's willingness to risk arrest to come to them with this invitation.

At the inn on the edge of Zollikon, Michael's white Benedictine garb brought a few glances their way during the evening meal. Today it was not unusual for a monk to appear with his wife at his side. Everyone knew that Zwingli had emptied monasteries around Zurich and that most of the monks had married.

Two men at a neighboring table were in a heated discussion. Michael caught enough to learn of a rash attempt by George Blaurock to take the pulpit of Nicholas Billter in Zollikon. In his own mind he wondered what Blaurock had thought he could gain by such foolishness.

"He stood right up in the church and told the pastor that he, Billter, was not sent to preach," said one. "That's nerve for you!"

"And to pound the floor with his staff. What did he mean by that quotation, 'It is written, My house is a house of prayer, but you have made it a den of thieves'?" said the other.

"It served him right to be put in jail," retorted the first. "A man has a right to his own beliefs, but it's not right to disturb the peace."

Michael was troubled by this evidence that not all was well among the Anabaptists either. He purposed to ask Wilhelm about this.

By the time they arrived at the Kienast home that evening the Sattlers knew they were involved in a program in which the peace within would not always be found without. But they were committed and had no plans to retreat. The public baptizings by the radicals had heightened the tension. Some people were convinced of the validity of the new call to discipleship, while others became more ardent in defense of Zwingli's program. The cleavage between the two movements was becoming increasingly more distinct in their minds.

Reublin met them at the door. In the Kienast living room a man in his early forties was speaking rapidly and enthusiastically. It was Felix Manz. Michael and Margareta stood in the doorway and listened.

"For those nine days we gave ourselves to prayer and studying the Scriptures. None of us knew what to expect next. George and I had been called separately to meet Zwingli and his men in defense of our position. Of course, we well knew the arguments from the disputations we'd had before. It is clear that Zwingli has gone back on his earlier vision.

"All were released but George and me. Later, George was released, being a foreigner, but as a local citizen I was to be used as an example. Last night the gate from dungeon into the long hallway on the upper floor was left unlocked. I discovered an open window, probably left open by one of the guards who is friendly to our cause. Climbing out, I hid until early morning, and then fled Zurich at once."

At this point Manz looked up to see Reublin standing in the doorway with the Sattlers. He rose and all eyes turned toward Michael and Margareta.

Reublin introduced them briefly, relating the events that had brought them to Zurich, and then telling of their baptism the evening before. A fervent "amen" was heard around the room. Conrad Grebel stepped forward to grip their hands, welcoming them into the fellowship as partners in Christ.

"Michael, when I was in Schaffhausen, I heard of your Bible classes and your endorsement of Luther's view. I hoped that someday I could meet you. We need men of your scholarship and ability in the free church movement. I'm glad you have followed the Master in this step."

The warmth of his words caused the Sattlers to feel involved in the brotherhood at once. Manz was next to shake their hands and he praised God for this sign of His blessing on the movement. His personality was friendly and aggressive, similar to Reublin's. Michael felt that here was a man who would rather die than give up the cause to which he was committed.

The group now resumed its discussion. Grebel, who had returned from St. Gall, reported on the conversations he had had with his brother-in-law, Vadian, whom he was trying to win for the cause. Michael was impressed with his boldness to seek the conversion of such a prominent man. As leader of the group that evening, Grebel led in a discussion of their strategy and future planning. His deep resonant voice was calm and deliberate.

"Zwingli is planning a new liturgy this month. The time seems to have come when he will finally cease the mass. However, it is clear that at this point he has gone back on his former statements against infant baptism, and they will continue that Romish practice. For the present I want to stay around Zurich and bid for an opportunity to defend the doctrines of the Word. I have already written to the council and would like your ratification of this petition I mean to submit to them."

He took a scroll from the folds of his garment and unrolled it in the middle of the circle. After explaining the contents, he read, "If it be found then by divine Scripture that we err, we shall gladly accept correction. We desire nothing more upon earth than to have these things decided according to the Word of God."

Manz looked around the group, each nodding approval. Then he turned to Grebel. "We support your statement.

How far you will get we cannot tell, but try we must. I have little faith in any further progress with Zwingli."

Grebel gave his word of encouragement to the leaders of the Zollikon Brethren, especially singling out Jacob Hottinger. He commended them for their growth and the numerous baptisms during the past month. Michael noted the reserved way in which Blaurock's attempt to preach at Zollikon was referred to. There was neither endorsement nor outright censure. It was Manz who spoke, "We must be sensitive to the Holy Spirit in our witness." Then with a smile he added, "Our brother George admits he doesn't always discern the difference between his own spirit and God's Spirit.

In the discussion of plans they decided that those who had escaped should come and go from Zurich rather than stay at one place. They were to carry the gospel into surrounding cantons in evangelistic missions. They would work in Aargau, St. Gall, and Appenzell, and then seek to penetrate into Austria and South Germany, especially Augsburg and west to Strasbourg.

Blaurock was already working to the east of Zurich since his release from prison in February. Grebel himself planned to go to St. Gall. Among others he would again seek to win his brother-in-law, Vadian. The winning of such an official to the cause would give it more recognition.

Grebel turned abruptly to Michael. "There is a divine commission resting on our shoulders, Michael. We are to carry the gospel into all the world. 'He that believeth and is baptized shall be saved.' We need your scholarship in the instruction of the Word. You aren't well known here in Zollikon as an Anabaptist, and you will be more free to work. Perhaps later you are the man to carry the faith back to Schaffhausen and to South Germany."

Michael nodded. "I did not break from Rome just for myself, but for the sake of truth. The call of God is clear in my own mind. He wants to see a pure church, a New Testament church again. I am ready to follow where He leads."

The group again voiced an audible "amen" and Michael had the feeling of being a longtime member of the fellowship.

The planning completed, Grebel asked Reublin to read from Romans six. As they entered into a discussion of this passage, Michael's hungry mind responded warmly to the depth of thought in the comments of the group. Grebel began, in contrast to Luther's interpretation, saying the high point of Paul's letter to the Romans was not chapter five but chapter six. With this emphasis he added Paul's words to the Corinthians, "If any man be in Christ, he is a new creature."

Reublin added his comments. "Man is not only a forgiven sinner, but in Christ he is regenerated, is born again. The Christian is a Christ-indwelt person. For us, faith is no longer a conquest of assurance but a demonstration of life in Christ."

Grebel picked up the discussion, addressing the Sattlers. "To be baptized into Christ means to be identified with Him. This involves a death to the old life, and a new life in the Spirit. The outer baptism is only a sign of the inner baptism with the Spirit. The Christian life is a discipleship in grace, a life of following Christ."

After the discussion the group knelt in prayer and many prayed, addressing God in a conversational style. They petitioned God "to teach them more of what it means to walk with Christ, to fill them with the Spirit for the mission to which He had called them, and to give them boldness to witness for the truth against all opposition."

After the prayer period when they were seated again, Grebel asked for the signs. Michael was hardly prepared for what happened next. Bread and wine were brought in and Manz gave a short discussion of the Lord's Supper as a feast of fellowship. He concluded with words that were already familiar to the Sattlers. They recalled them from Reublin's report, words spoken by Blaurock at the group's first celebration of the Supper.

"He who believes that God has redeemed him through His death and rose-red blood, let him come and eat with me of the bread and drink with me of the wine."

Manz broke the bread in pieces and placed it on a plate which was passed about the group in silence. Each one took the bread in silence and ate. Grebel next took the wine and poured it into a cup. He lifted it and offered a prayer of thanks for the sacrifice of Christ. They passed the cup around the group and each drank from it. There was a holy hush in the room as they closed the meeting with prayer. The group silently dispersed by ones and twos, slipping out of the house and disappearing into the night.

The Sattlers spent the night in Zollikon with the Hottinger family. After leaving the meeting, they spent another hour with the Hottingers before retiring, speaking about the nature of the church of Christ. They were discovering what it meant to be a part of a fellowship of believers. Jacob Hottinger testified to them of his joy in the Lord, and of the growth of the Zollikon brotherhood. He told them of numerous homes throughout the village where believers met for fellowship and shared the Lord's Supper in this simple New Testament manner. When the Sattlers retired for the night, sleep was slow in coming. They were both thrilled by this new association. The church was not just an institution for them now; it was a fellowship.

"We're a long way from the work of the church we knew in Staufen and St. Peter's, Margareta, but it has been a rewarding path. I wouldn't go back to the old life for anything. At last I feel I'm actually sharing fellowship with the people of Christ."

His words hung between them in the silent room. Then Margareta spoke softly, "I feel we have found our answer."

"Yes, my dear, but doubtless as much to a cross as to comfort."

"Michael, it is His road, and whatever lies ahead we'll face with Him. If it be a cross, we'll share it in His love."

"And in ours," he said, drawing her to himself.

Long after her even breathing told him she was asleep, Michael lay with her hand in his, thinking of the goodness of God in leading their lives together in this way.

Chapter XII

The little town of Zollikon was bustling with the new life of spring. The days were warm and bright, and spring flowers and blossoming trees colored the landscape. Fresh cool air blew in from the mountains and skipped across Lake Zurich. The days were invigorating and the nights cool and calm.

This was home now for the Sattlers. Through the courtesy of Jacob Hottingers they had their lodging in a section of the Hottinger household. Margareta found Frau Hottinger to be not only a gracious Christian but a wonderful friend.

Margareta enjoyed setting up housekeeping again, and each day some new touch added to the domestic atmosphere of the Sattler home. Her vivacious spirit soon won many new friends, and her regular visits to the market introduced the Sattlers into the social life of the town.

Michael engaged in Bible teaching and preached to small but eager audiences. The brethren were in hopes that the whole Zollikon community would turn to the Anabaptist belief. They met in homes or, when larger groups gathered, in a *Bauernhof* or in the open in some secluded area.

On a warm afternoon, March 8, a special service was called for the larger group. They met for their fellowship on a grassy knoll overlooking the lake in the orchard of Hans Murer, one of the brethren. Here in the open, in a very simple expression of their faith, the bread and wine were presented and they shared together in observance of the Lord's Supper.

Jacob Hottinger was in charge of the service, interpreting the Lord's table as a table of Christian fellowship. He reminded them of Grebel's words that, "Whoever partakes of the bread and wine must purpose thereby to live from henceforth a truly Christian life." Michael was deeply impressed by the spirit and simplicity of the service. He and Margareta walked home from the meeting with Jacob Hottinger. "Do you interpret the bread and the wine as divine presence or as emblems?" he asked.

Hottinger was quick to reply, "As holy emblems. Christ is present, but by His Spirit rather than in the bread. These are not the means by which we receive grace, but the testimony that we are living in grace."

Michael nodded. "That is my own conviction, and the same applies to baptism. Baptism with water is a testimony that one has an inner baptism with the Spirit, and a repentant and regenerate heart. The inner baptism is what really counts." He paused a moment as they walked then continued, "This conviction has enriched my relation with the Lord. It is a real joy to know the infilling of the Spirit."

Hottinger gave a fervent amen to these words. As they continued their discussion of the Spirit's work, Jacob concluded, "The presence of God's Spirit is a spiritual reality, an inner joy and power to all who truly follow Christ."

By the following Sunday there was real excitement in Zollikon. One of the bold witnesses for the doctrine of the Anabaptists was Jorg Schad, a farmer who lived in Zollikon. He had led a notoriously profligate life, but a few weeks earlier he had been soundly converted. The change in Schad was still the talk of Zollikon. In the recent days several persons had responded to his preaching and had asked to be baptized. They were of course members of the Zollikon State Church, and their baptism at the public well became the talk of the town. Schad was now waiting until Sunday, and if he found opportunity in the service to explain the baptism, he planned to do so publicly. He apparently hoped this would help others to make a decision.

Michael and Margareta attended the service this particular Sunday morning quite unaware of his plan. They wanted to get better acquainted with both the people of Zollikon and the tone of the Reformation there. The message of the pastor, Nicholas Billter, was a call to true faith in Christ that particular morning, a clear emphasis on the Protestant awareness of justification by faith. Michael was well impressed by the quality of the message. Billter was reserved and did not speak of the stirrings for a believers' church, nor did he emphasize saving faith as a voluntary commitment to Christ.

At the close of the service, Jorg Schad rose to his feet and courteously asked if he as a member of the Zollikon community might say a few words.

There was a rustle as the audience turned to see who was so bold. Billter nodded as he stepped down from the platform. Schad walked to the front of the auditorium and faced the audience. At this unusual action most of the

100

people stayed to hear, although the service was dismissed with Billter's descent from the pulpit. Recalling what Blaurock had done a month earlier in trying to take the pulpit from Billter, many were curious to see what Schad wanted.

He began with a warmhearted testimony to the message of the morning, affirming that the real joy of the Lord and assurance of salvation had come into his life when he took this very doctrine of justification by faith seriously and committed his life to Christ. This testimony itself was a radical innovation for a morning worship service, but more striking to the congregation was the change in the man from the Jorg Schad they had known.

After some careful quotations of Zwingli on the sacraments, that they were symbols of the true working of the Spirit, he started to discuss the meaning of conversion and the place of baptism as a testimony to an experience of faith.

As Michael observed the audience, he was sure that many others were as impressed as he with the sincerity and eloquence of Schad's statements. He glanced at Margareta and she was listening intently, a soft smile on her lips. But even while Michael's heart and mind were giving assent to Schad's message, his caution made him fearful. He wondered what would happen next. He did not have to wait long.

"I know there are persons in this audience," said Schad, "who need to place their sole faith in Christ for their salvation. I invite you to do so now, and to openly confess your faith in baptism. You are aware of some of your neighbors who have been converted and asked for baptism during this past week."

There were a number of knowing expressions which

passed between the members of the congregation.

"I have talked with these people during the last few days, and I'm sure they are truly believers. I want to ask others of you to repent and come for the sign of faith. What we are doing is reforming the church, and there is no better place for expressing this faith than here."

All over the audience people stood with clasped hands, some with tears, expressing their faith. Schad, seeing Michael in the audience, asked him to come forward and pray for the people. Michael greatly moved by the spirit of the meeting, rose and stepped to the front. He and Schad knelt in prayer, as those standing confessed their sins to God. Schad then asked that all who would testify of their desire to walk with Christ, follow him to the well for baptism. Some twenty persons followed him out of the church for the brief walk to the village well. The congregation followed, gathering around as Schad explained the meaning of baptism. He then took water and baptized them, while the audience watched silently, listening to the water poured on the heads as it dripped on the ground. Following the baptism Schad exhorted each of them to be faithful disciples of Christ.

Billter stood at a distance and watched the entire proceedings, but did not interfere. At the close of the service the congregation left in a solemn hush, pondering the significance of what they had seen. Michael joined Margareta and started toward their home; his eyes met Billter's for a moment. The pastor's expression was not hostile, but it said more than simple curiosity. Michael sensed that this would not happen soon again in Zollikon.

The Sattlers returned to Hottingers talking about the events of the morning. Jacob spoke pointedly to Michael.

"My brother, you are no longer unknown in Zollikon. From here on you are a marked man, a leader among the radicals."

Michael smiled, the thrill of the morning service still fresh in his mind. "Hottinger, we want a believers' church. This may be the beginning of one in Zollikon."

"Don't be too sure, Michael. Zurich can't run the risk of surrendering its authority here, and Zwingli isn't with us any longer. Billter may not be exactly sure where he stands, but you can be sure that in a showdown he'll side with Zwingli. We must move ahead on our own, calling men to repentance, and baptizing them into a brotherhood. We must be prepared for a crisis—a believers' church opposed to the people's church."

And for the next week they did just that. One of their men, Hans Bichter, a tailor, had come to Zollikon from the Black Forest. Having been converted to the faith, he was a very successful witness. During the following week he won thirty people to confess Christ as Lord, and baptized them as testimony of their commitment to discipleship. A free church, a fellowship of faith, was developing apart from the recognized church. It was more dynamic as well as more informal.

Bichter stayed at the Hottinger home during this time. Jacob Hottinger the younger had regarded this new movement with skepticism. They were nothing but enthusiasts in his opinion. But the conversion of one of his close friends upset his judgment. The evident transformation was too much for his honest mind, and seeking out Bichter he surrendered his life to Christ.

Jacob's conversion startled his sophisticated friends. One by one he spoke to them about his new life in Christ.

Within a few days seven of his circle experienced a spiritual birth.

Now the Lord's Supper was being observed in numerous homes across the village. The witness was spreading. Many were being stirred to repent and confess their faith in Christ. More were joining the movement from prominent political circles. The wife of the deputy bailiff, Hans Wuest, was converted. If they could not gain approval for the movement, this might at least help retard the opposition.

But while they rejoiced in the work of the Spirit and the success of their movement, there was growing apprehension. Margareta felt it, and brought it up for discussion. "Michael, this much success is not only noticed but is causing reaction. Today in the market I heard the word 'Anabaptist' hissed angrily at me several times, and this from people who had always seemed very friendly. We are in for serious trouble."

"Perhaps it is time for our group to move out. It may not be wise to keep stirring over the same territory."

Michael immediately inaugurated a new program. He encouraged the group to move out into areas around them. It would be better if they were not all in one location in the event of persecution. The village of Hoengg, only a few miles away, had already been prepared for them by the former pastor, Simon Stumpf. Michael went to Hoengg himself, and his earlier acquaintance with Stumpf enabled him to find friends.

No one knew whether it was this expansion, or the impact in official circles that stimulated the opposition. But direct action followed immediately. The Zurich Council meant to suppress their witness. On Thursday morning, March 16, 1525, a runner brought news that Hans Hot-

tinger, the watchman of the city, had been arrested for associating with the Anabaptists. Even now the officers were moving through the village, arresting all who had been rebaptized. By the time Michael received the news it was too late to flee.

Quickly he took Margareta to an upstairs room of the Hottinger apartment where she might hide. It was little more than an attic, but there he hid her. "I'll be back, Margareta," he whispered, taking her in his arms. "You must trust God and pray for us. I'll go to the door and surrender. Perhaps they won't search the house."

"Yes," she answered tearfully. "I will trust . . . and pray. Don't worry about me."

There was a loud knock on the front door. Michael kissed her quickly and released her.

The officers started with surprise when Michael opened the door and stepped out before them.

"You are Michael Sattler?"

"I am."

"By orders of the Zurich Council, you are under arrest. Come with us."

He fell into step, their feet ringing on the cobblestone street. Others were converging from narrow side streets. Several dozen persons were taken into custody. They were halted before the city gate while an order was read from the Zurich Council. It called for the arrest of those who had been practicing rebaptism. While this involved only a few who had actually baptized, the officers didn't know who were the offenders. They spent some time questioning them, and finally took nineteen men. The women were warned and berated, then released. Michael was relieved that they wouldn't be searching for Margareta.

The Anabaptists marched without protest and the strange procession began its journey to Zurich. The brethren cheerfully greeted farmers driving oxcarts along the road. Some were neighbors, who looked on in silence at this strange event. In Zurich, people lined the streets, some shouting at the officers for suppressing freedom of faith, and others mocking the brethren for rebaptizing. Tension mounted steadily in the crowd, and the officers, fearing an outbreak of violence, kept watching the people along the street.

The group was herded into the Augustinian monastery and imprisoned. The bailiff looked at them reproachfully. "An unthankful lot, I'd say. Why aren't you satisfied with the new freedom in Zurich? You can answer to Master Zwingli on that. You will be held for questioning, and the will of the council."

Michael sat in the prison with his head bowed in prayer. A few times the group attempted conversation, only to be silenced by the guard. After several hours the bailiff returned to place each one in a separate cell. The barren room was strangely reminiscent of his years in monastic life. At first Michael was concerned that each brother must face his interrogators alone. But his experience with the Zollikon group assured him of one thing: this was a group who not only took the Scriptures as final authority but who knew them. Their true strength would now be measured by the depth of their convictions.

Seven days passed, in which they were examined repeatedly. Councillors appointed by Zwingli put them through a grueling experience. There were threats and repetition of questions. Again and again they were asked what they had been doing since the last imprisonment of Anabaptists

107

on February 8—whether they had been baptizing, and why they themselves had been baptized. To the last question each would answer, "The Holy Scriptures have led us to baptism." Michael sought to engage his interrogators in discussion, only to be told they were conducting the questioning.

Gredig, a farmhand from an area called the Grisons, was in the next cell to Michael. At times Michael could hear his strong voice. His positive answers and his knowledge of the Scriptures were surprising. The answers were simple but firm, quoting the Scriptures, "He that believeth and is baptized shall be saved"; "Go ye therefore, and teach all nations, baptizing them in the name of the Father, and of the Son, and of the Holy Ghost."

Finally on the seventh day, the councillors asked each one, "Are you willing to be corrected by the Holy Scriptures?"

They gave assent to this, for the Bible was their authority. "This correction," they were advised, "will be conducted by Master Zwingli."

The day following Zwingli entered the monastery. Accompanied by several councillors, he went from cell to cell, questioning the prisoners. Most of the men were untrained farmers and no match for Zwingli. Michael feared that some of them would not be able to resist the influence of so great a personality. Finally his turn came and the bailiff opened the door to admit Zwingli.

He was an imposing figure, tall and well built. His voice was pleasant, and his way of conversation most gracious. Michael had heard him speak at the Great Minster, but this was their first personal encounter.

Learning that Michael was from Staufen and not a

citizen of Zurich, Zwingli began his interview by a discussion of the Protestant faith. Here Michael was on familiar ground with Zwingli; both confessed the supreme authority of the Scriptures, the priesthood of the believer, and the truth of justification by faith. But when Zwingli began discussing the relation of baptism to conversion, his voice became intense and his manner more sharp. It was clear that he saw beyond the sacrament to the greater issue of a free church. Obviously this was not a light matter. He meant to preserve the people's church at all costs.

"Sattler, I believe that the sacraments are scriptural signs. What more do you ask? They are symbols of the divine presence. What matters whether the sign of membership in the covenant-community is given to a babe or to an adult? Circumcision was given to babes in God's covenant; baptism is the same."

"But the new covenant," Michael replied, "is not the same as the old. We are now being baptized as an expression of our faith in Christ. Can a babe offer such an expression?"

Quickly Zwingli retorted, "Baptism doesn't save anyway, for one is saved by the electing grace of God. It is the inner baptism with the Spirit that accomplishes the salvation."

Michael nodded. "With that I agree, but in obedient testimony our Lord says, 'He that believeth and is baptized shall be saved.'"

Zwingli now argued at length for the parallelism of circumcision with baptism, a rite or pledge that one shares membership among the people of God. With this Michael could not agree. They approached the Scriptures from different perspectives—Zwingli from Old Testament analogies, and Michael from New Testament principles. In the deadlock Zwingli's tone changed. "Sattler, you'll never get by with this independent movement, this free church as you call it. How can a church exist without identification with the state?"

"Master Zwingli, it did in the days of the New Testament."

"But had it not been for Constantine it would doubtless have been crushed."

"Crushed? More likely scattered. Remember that under the earlier persecutions the Bible says, 'They that were scattered abroad went everywhere preaching the word.' "

"What wider influence could it have had than under the Constantinian empire?"

"Influence is not a matter of quantity but quality. The forcing of Christianity upon the populace was really the fall of the church. Faith is never coerced; it is voluntary. The free church will demonstrate this again."

Michael's voice rang with conviction, while Zwingli's expression revealed his anger. "Sattler," he warned, "if your group persists in rebaptism in this free church, you will all be banished from the canton of Zurich!"

Zwingli rose to leave. The conversation had only begun, and now it was over. At the door he turned as though to clear himself.

"Think this over, Sattler. Your training prepares you for something better than this radical movement. I believe—indeed I know—the sacraments are far from conferring grace; they do not even convey or dispense it. This far I can agree. But, by baptism the church publicly receives one who has previously been received through

110

grace. Baptism does not convey grace, but the church certifies that grace has been given to him to whom it is administered. The true church is invisible. Leave the proof of faith with God."

Michael well knew what this meant—the continuation of a state church, run by the council of two hundred. There would be no free church, no voluntary church of believers if they should follow Zwingli.

Next morning the entire group was released with a stern warning. Any more rebaptizing and they would be apprehended, banished, or restricted by more severe measures. Following the warning, there was a commendation for those who had cooperated and agreed to cease this unheard-of practice. This last note visibly affected the group. They looked at each other in silence, a suppressed group. Returning to Zollikon, they were greeted with warm enthusiasm by many praying friends.

Michael excused himself and went immediately to Margareta.

"Oh, Michael! God answered my prayers for your release."

"And mine for you, *Liebchen*. Each day in prison I prayed for your safety and for God's presence to be with you."

He reviewed the nine days in prison, the trying interviews with the councillors, and the final meeting with Zwingli. He hesitated before telling her that some had given Zwingli reason to believe the group would relax its program.

"And what now, Michael? What do we do?"

Michael was silent for only a moment. "My dear, we have a commission from Christ that tells us to reach the world with the gospel. I intend to call men to repentance and faith though there be a thousand city councils. Zwingli can stand by them; we will abide by the Scripture alone. The work of the Spirit is invisible, but where He works the church becomes visible. Within that visible brotherhood we shall pray and study the Word, discerning the leading of the Spirit."

Michael paused a moment, then continued, "There are other areas besides Zollikon. We do not want to be interpreted as merely reactionary, nor do we want to confuse the impression of the truth of our mission. There are many people in the church who do not know what conversion is. Perhaps we can satisfy Zwingli by not fighting his program, and engage ourselves in missions to areas beyond. We have bound ourselves over to the Holy Spirit and we cannot go back."

Chapter XIII

For the next several weeks the brethren in Zollikon were quiet. Michael was very careful in his trips to Hoengg. In gatherings arranged in different homes he taught the gospel and called for a believers' church. Baptizing was left to some who were not known as leaders in the congregation.

Springtime came early in the lowlands around Lake Zurich. Green carpeted meadows studded with bright blossoms contrasted to the distant snowcapped mountains. But under the peaceful facade strong undercurrents of tension surged.

Michael gave much thought to Zwingli's statement. Was the church really invisible, made up of the elect known only to God? In turn he had to ask, Was not the New Testament church made up of committed disciples? Does not the true church, by its expression of fellowship, become visible? The new church must be a brotherhood of committed disciples, of true believers who walk with Christ—by this he would stand.

The conflict was increasing around Zurich. Manz was preaching in surrounding areas. Blaurock joined him in early April and together they held services in the forests, always on the move. Grebel's family responsibilities kept him at home considerably more in the past weeks. Jacob Hottinger, who knew where he was hiding, sold some of Grebel's library for him to help him financially. He told Michael that Grebel was anxious to be out preaching, but due to his health his wife wanted him to stay in. To force him to stay, she threatened to tell the authorities where they could find Manz if Conrad left. Michael suspected that Grebel's wife did not share his convictions. Relating this to Margareta, he expressed again his joy that they were one in faith as well as in love.

Early one morning Michael left Zollikon for a trip into the forest area to meet Manz and Blaurock. He had been told by a brother in the market where he might find them. As he walked briskly along, he breathed deeply of the cool morning air. It was good to be out of the city again, and his love of nature stirred within him a response to the awakened spring.

He passed neat little farms nestled close to the forest. He was now beyond the open fields, farmed by families living in the city, in the area where farms were a unit in themselves. The tinkle of cowbells floated down from the little meadows in the hills. The smell of fresh manure forked onto a pile before the barn rose with vapor into the crisp air. The house and barn stretched out together, connected under one long thatched roof. Passing one home, he smiled to himself at the change of aroma as he moved beyond the manure pile at one end of the building to smell fresh bread from the brick oven at the other. The morning was well past now. He was tempted to stop for rest, and perhaps a fresh biscuit, but thinking better of it if he was to reach his destination by noon, hurried on his way.

In the forest the path narrowed to a simple cart-track winding through the trees. It was several hours later that he heard the ring of a woodsman's ax in the forest. He hastened his step, knowing by the sound that he must be nearing the village. He came upon a beautiful little valley, with circles of houses sheltered from the outside world by a ring of hills. He noted that his destination was the house highest on the hill to the north. Having approached from the west, he moved down the left side of the street, nodded to the few persons about, and climbed the hill to the house.

He had scarcely knocked at the door when it opened and he was greeted by a pleasant-faced man who was a stranger to him.

"I'm Michael Sattler and have just come from Zollikon."

The man smiled broadly, "Welcome, brother, I'm Hans Ziegler. It seems I already know you from the comments your friends have made about you. Come in, they are expecting you."

Following his host Michael stepped into a second room. Felix Manz turned quickly as the door opened, and seeing Michael, stepped across the room and clasped his hand warmly. "You did get our message. Praise the Lord for His care; He brought you safely here."

George Blaurock's towering frame was just behind Manz. Extending his hand to clasp Michael's, he added, "Our answer to prayer. We needed you. We asked of God, and you've come." His voice was firm, assured, although he spoke with gentleness.

Michael's reply was immediate. "Brethren, it was I

115

who needed you. When I heard where you could be found, it seemed imperative that I come. I've had only secondhand contact with Grebel, and for weeks no direct word from you. Our movement must stay together and one of the greatest keys to unity is in understanding one another."

"Our thinking exactly," declared George. "We want the news from the brethren in Zollikon, but we want above all to increase our strength by enhancing the understanding within the group."

Felix added, "Michael, we don't know how long we can continue to preach and baptize. No matter what happens, this work must go on. George and I feel you are the man to shape the thinking of our group, a ministry that must be performed by the printed page in addition to public preaching. There is power in the printed word. This invention is too great to leave it for the devil's crowd."

All afternoon they talked, sharing ideas and plans. Michael was enthusiastic with their convictions and dedication. They prayed over their conversations and retired for the night. Michael, tired from the long trip, was soon asleep. But he awoke early, ready to leave for Zollikon. As he bade his brethren farewell, it was with a sense of foreboding. When and where would they meet again?

The trip back to Zollikon was uneventful, but his report to the brethren there added new encouragement. There was a new sense of destiny, a general attitude of repentance for the failures before Zwingli.

In mid-April the Zurich Council struck again. Grebel was arrested in Zurich. Manz and Blaurock were discovered and arrested in the forest east of the city. This was a well-planned attack on known leaders of the movement. They were imprisoned in the Witch Tower, with eleven other men and seven women.

Michael and Margareta feared for their friends, and met with other brethren in prayer for their safety. They rejoiced that this time they had not been apprehended. Through one of the guards it was learned that the prisoners sent requests to the Zurich Council for a public disputation, only to be flatly refused. Evidently, the council did not intend to open the issues to public discussion.

Near the end of the month the community was electrified by exciting news. The entire group had escaped! Zwingli was enraged. The council called the magistracy to account, but the prisoners were gone. Several from the Zollikon community shared the details with Michael. Now Grebel had gone to St. Gall, and Manz and Blaurock to Appenzell. Others had made plans to leave the canton of Zurich and journey to Strasbourg. There the political system was divided, and at least a temporary asylum was possible. To many of them Strasbourg was a city of hope.

Michael had now added writing to his ministry. It was a new satisfaction to put his beliefs in print which could be circulated. Convinced of the New Testament call to create a believers' church, he was urged by the inner witness of the Spirit to promote this in every way. Rarely did he preach at Zollikon, but traveled much in the surrounding cantons, ministering the Word. The movement was spreading like fire, fanning out into the lowlands, and hundreds were being baptized into the brotherhood. They would take the land yet!

Zwingli had finally discontinued the mass during Holy Week, 1525. With the growth of the Anabaptist movement he was even more vehement against them. "The Anabaptists," he said, "are a more dangerous threat than Rome." He went before the city council to advocate more strict handling of those who rebaptized.

With the spread of the movement and activity of the leaders, the group in Zollikon lost much of its original dynamic. It was evident that conversation with Zwingli had meant compromise for some of them. Elsewhere the movement was making a more striking impact. Since his escape, Grebel was having great success in evangelistic work in St. Gall and Appenzell. He preached with boldness and sincerity, and many responded in repentance and faith.

The very boldness of the program helped it catch fire among the populace. A public baptism of over five hundred at one time made quite a stir, and brought increased enthusiasm for the new movement! Grebel, encouraged by this success, sent glowing reports of his ministry to Michael. But the opposition was growing also in St. Gall. The leading reformer here was Vadian, Grebel's brother-in-law. Grebel sought to win him for the free church movement, but his loyalties remained with Zwingli. He warned Grebel that his views were heretical, and a menace to the state church. As a man of repute, a scholar, a physician, and a political leader, he had a reputation to defend!

In neighboring Appenzell the populace took to the Swiss Brethren emphasis, and responded enthusiastically. Zwinglian doctrine was preached there, but the Catholic practices had so far been continued. The people were ready for a change. They flocked to hear the Anabaptists speak of assurance of salvation and of freedom in Christ.

It was late May of 1525. At the close of a meeting in Aargau a stranger made his way through the group to Michael. "Brother Sattler, may I have a word with you?" Michael nodded and the two stepped to the edge of the group. The stricken look on the man's face revealed serious trouble.

"Is it ill news?"

"Ill indeed. I have just come from St. Gall. We have been struck a deadly blow. Bolt Eberli, one of our brethren, was arrested and executed with scarcely a trial—the first martyr for the cause! Although the canton of Schwyz is in Catholic territory, we fear the same severity in the Zwinglian areas!"

Michael was stunned. Although they had anticipated violence, the abruptness of this execution was staggering. This was a deliberate stroke to stop the free church, to crush the Anabaptists. From here on the struggle would increase, the gap widen. There could be no compromise— no halfway program. The people's church had by this act proclaimed itself the open enemy of the free church.

With an effort Michael's thoughts came back to the immediate problem. To the waiting brother he said, "The cup which the Father gives us, we must drink. Eberli's martyrdom will strengthen our cause. The human conscience stands with us and freedom. Take heart, my friend. As you spread this news, be sure to add that our mission goes on!"

To the small group standing in silence awaiting his final word, Michael related what had happened in St. Gall. "The free church will live or die depending on how

119

we face persecution." He called them to prayer for grace to face what must surely be ahead. Then the group slipped away silently, each with his own thoughts.

Michael responded to this blow by openly advocating a separation of the believers' church from the state church, from the state in general. This was a bold response to the martyrdom of Eberli. But in Michael's mind, for the state to execute a man for doing good was a violation of its God-given role. The state existed to protect the good and punish the evildoer. To use the sword to settle issues of faith was incredible. For the people's church to identify itself with the state in such a way was to demonstrate that it had indeed compromised the gospel, and its mission had sold its very birthright.

On his next mission Michael took Margareta along to the Aargau area. The tensions in Zollikon and Zürich made him fear to leave her. Working with Konrad Winkler, they reached into the lowlands with the gospel. In late June while in Zürich Winkler was arrested. The council tried him for his doctrine, with stern warnings against the Anabaptist activities. He was able to say in answer that he personally had not been baptizing. He was finally released, but with a fine for contradicting one of Zwingli's councillors.

Michael and Konrad were certain this arrest was warning of more to come. They would return to Zollikon for a brief stay with the group, but he and Margareta agreed that their time there was nearly over.

Grebel had left Zürich for a time, having gone to Waldshut to converse with Dr. Hubmaier. The congregations would soon need to function without the present leaders. Planning for their direction when he would be forced to leave, Michael spent many hours developing congregational guidelines for the churches. Under the shadow of persecution, his training as prior of St. Peter's was put to work in organizing congregations.

In Michael's evangelistic work, Jacob Zander of Bulach was converted. Instructing him in the faith of the brethren, Michael baptized him into the brotherhood. Zander was a man of high social position, and in spite of the danger of persecution for the baptism, he showed promise of becoming an effective leader. His assistance added much to Michael's work and gave Michael time for more study and writing. Zander, known as Schmid among the brethren, was soon known as an effective lay leader in the management of a congregation.

The rapid spread of the movement appeared to Michael as the evident blessing of the Holy Spirit. In spite of persecution he was sure the free church movement was on its way to success! The New Testament church was becoming visible again. "The church of Christ," he taught, "is a believers' fellowship, repentant and regenerated by the Spirit, a people committed to a life of discipleship and peace."

The movement had now achieved all the characteristics of a true church: preaching, baptism, the Lord's Supper, and a disciplined congregation. The brethren had reason for a growing confidence.

At Zollikon, the discouraged group caught enthusiasm from the rapid spread of the movement. But a number of them suddenly became overly zealous. They were going to win Zurich in spite of the former persecutions. They would redeem their own reputation and correct the compromise with Zwingli! A few of them began calling for a renewal of the prophetic gifts of the Spirit. They made up a procession of men, women, and children, dressed in skins for garments with willow belts. They attempted a John the Baptist role. Entering Zurich, they started running through the streets, calling for repentance. They denounced Zwingli as the dragon of John's prophecy in Revelation. Some of them, like Jonah, cried out, "Woe, woe, woe to Zurich. Zurich has only forty days to repent." Others were crying, "If you repent not, a dreadful calamity will befall the city."

This boldness of the Zollikon farmers startled some and aroused intense feeling against the brethren. Michael was greatly disturbed. Such behavior only added to the accusation that the Anabaptists were fanatics. Such behavior could not be reconciled with the spirit of Christ. The brethren needed his guidance, as Grebel expressed it, "to give structure to their faith." If this group was to become a strong church and communicate a clear witness of true faith, it would need to have both purity and order.

The blow fell with startling severity in response to the Zollikon fiasco. The Zurich Council had deliberated several weeks about where and how to move first. When the move came, it was aimed at the head of the movement. Felix Manz was arrested and imprisoned on July 18, and put in the Wellenberg Prison. The council in Zurich meant to use stern measures of suppression!

Weeks followed with no sign of release for Manz. Tension mounted and the Sattlers found it necessary to be very secretive on any trip to Zurich. A strained silence regarding the Anabaptists seemed to blanket Zurich. Grebel returned from St. Gall and was hiding in the city. A foot ailment limited his ability to travel, and his family and friends had a covenant of secrecy on his whereabouts.

While Michael was increasingly concerned for Margareta's safety, her courage was unshaken. He never doubted her willingness to risk all in following the Spirit's leading. Yet he felt that being on the move so much was unfair to her. He must open the subject in one of their times together, and, that evening, when they sat alone with their thoughts and their love, Michael asked, "Margareta, why couldn't we return to Schaffhausen and find lodging for a while? I could work from there and you would be among friends when I'm absent."

"I don't mind traveling with you, dear," she replied, "but there is little security here. We ought to have a place we can call home for ourselves and—" she paused and the color in her cheeks heightened as she added, "a family if God so wills."

"That would be wonderful." His arm tightened around her waist in response. "Perhaps God sees that we are hardly free to raise a family in times like these." He smiled contentedly, "But we can plan and pray." And as on other evenings, the world was closed out, and two persons found in each other the fulfillment of a love bordered only by eternity.

They journeyed to Schaffhausen and found a dwelling at a modest rate through the kindness of the Meyers'. From this center Michael could have a continuing influence in the canton of Zurich and also be involved in new areas to the north of their home, areas of South Germany with which he was quite familiar. A new frontier lay open before them, a frontier of people, of minds, of souls to be enlisted in the kingdom.

Chapter XIV

Michael and Margareta stood watching the flail in the
hands of the farmer, as he beat out the grain. It was
threshing time, and across the fields were shocks of grain,
sheaves tied with strands twisted about their waist like a
belt. Here and there piles of straw gave evidence that
threshing had begun. Much threshing was done by driving
cattle round and round in the straw while it was turned
by farmhands. But the common method by small farmers
was the flail being used before them.

They watched in silence, caught up by the rhythm in
the farmer's swing, the flail striking the grain with a
thud as it swung in a circle from the leather thong on
the end of the bar in his hands. His wife deftly forked
straw away and added more while he adjusted his blow
to another spot—never missing a beat. After some time
he stopped, wiped the sweat from his face, and spoke
to the Sattlers.

"You swing that flail like an expert," Michael remarked.

"I ought to, my friend; I've been at it all my life.
Between my wife and me we can put out as much grain
in a day as the next couple," at which compliment she

smiled appreciatively.

"I'm Michael Sattler, lately of Zürich. I'll be at the inn of Herr Meyers tonight for Bible study. You folks are more than welcome."

"We may be there, Herr Sattler; we've heard of your class and would at least like to know more before we judge you."

Michael nodded his head in approval of the answer, and with the mutual exchange of "*Auf Wiedersehen*," he and Margareta were on their way.

So it was in August of 1525, a wonderful month for the Sattlers. Six months ago they had joined the Swiss Brethren movement. Those had been six months of happiness and spiritual blessing. Both knew a deep peace of mind and soul amidst the persecution which threatened them. The past weeks in Schaffhausen, a bit removed from Zürich, had been a real respite.

Margareta was especially buoyant, pleased to be back with Frau Meyers, and radiant in her love for Michael. They had time here for evening walks together, time to converse and plan concerning the future. The Rheinfalls again became their tryst; the cascading waters were something of a symbol of the ongoing of God's purpose in which they shared. Even with the awareness that Providence might not have in store for them all that their hearts craved, they knew they were a part of something momentous.

Michael spent much time with his books and pen during the day. But there was a restlessness about him that Margareta knew was caused by his concern for Felix in prison. Slipping up behind him, she placed her hands on his shoulders. "My husband, leave it to the Lord.

125

We serve only where and as He wills."

She had read his thoughts.

"If only they'd release him. I feel I must do twice as much with the loss of his service."

Early in September Michael received a communication from Grebel. He had left Zurich and gone to St. Gall again. But now he was back in the Gruningen area of the canton of Zurich. Here the peasants had earlier revolted against the magistrates. They were complaining over the reticence of Zwingli's movement to provide opportunities for the common man. This unrest opened the door for a new emphasis, and Grebel was utilizing it. His letter was asking Michael to come and help shape these new converts into strong congregations.

Michael well knew the danger of working in the canton of Zurich, yet this appeal could not be ignored. He presented it to Margareta without hiding the implications.

"Oh, Michael, so soon—we've enjoyed our new freedom only a few weeks. Must you? And the danger—"

"We're committed, my dearest; we can't ignore this. Let's pray about it, and if the Spirit witnesses that this is His will, I can do nothing else but go."

They prayed together and discussed it again the following morning. Actually, there was little to discuss. Both sensed that he would go. Margareta was reserved about her fears, but Michael sensed her deep concern. She clung to him an extra moment as they kissed good-bye. There was a sense of foreboding resting on each as he left.

Michael found Grebel in Gruningen, a town with a population of a little over two thousand. The people of this area were a hearty lot, peasant folk interested in a religion they could experience. Grebel was having good success. The government here was "by the people" in contrast to the Zurich pattern. The spread of the free church concept was becoming a movement of the people!

Grebel was lodging with a family who had recently accepted believer's baptism. He invited Michael to share the one little guest room with him that first night, and related the success of his past weeks of preaching. Over two hundred had been baptized into the fellowship.

"Our next task, Michael, is to lead these people in the study of the New Testament. If the Scripture is to actually function as authority, it must be taught and understood by the people. The only security for our movement is in developing deep convictions."

Michael nodded his assent, and Grebel continued. "This is where you are needed in the program here. You'll meet Jacob Gross. He will assist you in meeting the groups in the forests and teaching the Word. I shall continue meeting community leaders and seeking to win them for the cause. Their guilt over Eberli's execution and the reaction of the populace causes them to listen, even though sullenly."

Michael set about outlining a strategy for church life, following Grebel's advice.

"Conrad, the best thing for us at this point is to structure our pattern for congregational life and faith in a very simple manner. One of the important things is to arrange for leaders in each congregation, perhaps a brotherhood council. And we must prepare our congregations to replace any leader that may be arrested. This could be by an immediate vote for a new leader. The work must go on. We cannot afford to have a failure because a group is without a pastor."

Grebel agreed with this. "We must build congregational spirit, and a loyalty that will last through the persecution that has begun in this area."

During the next weeks the task was not easy, but it was rewarding. All over the area new fellowships were formed. Sattler's work was a marked success.

In early October who should come to the canton of Zurich but George Blaurock! He began ardently assisting Grebel in evangelistic work, with noted success in Hinwil and Baretswil. His presence and aggressiveness added new impetus to the work. In public presentation he was a fluent and dynamic speaker. Large crowds gathered to hear him preach and enthusiasm for the movement was high.

But the real test was the free church issue; the chief difference of the Swiss Brethren teaching from that of the state church. Their emphasis on separation of the Christian from the magistracy caused question and then tension among the people. Two brethren, Jacob Gross and Ulrich Teck, were arrested for refusing to bear arms. They were tried in an open court, fined by the magistrates, and released with a warning not to propagate their doctrines. The brotherhood was now being closely watched by the authorities. In response Michael, with Grebel and Blaurock, preached much against violence. Each of them instructed the converts in the way of love, lest they be misinterpreted as political revolutionaries. But the local magistrate, Berger, was loyal to Zwingli and suspicious of their program. He was in direct contact with the Zurich officials and rumors were afloat that a more intense persecution was imminent.

Michael and Conrad went together to Hinwil for services early in October. It was a beautiful fall day and they took the path through the forest. Their feet scarcely made a sound on the carpeted earth. Conversation flowed freely concerning their work in Grüningen. Grebel was relating his conversations with the local pastor, Hans Brennwald.

"After we had discussed justification by faith as a personal trust in Christ, I asked him finally if he didn't see that the Scriptures meant baptism to be administered only when children come to reason."

He replied, "My lords have issued a writing on the question of baptism, and I intend to be obedient to my lords."

Michael shook his head, "Conrad, that is the same problem wherever we go—the choice between the authority of Scripture and the authority of tradition and the state church. The only hope is a free church, a brotherhood of believers, persons who will follow Christ in newness of life."

Grebel struck his fist into the open palm of his other hand—"And this is what they say must never happen! They mean to prevent the church from ever being free from the state. But they will see—Jesus said, 'My kingdom is not of this world: if my kingdom were of this world, then would my servants fight.' "

Arriving at Hinwil, they met George Blaurock whose greeting was warm and enthusiastic. "Brethren, the door is open in Hinwil to the gospel. I expect to preach in the village church this Sunday morning. Perhaps we can win a whole church at once!"

Grebel smiled, "If I recall, you tried this a few months

ago in Zollikon with little success."

"Yes," replied Blaurock. "I was too hasty. But you know what happened since when Schad spoke in the Zollikon church. It could happen here!"

"But, George," Grebel cautioned, "the freedom we seek for the church of Christ is more than organizational; it is spiritual. Jesus said, 'The kingdom . . . cometh not with observation,' that is, it doesn't move in by force."

Blaurock nodded, "True enough, I seek nothing other than conversions wrought by the Spirit."

They retired for the night, agreeing to spread the news in the morning that they would hold a public meeting in the open field east of town Sunday afternoon. This pleased Blaurock, for he was sure that if he could speak to the Hinwil congregation in the morning, the cause would get attention and draw a larger attendance in the afternoon.

Saturday was spent meeting with the brethren, encouraging them in the faith and calling them together for an evening service. They met others whom they encouraged to repent and testify to faith in Christ by baptism. In the evening the group gathered in a village home for fellowship. Following a message from Grebel, Michael discussed the Lord's Supper and the witness-character of Christian ordinances. Their sharing the bread and wine was a testimony of experienced grace, not a sacrament to mediate grace. The believers then joined in the breaking of bread and in the cup as testimony to their faith. The emblems of Christ's death were passed to each in turn for all to share—a brotherhood of the redeemed.

The group was about to separate when there was a knock on the front door. The host opened it a crack to peer out, then threw it wide open with a shout of amazement. Felix Manz stepped across the threshold and into the circle! A fervent "Praise the Lord" was heard around the room. Grebel and Manz stood for a few moments with their heads on each other's shoulders.

Felix stepped aside and looked over the group with a smile. He was pale from long imprisonment, but the three months in a cell had not daunted his spirit. As he began to speak, the group was awed by his strength of spirit.

"I was released this morning with a stern warning not to rebaptize anymore. The council has reaffirmed its mandate that any person doing so will be exiled. I left Zurich immediately, hoping to find you here."

He paused briefly, then added, "I have planned to move on east into St. Gall or Appenzell for a time. Brethren, the opposition increases, but the Spirit of God calls us to work on."

His deep conviction spoke to each believer present. It was a call for their best in loyalty and service. For the present, Manz would be an added attraction in their meetings here.

Sunday morning dawned bright and clear and people from all over the village streamed to the church. Blaurock was there early. Immediately before the appointed hour for the service to begin he mounted the pulpit and began to preach. His strong voice claimed the attention of the entire congregation, and his eloquent delivery held their interest. He spoke with conviction on trust in Christ for salvation by faith alone. He followed this by emphasizing the privilege of every believer to be a priest, to have direct access to God.

The pastor arrived to find Blaurock preaching, and noting

the interest did not interfere until George began to speak about baptism. At this point he interrupted. "You are violating the mandate of the Zurich Council," he shouted.

At once the entire congregation stood up, some arguing against the pastor for interrupting and others heckling Blaurock. The pastor ran to find the chief magistrate and Blaurock continued to speak as best he could. He had just told the people of the meeting to be held in the field that afternoon when the bailiff arrived to arrest him. Now the mood was with the brethren, and the bailiff backed off, shaking his fist—"There will be another time," he called. "I'm not through with you!"

Lunch was practically forgotten that eighth day of October. Soon after the morning service the whole town was alerted to the arrival of Magistrate Berger from Grüningen. Hearing of a proposed meeting in Hinwil, he had come to arrest the leaders. Berger stationed his forces between the village and the open field and sought to dissuade the people from gathering. This was too much. The peasant spirit surged to the fore, and the crowd declared itself on the side of the brethren. They streamed onto the field from every direction. Berger's attempts to stop the meeting were frustrated for the moment.

Michael, Grebel, Manz, and Blaurock entered the field from the forest side. Blaurock began to sing as he walked, and the people caught it up, astonishing the bailiff who was now helpless before the crowd. Between the songs, Blaurock's strong voice rang out, calling the people to gather round. The crowd surrounded the leaders in a tight circle. Grebel next took the lead, and after a pointed introduction, called on Manz to speak.

The testimony of Manz caught fire in the crowd. After

his words Michael spoke on God's call to a new life in Christ. He emphasized a death experience to the old self, and a regeneration in the Spirit. He denounced both sacramentalism and works-righteousness, speaking of baptism as a symbol. Suddenly there was a disturbance at the edge of the crowd. Berger had secured a horse and was forcing his way through. As the people fell back, step by step he advanced on the circle of leaders. Michael was penned in by the press of the people. Manz, quick-witted and smaller than the others, was making his way through the crowd to escape into the forest.

A group of officers followed Berger's drive through the crowd, and Michael watched helplessly as they seized Grebel and Blaurock. Suddenly rough hands grasped him by the coat and jerked him roughly after them. Amidst the jeers of the crowd, Berger bound the men and led them out of Hinwil. For some distance a large crowd followed, voicing their support of the brethren. Berger marched them before the soldiers all the way to Grüningen and jailed them in the castle. "And now," he said, "I'll tell Zwingli his bastards are in chains. This new movement has too many children."

Arrests continued the next several weeks until over a hundred were imprisoned in the castle. With these arrests a spirit of antagonism developed among the peasants against Zurich. This was increased by the fact that freedom was short-lived for Manz as well. On the last day of October he was arrested in a forest meeting in Appenzell. They marched him through the area as they brought him to Grüningen to join the others in prison.

Berger was feeling quite successful. He had now imprisoned the major leaders of the brethren along with a large number of their followers! The Zurich Council commended him highly and ordered the leading prisoners sent to Zurich for trial. But now Berger was on the spot. The public spirit in Grüningen was such that he couldn't comply with the order. He well knew that such an act would only antagonize the populace the more. They were calling for a public disputation on the issues that caused such intolerance from the council.

Inside the castle the prisoners encouraged each other in their suffering. Their buoyant faith, the prayers, and the discussion of Scripture kept their spirits up. Michael and Blaurock composed simple songs which the group sang to familiar tunes, echoing through the halls of the old castle. The courage of the brethren increased the respect of the magistracy, and responding to public opinion the local authorities refused to bow to the Zurich Council. The prisoners now gained hope and boldly stated their desire for a public disputation with Zwingli.

With the growing pressure of public sentiment, the magistracy began petitioning Zurich: "We feel constrained to ask that you give the Anabaptists a public debate. You must get Zwingli to let the men of the opposing party have their say in the debate, and refrain from interrupting or stopping them, so that this issue can be finally answered."

The Zurich Council was now required to answer. In early November the word came that the privilege of debate was granted. Michael and Grebel were thrilled by this news! They were sure their position could be presented convincingly if they had opportunity. This was an answer to their prayers.

On November 6 the Anabaptist leaders were led into

the city hall of Zurich to be faced by appointed judges in an open debate. At the judges' table sat Zwingli, Joner of Cappel, Vadian (Grebel's brother-in-law), and an earlier acquaintance of both Michael and Grebel, Dr. Hofmeister of Schaffhausen. The debate opened with the room packed and several hundred people outside the hall trying to get in to hear the proceedings. Nearly a thousand men were in attendance, and the city hall was far too small to accommodate them. The council decided that for the sake of better order they would move the sessions the next day to the largest church of Zürich, the Great Minster. The Anabaptist leaders were back at home base; they had started from here, and now they were here on trial!

They had been moved from Gruningen to Zürich and were imprisoned in the Witch Tower. Each day the Anabaptists were brought for the public sessions. For three days, from November 6 to 8, Grebel, Manz, and Blaurock, the leaders best known in Zürich, defended the position of the brethren against Zwingli and his associates. Michael and other of the prisoners sat back of the three leaders, conversing with them on occasion and watching for opportunity to share in the debate. The open discussion was carried on largely by Grebel and Manz. Less than a year earlier these men had been Zwingli's associates.

Zwingli opened the discussion with a defense of infant baptism. "Children born in Christian homes," he said, "should be baptized into the people of God. This is clearly taught in the Old Testament practice of circumcision. Here God inaugurated a practice identifying infants as His own."

The brethren answered, "God claims infants as His

135

own, but through the work of Christ rather than circumcision, which is an Old Testament practice, necessary in identifying a people as a nation. We are dealing with salvation by faith in the New Testament. Baptism is a sign of prior faith, of believing on Christ, that one has converted." The discussion shifted. Zwingli became more critical in his approach.

"Two years ago," he said, "Grebel, Manz, and Stumpf urged radical reforms in the church. Now Martin of Berne tells me the Anabaptists in Zurich believe there should be no magistracy, that all things should be held in common, and that there is a security of the saints! And Brennwald heard Blaurock tell an Anabaptist in Zollikon already last February that when they are strong enough they should resist the magistracy. From all this," he said looking carefully around the room, "nothing can be inferred but that they have as their final goal to increase their number until they can free themselves from the authorities." Heads nodded in agreement and a murmur ran through the audience.

Hofmeister and Brennwald in turn each supported Zwingli's charges.

The Anabaptists looked at each other in disbelief. Zwingli was turning the debate from the real doctrinal and ecclesiastical issues to imply a social revolution! Manz rose to his feet and asked for the floor. "My lords, we are not involved in political revolution but in spiritual reform! In regard to your charge that we are calling for a separate church, that we deny the magistracy, we hold that those who desire to accept Christ and to be obedient to His Word and to follow His example should seek to unite themselves by the sign of baptism as citizens

136

of Christ's kingdom, and should let others answer to their own faith. As to community of goods, we mean that a good Christian should share with his neighbor when he is in need. We do hold that no Christian should be a magistrate, nor use the sword to punish or to kill anyone, for we have Scripture for this position—the sword belongs to earthly kingdoms."

Michael thrilled at his answer and uttered a bold "amen," as did other of the brethren. They were silenced by the bailiff, who ordered that only those should speak who were recognized by the bench.

Grebel spoke next, calling attention to their earlier discussions on conversion. He spoke to the charge on baptism: "From the teaching of Christ, who said we must be born again to be saved, anything which gives a false hope, such as infant baptism, is of the devil, and re-baptism is right. In fact, we are not rebaptizers, for the baptism of infants is no baptism. You are the ones guilty of false teaching, for Master Zwingli, you once said the same as we teach." Zwingli blushed nervously as Grebel continued, "Further, we have never taught that one should give away his own wealth for nothing. As regards the church, whoever is covetous, a gambler, or a usurer, or guilty of vice, should according to the Scripture in no case be considered among the Christians but be excommunicated by the ban."

Again the brethren echoed their "amen," and similar whispers were heard in the hall. But it was clear from attitudes at the bench that their arguments were not respected. The case had been determined before the trial!

On the final day Grebel refuted the charge that he had spoken to Martin of Berne against authorities, and the charge that the brethren held things in common. Dr. Hofmeister charged the brethren with wanting to abolish the state. To this Grebel replied, "Our desire to see a voluntary church within the state and our rejection of the magistracy as a vocation for the Christian does not mean that we reject the role of the state in its order. I have never said, as Dr. Hofmeister charges, that the state should be abolished."

Vadian raised his hand toward Grebel to ask, "Why, if baptism is a sign, must you make so much of this?"

Grebel replied, "Baptism belongs to those believers who devote themselves to the Son of God and separate themselves from evil. The believers who bear the fruit of the Spirit, which is love, joy, peace, goodwill, trust, meekness, humility, patience, righteousness, truth, and those who walk therein, they are the church of Christ and the body of Christ, and the Christian church. And now you want to force us out of the truly Christian church into a foreign church!"

The last session closed and there was no evidence of understanding nor of closer harmony. There was no sign of mercy on the part of Zwingli or the Zurich Council. The brethren were all taken back to the tower and imprisoned. For ten long days the prisoners awaited some word. Finally a delegation was sent by the magistracy to the tower and the bailiff read their sentence: "Because of their Anabaptism and their unbecoming conduct, Grebel, Manz, and Blaurock will lie in the tower on a diet of bread and water, and none shall visit them but guards, as long as God shall please and as it seems good to my lords.

"Others, from outside the canton of Zürich, shall be

banished from this time and forever."

Michael gripped the hands of Conrad, of Felix, and of George in turn. "Good-bye, my brethren, and God keep you. By His grace we'll carry on."

Bidding farewell to Manz and Blaurock, he turned and joined Ulrich Teck and Martin Lingg, with whom he was being banished from Zurich. As the three were led to the edge of the city, the bailiff read the orders, standing in the gate with a stern word, "Go, you heretics, and don't come back. Just be thankful you are alive."

As the three men started down the dusty road, Michael heard the echo of Grebel's words: "Those who bear the fruit of the Spirit, they are the church of Christ, the body of Christ, and the Christian church."

Though this might be a martyr road, Michael Sattler was convinced even more deeply of the call to discipleship. He had found the way of the Spirit to be the satisfying one, even while it was a way of suffering. At the moment his heart was warmed now with the joy of his release— he could go home, back to Margareta. And that was home, even though it meant being "pilgrims in an alien land." The words came to him from the Scriptures, "pilgrims" . . . "strangers in this world" . . . "citizens of another kingdom."

Chapter XV

The long weary trek from Zurich was nearly over. Michael trudged down the road and entered the little village of Schaffhausen. It was late November 1525. He had passed another milestone on his road of life. Behind him lay bridges that had been burned. He had left the monastery and married a wife. He had gone to Switzerland, had met the Anabaptists, and had joined their movement by being rebaptized. For nearly eight months he had given himself to the preaching of the Word and to the building of churches. During that time he had seen the church spread through the canton of Zurich and the surrounding cantons. Twice he had been arrested and imprisoned. Now he was banished from Zurich and told never to return.

Left behind in Zurich were close friends; friends who had shaped his life and contributed to this faith; friends who had strengthened him in his understanding of discipleship and had called him to help build a believers' church. What lay ahead for Manz, Grebel, and Blaurock in the tower prison was anyone's guess. At best they were sentenced to lie in prison until the lords of Zurich should be pleased to release them. Persecution of Anabaptists in other areas was warning enough. The death of the first martyr in St. Gall stood before them as a haunting specter, a reminder that it could happen to any of them.

Now Michael accelerated his step. He was in the familiar streets of Schaffhausen, and nearing home his heart quickened with the anticipation. It seemed so long since he had been with Margareta. There had been days when loneliness had weighed upon his spirit like fog settling upon the hills of the Black Forest. At other times he had hungered to be with her as only a husband can long to be with his wife. And now the separation was almost over, five long weeks that seemed like years.

He had scarcely lifted his hand to knock when Margareta released the door and flung herself into his arms. "Michael, you're free—you're free!" She was almost hysterical with joy and relief. The long days and nights of sleeplessness had taken their toll. Margareta had fought a real battle between faith and despair that he would ever come home. Holding her close, he whispered, "Yes, my love, I'm free. Free to come home—to you!"

It was some time before either said much. Words were unimportant as he held her in his arms. Michael was alarmed by the evident change in her appearance, but said nothing about it. Deep circles shadowed her eyes and she was noticeably thinner. She clung to him desperately, and tried to control her weeping.

"Michael, I love you so—and when I heard that you had been captured, I wasn't brave at all. Frau Meyers can tell you—but she said she won't. I don't want us to die. I want us together until we're old. I want you for years and years and years—" She broke off and began crying again.

"Yes, my dearest—I want that, too, more than you know. But only as God wills it."

Margareta's chin lifted almost defiantly. She started to say something further, then paused a moment, taking a deep shuddering breath. "Tell me all about it—all about—everything. What did they do to you?"

Michael began to reconstruct the events of the past weeks carefully. He told of his trip back to Zurich and on into Grüningen. He told of meeting with Grebel, of the spread of the gospel in that area, and of his part in organizing the churches. His eyes shone as he related the events that led up to the morning of October 8 when George Blaurock took over the pulpit in Hinwil, and of the afternoon meeting when the crowd listening to the gospel was interrupted by Magistrate Berger. He told of their arrest, and of being led back to the Grüningen castle for imprisonment. He tried not to describe too vividly the trying days in the castle prison while they waited for the disputation to be agreed upon in Zurich. He followed with the imprisonment in the tower and the three-day meeting when they debated with Zwingli and his authorities in public.

Margareta's vivid imagination filled in the rest. She could almost feel the tension of the surging crowds that thronged the city hall and packed the Great Minster for the trial, could almost hear the accusations and the defense of the men on trial. Her anger mounted at the total injustice of the authorities, deliberately sidestepping the central issues when they were obviously cornered and accusing the men instead of political revolution.

". . . back to the prison for ten more days until sentence

was pronounced." Michael's voice continued. Margareta had been mentally sitting in the packed courtroom, glaring at Zwingli and the false accusers. She tried to concentrate on what he was saying.

"Those were not wasted days. We had a ten-day Bible session, examining our views with the Word and discussing our course from here on. The free church still moves on, Margareta. The cause will triumph."

"What was the verdict, Michael? Were they all released?"

"No, the sentence was more severe than we had expected. Grebel, Manz, and Blaurock remain in prison, in the council's words, 'as long as the lords should feel it pleased God, in their understanding, to keep them there.'"

Margareta gasped. "Michael, that could be for life." Her anger flared again. She had always resented injustice, whatever its form. This was incredible.

"The lords of the Zurich Council! What do they know of 'pleasing God'? Indeed—a pious-sounding verdict! It's nothing but their own blind prejudice."

Michael was confronted with a new facet of his wife's personality. Coming to light in adversity, Margareta's impassioned reaction to what she had heard of the Zurich Council's perversion of justice revealed a spirit scarcely hinted at before. Her weariness had vanished and color flamed in her cheeks. She had never looked more lovely.

"Michael, what does this mean for you—and for me?"

"More than ever, the work rests on us. We must shoulder more responsibility now."

"But must we go to Zurich to carry on?"

"No. We are banished from the city, never to return. That's an order from the council. To disobey it will

143

mean arrest, life imprisonment, or possible death. I'm through in Zurich, Margareta. There's no point in a risk there. We'll work in South Germany, perhaps Staufen!"

"No, Michael. All is not well in Staufen. The government has announced that it will follow the mandate of Rome to suppress the Reformation at any cost. And this opposition is even more severe than the tension in Zürich. Oh, why can't that stubborn Zwingli see? We ought to stand together against Rome."

This new development meant that Michael and Margareta were in grave danger on two fronts. The renegade prior of St. Peter's was a marked man. In defiance of the Roman system he had married the Beguine Margareta. Michael knew they were in danger of arrest, for this apart from their having joined the hated Anabaptists. They might go to Staufen—but for how long?

But now they were together again, and both were aware of the thrill at being in each other's presence. Margareta set the table with special care for their evening dinner. Lighting the candle she had kept for just such an occasion, she placed it in the center of the table. Michael reached across and clasped her hands as they bowed their heads for prayer:

> "Blessed Lord Jesus, we thank Thee for this hour, for each other and the love You have quickened between us, and for now bringing us together again. Bless those of our brethren who suffer, even now, and grant each of us grace from Thy Spirit for these days. Amen."

Dinner was over, and the shadows of night closed them in from the outside world. Margareta took the candle and led the way as they retired for the night. From outside came the cry of the night bird in the wood. In the privacy of their cottage they were alone with each other again and their love. Michael drew her to himself, the fire in her body matching his own. Much later, her regular breathing telling him she was sleeping, he thanked God for the wonder and purity of marriage in love.

They chose mid-December to visit Staufen while the city was caught up in its holiday gaiety. Renewing former acquaintances, they soon formed an active fellowship. They were fully aware that it could not be long until the Roman authorities would find them. Michael worked with groups in the hinterlands he referred to as forest-churches, strengthening them over against the day of his departure.

The city of Strasbourg in Alsace, halfway between Luther's Wittenberg and Zwingli's Zürich, had a measure of neutrality with some tolerance of Anabaptists. Many Swiss Brethren had found asylum there. The leaders of the Reformation in Strasbourg, Bucer and Capito, had been calling for more tolerance between the groups including those who rebaptized. The city became known among the Anabaptists as the city of hope.

Many of the brethren were going to Strasbourg for more freedom and protection. Martin Bucer appeared to be a mediating voice and had spoken of baptism as an external thing not bound to any particular age in life. One man quoted him as saying, "There are two baptisms, the inner and the outer, of which only the inner is of decisive importance. One should not overstress the time of baptism."

Michael recognized that with this position it was possible for Bucer to stand between the reformers and the Anabaptists. The reformers were insisting upon infant baptism in the building of their people's church, and the

Anabaptists insisted upon adult baptism in the building of a believers' church. Perhaps Strasbourg was the place for a development of the free church program!

By the end of January Michael's and Margareta's stay was over in South Germany. The area was being searched for any Protestants by the authorities of Ensisheim. The persecution was directed against any and all non-Catholics. The Holy Roman Empire, seated in Austria, was intense in search and very severe in its persecution. Eberhard Hofmann, the clerk of the city of Ensisheim, was venomously hostile when he discovered that the hated Anabaptists were to be found in his area. Knowing that persecution endangered their lives, the believers urged Michael and Margareta to flee. They would travel north, down the Rhine to Strasbourg. There in a more neutral surrounding, they hoped to find the kind of peace where he could write and preach of the true kingdom of Jesus Christ.

The last few weeks of their time in South Germany Michael used to meet with leaders of the groups in the Black Forest. There were many in this area who responded to his preaching of the Word. Some asked for baptism before his leaving, and he organized them into small congregations. With the increase of persecution some, especially in the Swiss cantons, were giving more consideration to the state church program. He wrote a brief but sharp tract entitled, "Concerning Evil Overseers," as a warning against unconverted priests, including those who had joined the Protestant cause and could adjust to the powers of the state with little conscience. This tract was printed and circulated among the brethren:

Grace and peace from God our Father and our Lord Jesus Christ. Among so many tribulations, dearest brethren and

146

sisters in the Lord, which arise in our times is also this, as it appears to us, that so many overseers have become hindseers, proclaiming that without being called they have arrived at an achieved service, running without the command of the Lord. Meanwhile the tribulation against the truth rises daily, and the Lord, as man sees it, delays His coming. . . .

They say that one may without harm hear the papish sermons, since they demand it, and in order not to offend anyone. Nevertheless, in Matthew 24 Christ earnestly commands us to flee from such desolation and abomination, and in no sense to turn back to them, but with true warning to meditate on Lot's wife (Luke 21). And Paul speaks with clear words in II Corinthians 6: "Be ye not unequally yoked together with unbelievers, for what fellowship hath piety with impiety," etc. I will forbear to mention how John, together with the prophets, so earnestly commands us to withdraw from such a Babylon that we may not be partakers of her plagues (Apocalypse 18; Isaiah 52; and Jeremiah 51).

They also teach, against themselves and against the truth, that infant baptism is an indifferent matter and that one can baptize infants without detriment to the truth. It is certain that such, in league with the Lutherans, hope to escape the cross in the future—just as if infant baptism were not flatly contradictory to the baptism of Christ (Matthew 17) but belongs to the antichrist or hireling (John 10). I will not mention that the commandments of men are many times condemned (Matthew 15; Colossians 2; Titus 1; II Corinthians 6; Galatians 5). But is this not as Peter says, according to the proverb that the dog has again devoured his vomit (II Peter 2)? God however will root out and cut off such (people) since they have erred with such wantonness in the house and temple of God.

In the fear of the Lord,

Michael Sattler

Chapter XVI

Late in February Michael bade farewell to the little congregations at various forest gatherings where he had ministered the Word. He and Margareta would make their way north, visiting Freiburg and Lahr, and then on to Strasbourg. He expected to do some more writing and to have it printed and distributed across the country. Called of God to use his talent and scholarship in writing, he planned to outline a Confession of Faith for the church in addition to his suggested polity and help the churches to stand firm even under the fires of persecution.

Knowing that the blow would fall first upon the leaders, Michael explained to each of these congregations what it would mean for them to operate as a brotherhood of believers without an official leader. He outlined a plan for lay brethren to serve as spiritual advisers. He spoke frequently on the great Protestant theme, "The Priesthood of All Believers."

"Every person has the privilege of coming to God through Christ with his own prayers, of baring his own soul to God. In turn each Christian serves as a priest to his brother and to his neighbor."

The Sattlers arrived in Freiburg during the bitter cold of the dying winter. For several weeks they met small groups of Anabaptists in the city, teaching the Word and encouraging them. By late spring they turned north, traveling down the Rhine. Crossing to the west side, they followed the canal into the city of Strasbourg.

The spire of the Gothic cathedral jutted above the horizon and beckoned them on for the last weary miles. Margareta was especially tired from the hard journey and the long months in hiding. Having heard that Wolfgang Capito was a friendly and gracious reformer, they asked for directions to his home. It was situated just a few doors from the cathedral. Standing on the narrow street, they paused to admire the beautiful Gothic architecture, the tower soaring more than 460 feet toward heaven. Approaching the great doors, they stood silent, studying the sermon in pictures of the youth of Christ, the Seven Cardinal Virtues and the Seven Christian Virtues. Michael's hand closed tenderly on Margareta's shoulder, and as they moved away, he said, "It's wonderful to experience what those pictures express, isn't it?"

She smiled through her weariness. "Indeed it is, Michael, to know His love enriches ours."

Arriving at the Capito home, they were met by Wolfgang himself. He opened the door and appraised them a moment in silence. Then a smile began at the corners of his eyes and spread slowly across his face. "Travelers, if I can discern aright, and weary ones too. Who, may I ask, and from whence?"

"I'm Michael Sattler, Herr Capito, and this is my wife, lately from Staufen, south of Freiburg. We'd like some counsel as to a good lodging in your fair city."

Capito squinted his eyes a bit and scrutinized them more closely. "You are Michael Sattler, the man who was expelled from Zurich."

Michael nodded, "How did you know of that?"

"News has a way of spreading, and Master Zwingli let us know what we might expect of the former prior of St. Peter's. But come in, we shouldn't talk with you standing out here, and I do want to talk." He chuckled a bit and added, "and Martin Bucer will be as anxious to meet you as I am."

Michael and Margareta looked at each other in a moment of mutual surprise that their reputation had preceded them to Strasbourg. They followed Herr Capito's gesture and stepped into a spacious living room.

Frau Capito came bustling in from the kitchen and welcomed the Sattlers with unusual cordiality, inviting them to spend the night. She radiated friendliness and concerned hospitality. Following the evening meal, they were soon engaged in discussing the Reformation. Capito shared Michael's views in many areas. They were agreed on the necessity of personal faith in Christ for salvation. "I have on numerous occasions given expression to my uncertainty about the validity of infant baptism, Michael. There seems to be a contradiction between this rite prior to one's faith and our belief that saving faith means personal trust in the grace of Christ."

Capito told them they need look no further in Strasbourg for a lodging; he would be very happy to share a part of his home with them. They soon discovered in his gracious hospitality why Capito's home was called, "The House of Peace." His wife, a friendly lady, soon had Margareta involved as though she were a daughter.

Capito and Michael engaged in dialogue to resolve their differences. Both had achieved a degree of scholarship and insight into the Scripture. They spent many hours discussing the Word, finding many areas in which they were in agreement, areas of mutual concern for the life of the church.

"Michael," Capito said, "the ideal would be to have a church of converted persons who trust personally in Jesus Christ for salvation by faith. . . . But how can this be done at the present time?"

Michael replied, "By emphasizing personal responsibility, individual decision, voluntary response in a free church."

"But we need the magistrates to carry the Reformation on."

Michael shook his head negatively. "Then you have an ecclesiastical structure, attempting to force faith upon persons by the power of the state."

"But," said Capito, "if each would adopt a creed satisfactory to both groups, if each group would give a bit, you Swiss Brethren could end the tension. By uniting with the Lutherans both would be stronger to face Catholicism."

Michael smiled. "It is not by size that God's program will win but by faithfulness to His Spirit."

"I'm eager for you to meet with Bucer, Michael. He's the strong voice in Strasbourg. He, with Caspar Hedio, Mathias Zell, and myself, has given direction to the Reformation here. If you would change one of us, you must change all."

Michael had already heard of Bucer's extraordinary qualities of leadership and his skill in ministering the Word. He knew of Bucer's goal to bring about the unification of Protestants and that he was known as an arbiter between disputing parties. And so he was pleased when the meeting with Bucer was arranged. His warm love for the Protestant church impressed Michael as well as his desire to strengthen the cause by better understanding between Luther and Zwingli.

Bucer said, "Michael, perhaps you can help me in this. If we could help them both to be open to the views of the other, they could both be enriched by the varied interpretations. Their agreement could unite Protestantism!"

Michael smiled at this: "I'm not sure from my encounters with Zwingli that he will adjust his views any more than Luther has adjusted his."

Bucer replied, "That's one reason I want to talk with you, to learn more directly of events in Zurich. Give me your account of the radical wing in Zurich and of the ideals and vision of your Swiss Brethren. What really happened in Grüningen, and at your trial?"

Capito, as if to explain the question, added, "You see, one of your men, Wilhelm Reublin, was here in March and debated with us on this question of baptism. He seems to have had great success for your cause at Waldshut—says he baptized three hundred. He's the one who converted this fellow Hubmaier who writes against infant baptism and defies all Austria. They're both in for trouble! He told us of your arrest and trial—now let's hear your story."

Michael was pleased to get this word on Reublin. He would learn more later. At the moment he needed to share with these men on his own ground. Expressing appreciation for their interest, he carefully discussed the position of the Anabaptists, their faith in the authority of the Scriptures, and their deep conviction for a believers' church that called for rebaptism.

Bucer shared his own view on this. "I agree that baptism is only an external sign. But for this very reason infant baptism can be justified, permitting this external sign in anticipation that as the child becomes older it will be led to an understanding of the meaning of baptism administered through the faith of its parents."

Michael was surprised when Bucer said, "Early in my work as a reformer I wrote to Luther about this very matter. My position was very near to your Anabaptist position." He smiled in reminiscence. "That was back in December 1524. I wrote rather pointedly: 'Mere water baptism does not save. Where anyone wishes to postpone baptism and is able to do this without destroying love and harmony among those with whom he lives, we will not quarrel with him or condemn him. Let each be sure of his own opinion.' "

He looked up into Michael's eyes. "You seem to be pretty sure of your position. Sure enough to be jailed for it. But isn't this a minor point on which to take such an inflexible stand?"

"Minor enough, I suppose, that the state church saw fit to arrest and imprison us over it! We make less of the rite of baptism than does Luther or Zwingli. For us it is only a testimony of our new life in Christ. It is the new life, a real conversion, that we are really concerned about. We would ask of you, Why insist on the baptism of infants and thereby give people a false hope, an assurance of salvation which they have never appropriated? You see, Martin, it is no wonder there is so little spiritual life and obedience among the people."

153

As they discussed this, Michael saw that while Bucer was expressing tolerance toward rebaptism, his tolerance was largely tact. He still held that it was justifiable by the Scripture for the church to require all parents to baptize their children and to bring them into the church.

Michael responded, "But, Martin, what about the nature of the church itself, its character, its very essence?"

"Michael, the church is people, the total people who hear the Word and share the sacrament."

"No, my brother, the church of Jesus Christ is made up of those who walk in the Spirit and who live in the Spirit. Can those who have never experienced His regeneration be called the church?"

"But how can you judge the true believer? You must let the wheat and tares grow together."

"But such is not His pure church, washed in His blood, correcting each other in grace. Is the church really demonstrating the new life in Christ if there is no discipline, if there is no fencing of the Lord's table, no demand for purity of life?"

Bucer assented, "We need a certain church discipline because of the imperfect, that is true. As it is, we are without any order. Through this very fact you Anabaptists, though we disagree with your position, have been able to win your way into many hearts and call them to a different church. But can we not add this to our program as we develop?"

Michael pondered this conversation during the next days and shared his concerns further with Wolfgang Capito. In Michael's mind there were important differences which could not lightly be explained away. Bucer had used the text, "The end of the commandment is charity," holding that Christian love should overlook and ignore differences. He even urged that love on the part of the brethren should create in them a willingness to unite with the state church despite these differences. But Bucer had not spoken about the need for love on the part of the state church leaders for the brethren. He left the matter of their intense intolerance and persecution go unanswered!

Michael had by now discovered that Bucer was himself intolerant toward the brethren in Strasbourg. He sought to get Bucer to admit this and become just as tolerant as he expected the Anabaptists to be on their side. He could not let Bucer interpret the Anabaptists' refusal to consent to union with the state church as a lack of Christian love!

Michael said, "Martin, the very spirit of the Anabaptists, our way of peace and forgiveness, our refusal to bear arms and to harm our enemies, and our willingness to share in conversation are evidence enough of our way of love."

Bucer acknowledged, "Yes, Michael, at least I can say this of you, if not of all your group. They aren't all saints, you know!"

During the summer Michael was the recognized Anabaptist leader in Strasbourg. He worked hard at training lay leaders to carry forward their witness. By patience and understanding he promoted a spirit of unity and strength among the brethren. Gentleness paid off, and the depth of his convictions helped ease the tension while clarifying issues between Anabaptists and other Protestants about them. Mathias Zell, an influential reformer, was gracious toward the Anabaptists, a tremendous encouragement. Mrs. Zell was especially interested and impressed by a movement which gave their women such a role of equality. Many times she sat with Margareta to discuss the meaning of being a disciple of Christ.

Bible groups met in various parts of the city, gathering in the neighbors to study the Scriptures, witnessing to the new life in Christ. A year earlier Balthasar Hubmaier had published a work in Strasbourg entitled, "Of the Christian Baptism of Believers." He had written the work as an Anabaptist reply to Zwingli's book defending infant baptism. Having written it in Waldshut, Hubmaier had sent it to Strasbourg for printing so that it could be spread across the South German area. The Anabaptists used this book as a ready text to express their faith.

But the building of a faithful church was not an easy task. The application of the "ban," a disciplinary measure excommunicating the unfaithful from the brotherhood, was often misunderstood. The reformers accused Michael of sitting in judgment. The mystics said he was majoring on the external aspects of faith rather than the heart attitude.

Michael insisted, "While true Christianity renounces works of merit, there are works of faith. These are necessary expressions of loyalty to Christ."

A most difficult problem arose when several marriages broke up in a separation over the issue of belief. Several spouses were divorced rather than be yoked to one of differing faith. When several persons involved in such a divorce asked to remarry, he sought to keep the way open for a reunion through the conversion of the partner. But in some cases the departed spouse had closed that

156

door by another alliance. When he learned of converts being misused by a spouse who had left them for another, it was time to act. "Divorce," he said, "may be granted only where one party has been unfaithful and gone into sin, for the immorality has violated the marriage vows, making divorce in such a case expedient to free the steadfast believer from an unholy alliance."

To explain his position he then wrote a tract to be printed and circulated among the brethren. This tract, "Concerning Divorce," was also an opportunity to apply his conviction of the superiority of the New Testament over the Old in expressing the full will of God.

Hence we, like Christ, do not permit a man to separate from his wife except for fornication; for when Christ in Matthew 5 often says, "But I say unto you," He thereby annuls the law insofar as it is grasped legalistically and not spiritually. (Ephesians 2; Romans 10.) As He is also the perfection of the law, therefore He is the Mediator of a better Testament which hath been established upon better promises. (Hebrews 8.)

Therefore He does away with the old divorcing, no longer permitting hardness of heart to be a valid occasion for divorce but renewing the regulation of His Father saying, "It hath not been so from the beginning, when God ordained that man and wife should be one, and what God hath joined together man shall not separate." Therefore, one may not separate for trifling reasons, or for wrath, that is, hardness of heart, nor for displeasure, aversion, faith or unbelief, but alone for fornication. And he who separates or permits to separate except for the one cause of fornication and changes (companions) commits adultery. And he who marries the one divorced causeth her to commit adultery, for Christ saith, "These two are one flesh."

Marriage is indeed a bond and an obligation as Paul calls it (I Corinthians 7), so that one hath not the control of his own body, but the other, and neither may depart from the other. Yet the obligation is not so strong in God's sight that the believer for the sake of the marriage must do wrong, the man rendering greater obedience to his wife, or the wife greater obedience to her husband, than to God, so that the unbeliever may remain one flesh with me. But now the spiritual marriage and obligation to Christ, yes faith, love and obedience to God (so that no creature can separate us from God and the love of Christ, Romans 8), takes precedence over the earthly marriage, and one ought rather forsake such earthly companion than the spiritual Companion. And by not removing the designated one from the bond of marriage we give evidence that we care more for earthly than for spiritual obligations and debts, as it is written, He who loveth father or mother, wife or child, more than me, is not worthy of me (Matthew 10); yes, also he who doth not hate and forsake all, even his own life, and renounce all that he hath. (Luke 14.)

From his own experience of grace and his study of Scripture, he was certain that knowledge of God is known fully in Christ. But he wanted to make clear that he did not minimize the prophets, who spoke about God. He saw in Christ, as the Nicene Creed expressed it, "Very God of very God." He longed for time to work out a theology around this central point—the ultimacy of Christ.

This conviction burned like a fire in his bones; he saw it in every page of Scripture as he studied the Word. Alone with his thought, in prayer with his God, the truth gripped him again—Christianity is to walk with Christ, to be a disciple, to share His life! A sense of divine presence filled his soul. He stood with his eyes lifted toward heaven; a warm glow filled his heart as the fire of Pentecost burned within. He was a pilgrim aflame!

Chapter XVII

The Word had become flesh—Michael knew this, for he had met Him. Christ, his Lord, had called him into a new life of association. To be a Christian meant walking with the Lord, to be a person in relation. For Michael this meant a mission to his fellows. Writing a theology could come later. Now persons needed to be won for Christ. Like his Master, so he must go "to seek and to save" the lost.

The believers had been generous with the Sattlers in Strasbourg. It had been possible for them to live without spending very much time in work for material needs. But burning in Michael's soul was this conviction for evangelism, the commission of Christ. He well knew that if a believers' church was to spread across the world, it would have to spread by the hard work of evangelism.

"Margareta," he said one evening, "there are so many souls that we aren't reaching. If what we believe is true, then I owe something to the thousands across South Germany who have no assurance of salvation."

"I know, Michael, and I think I know what is on your mind. You're yearning to go preach in the hinterlands, aren't you?"

Michael nodded as he looked into her understanding face. "You seem to have read my mind. I'd at least like to work more widely here in Alsace, and perhaps in a few months I could visit the areas again in which we worked on our way to Strasbourg, Lahr, and Seelbach."

The days that followed found Michael and his associates preaching in the forest area below Strasbourg. Margareta shared in Bible studies with the women. They conducted meetings in villages and in forest sections where their gatherings were not so conspicuous to the rulers. Little congregations soon developed in the forests at Echboolsheim, at Lingolsheim, at St. Oswald, and in the region of Schnakenloch. The populace, soon aware of the gatherings of Anabaptists, now spoke of the "forest church" of the Anabaptists! Persecution immediately followed and as it became more intense, they found it necessary to withdraw into more remote areas.

With this increased danger Michael decided it was urgent to draft a confession of faith. Such a confession could be put into the hands of the people, copied and passed from one to another. The brethren must be united to be a strong though a voluntary movement. It was clear they would need spiritual strength to face persecution and stand the tests of the hour.

The seat of government of the local regime was Ensisheim, south of Strasbourg. The magistrates ordered the arrest of the Anabaptists wherever they could find them. This drew more attention to the movement and many a convert was won whose interest began with sympathy. Sattler now faced daily pressure from Capito and Bucer to bring the movement into an acceptable relationship with the magisterial Reformation.

In the summer of 1526 Wilhelm Reublin suddenly arrived in Strasbourg, without any word of his coming, Michael was thrilled to meet his old friend. Briefly they shared news of what God had been doing through their respective ministries since they had been separated. But Michael's main concern was to learn of the fate of the leaders he had left in Zurich.

"Tell me, Wilhelm, what of Conrad, Felix, and George? Are they still in prison?"

"You mean you have heard nothing from them?" Reublin appeared surprised. "Our brethren have gone through a long and trying imprisonment. For four months they lay in the tower with scores of others. Finally, on the fifth and sixth of March, the entire group was given a second trial. On March 7 they were sentenced to life imprisonment, but—"

Wilhelm noted that Michael received this news gravely—his head bowing in sorrow—and reaching his hand, he gripped Michael's shoulder and shook it gently as he said, "They've escaped!"

At this electrifying news, Michael stared in surprise. "All of them—are they all right?"

"They are free. Fourteen days after they had been sentenced to lie in that tower and rot—all escaped. A window was found unlocked, and one of the prisoners found a rope. They lowered themselves through the window. Conrad and Felix were hesitant to flee, but not George. The group soon convinced them that this was by God's providence. Even the drawbridge was down! They crossed the moat and fled, but," and here Wilhelm paused, before adding, "they aren't all well. Conrad's health is broken. His condition is poor; his contribution will be greatly limited. Much now depends on us."

Reublin's presence was an encouragement in the work. He stayed with the tailor, Jorg Wenger, who was a staunch Christian and effective lay leader, a ready host. For several months Reublin served with Michael, preaching the gospel and baptizing converts. His testimony of the conversion and baptism of converts at Waldshut and in the Rottenburg area seemed to offer encouragement to persons who were counting the cost of this faith. The men rejoiced over the many responses around Strasbourg, although they well knew this would bring increased persecution from the state church. Margareta was concerned for Frau Reublin who had remained in the Rottenburg area.

The call to personal conversion was a verbal slap in the face to those who stubbornly held that a person was a Christian by virtue of having been presented for infant baptism. The Anabaptist fears were not groundless. A few days later some of the group were arrested, and a number were imprisoned by the Strasbourg city council. Bucer had become more withdrawn, and Michael had little satisfaction from calling on him.

Matthias Hiller arrived in Strasbourg from St. Gall. He had more news of Felix, Conrad, and George. Conrad Grebel was in Schaffhausen where he had written a tract on baptism. Hiller had brought it along to Strasbourg. They made arrangements to have it printed and distributed at once. Hiller also informed them that Felix and George were evangelizing in Kyburg, and had even dared to work in Grüningen again! Michael expressed his concern to Margareta that although such boldness was noble, it wasn't wise!

"They are playing with fire. The peasants may be for us, but there are many revolutionaries among them. The magistracy will be on them again."

Near the end of August news came that Conrad Grebel had died. This was a schock to the group in Strasbourg who had known him during their days in Zurich. He had been with Manz in Appenzell. From there he left for Maienfeld in the Oberland for a period of rest. He needed an opportunity to recover his health. Shortly after arriving at the home of his sister he was stricken with the plague and died!

Grebel's wife had taken the children and declared herself with the state church, going back to her people. This was not surprising, for they knew she had never really shared her husband's faith.

The group expressed their grief in the passing of one who had been a great saint, a trusted leader, and a close friend. The founder of the Swiss Brethren movement was gone. Grebel had served briefly but well. Having been converted from carnality to Christ, Grebel had boldly launched a program that Michael was convinced would affect the whole world. He summed up his own feelings in the comment to Margareta, "If my service is as brief, I hope it is rendered as well."

The quarters the Sattlers occupied in the large rambling home of Capito had provided them with a degree of security. Michael had been able to continue his work under the benevolent protection of his host. But early in November things changed.

A reformer who already in 1525 had been expelled by the Lutherans at Nürnberg arrived at Strasbourg. Hans

163

Denk found his way to Capito's house and was shown similar hospitality. Discussions on the Christian faith became a daily affair again.

Denk held beliefs which challenged some of the reformers' basic theological premises. With respect to man's sinfulness he taught that man is not totally depraved, for within him there is yet the light of the Spirit of God. As a consequence he proposed that a revelation of God is to be found in the human spirit, an "inner light" which has equal authority with the written Word.

A marked difference was evident between Sattler and Denk. Michael found himself closer to Bucer and Capito, especially regarding the authority of the Scripture. Against Denk, he insisted on the necessity of the atonement in forgiveness. He reminded Denk of Paul's reference to Christ, who "gave himself for us, that he might redeem us from all iniquity, and purify unto himself a peculiar people, zealous of good works." But Denk held that Christ gave Himself as an example rather than as a substitute on the cross.

It seemed providential to Michael that at this very time his friend, Wilhelm Reublin, returned. He had left for South Germany weeks earlier. They met at one of the forest gatherings to the west, and following the service walked to Strasbourg together. Reublin had come to ask Michael to return to South Germany. While this stirred his convictions afresh to be extending the church, he hesitated to leave the brethren in Strasbourg under the influence of Denk.

Since both Michael and Hans Denk were outside the state church, their differences soon became a debate. Each attempted to clarify his position. Michael wanted to build a church of Christ, voluntary, God-fearing, genuine, cleansed by the blood of Christ, to be holy and blameless before God. The members of this church were to be God's obedient children who had been truly regenerated by the Spirit and separated from the world. Denk was somewhat of a spiritualist. He regarded the sacraments as nothing more than the early symbols, unnecessary to the life of the church. On the other hand, Michael insisted on the practice of ordinances as testimonies of obedience to the call of Christ; and that through baptism the believer is admitted into the church of the saints.

Capito and Bucer were deeply interested. They rejected Denk because his views were not true to the Protestant spirit and to the norm of the Scripture, and they stood by Michael in much of the debate. This placed Michael in a new difficulty, for it appeared that he was agreeing with the reformers at last!

A former acquaintance, Ludwig Haetzer, came to Strasbourg, seeking a place to work on translations of the prophets. He was offered lodging by Capito and used this opportunity to advance his views. He was hostile to Michael, for he remembered him from having attended Zwingli in the Zurich disputes of November 1525. Michael didn't trust him, and was repelled by his restless spirit and his low moral standards. Haetzer was obviously indifferent to the gospel call for a life of holiness.

The increased disputes led Michael to wonder how much good his continued stay in Strasbourg would accomplish. He resumed conversation with Wilhelm Reublin and began seriously to consider Wilhelm's invitation.

"Michael, the churches at Horb and Rottenburg need guidance. You're acquainted with that area and your ministry in South Germany could be the means both of strengthening the church and of helping to bring about greater unity. There must be a greater understanding of the position we clarified in Zurich. The new converts brought into the faith have had little instruction. I'd like to see you and Margareta go back to Horb, and build a congregation that can be a witness in the South German area. I know that community—I was born at Rottenburg, you know—but I'm a marked man by the Hapsburg regime and can't work as freely as you could."

Michael thought for a few moments, then replied earnestly. "Reublin, we are praying about this. For some time I have felt that my stay here is not fulfilling my entire calling. It may be that I should devote my energies to developing the congregation you suggest. Such a program would show what we mean by the necessity and character of a believers' church."

That night in their little room Michael shared Reublin's concern again with Margareta. He could not spare her from facing what this could cost. Anyway, there was no escape—even here.

"Michael, if the Spirit of God is leading you back to South Germany, I am ready to go with you. This is His work, and we are in it together. You must not stay here if you feel God is leading you there. The only safe place for us is in the center of His will."

Michael placed his arm over her shoulders and held her close. "I shall never be able to thank Him enough for this—that He brought us together. He knew how I needed you. You mean more to me and to the work of the kingdom than you will ever know—because I cannot tell you . . . with words," he finished softly.

"He knew I needed you, too, my darling. Somehow I feel that neither one of us will ever be asked to go on alone, for very long."

Late that night Michael lay awake. Leave Strasbourg, he must. To stay here enjoying the protection of Capito and Bucer while Anabaptist friends endured imprisonment in Strasbourg appeared to be a compromise. To leave meant a definite break with the Strasbourg reformers and would place him outside of their protection as he carried on the work.

Margareta was asleep at his side, an expression of absolute peace on her face. He kissed her lightly, watching as she stirred but did not awaken. The joy of her love thrilled him, and he thanked God again for having led them together. Perhaps someday God would grace their home with children! He smiled at the thought— lives through whom he and Margareta could further share the faith they had come to enjoy. But if their lot should be to continue on the move, hunted and harassed by persecution, strangers and pilgrims . . . "I delight to do thy will, O my God," he whispered and fell asleep.

Chapter XVIII

The Sattlers and Capitos went to the Bucer home together. They had been frequent visitors here. Not every couple married for love in those days, but no one questioned the presence of love in the Bucer marriage. Frau Bucer was a beautiful woman, both in form and spirit, and it was common knowledge that Martin and his wife loved each other deeply. Her disposition was very gracious and cheery, and the five children that graced their home radiated their happiness. Their home was known in the city as the "House of Righteousness."

Having spoken freely to Martin Bucer about his differences regarding the church, Michael didn't feel rejected by him. Instead, they had developed a very satisfying friendship.

"Welcome, my friends, to our humble abode." Warm friendliness spilled over the doorstep and enveloped them as they entered the spacious hall.

"We always feel as though we've just come home." Margareta greeted her hostess.

"Many of our friends say that—I'm not quite sure why," laughed Frau Bucer. "It's so good to see you . . .

and we want you to feel that way."

The men soon excused themselves and went into the study.

"Michael," Martin began, "it appears that having Denk and Haetzer in Strasbourg has been to our advantage, and I don't mean just for their work in translations from the Old Testament. Their heresy seems to have led you to see things more our way!" Martin and Wolfgang chuckled, and Michael smiled.

"That is what I want to talk about today. It appears that I can scarcely be honest about my convictions in this setting. Our common ground is the Scripture, from which I've outlined a confession of my faith which I would like to discuss with you yet once more."

Martin nodded. "That sounds reasonable; let us hear why if you still can't agree with us."

Michael presented his faith without apology. "I have here a series of twenty theses that explain my position.

"Christ is come to save all who believe in Him." The men each nodded assent.

Michael continued, "He who believes and is baptized will be saved, but he who does not believe will be condemned." Again there was a nod of agreement as Martin and Wolfgang looked at each other.

"Faith in Christ reconciles us with the Father and gives access to Him.

"Baptism seals all of the believers into the body of Christ who is now their Head.

"Christ is the Head of this body, that is, of the believers or the church, and as the Head, so shall the body be."

There had been general agreement to this point, but

169

now Martin asked, "What do you mean by that last phrase?"

"My next point will answer you, Martin. The predestined and called believers shall be conformed to the image of Christ."

Capito broke in, "A wonderful ideal, but how can it be realized?"

Michael answered, "This is the character of the new creation. We seem to have no problem agreeing on salvation by faith, but you brethren say too little about the character of the new life in Christ. This point and the next four speak to holiness of life."

Martin said, "Read on. We'll hear you out."

"Christ despises the spirit of the world; His children shall do the same." Michael paused, but there was no comment.

"He has no kingdom in this world; the world is against His kingdom.

"The believers have been chosen out of the world; therefore the world hates them."

Capito shook his head in rejection. "An impossible position, my friend. What is this, a mobile monastery you are trying to create? I thought you were a reformer and this sounds like a new monkery!"

Michael retorted, "I am a reformer, a reformer in depth. To break with Rome is not enough; we must break with sin, with the world, and with the idolatry of the state."

"But why with the state?" asked Martin.

"You know Augustine's words that the state is the ultimate expression of pride—we have a spiritual security, not a physical one! We are separated from the false securities of this age."

"The devil is the prince of all the world; through him all the children of darkness reign."

"Is this just a question of security then?" asked Wolfgang.

"No, this is a matter of loyalty and of character. I have five points to explain how this position is a consequence of being in Christ:

"Christ is the Prince of all spirits; through Him live all that walk in the light.

"The devil seeks to destroy; Christ to save.

"The flesh is at enmity with the spirit; the spirit with the flesh.

"The spiritual are Christ's; the carnal belong to death and the wrath of God.

"Christians are quite at rest and confident in their Father in heaven without any external worldly armor."

"Michael, you can't ask such a position of a total society," Martin broke in. "What if all would reject the sword?"

"It would be better for our world, Martin, if all lived by love and forgiveness!"

"Yes, but since they don't, we can't avoid the sword."

"But the church is to live by a higher ethic; we stand within the full will of Christ. Let me explain.

"The Christian's citizenship is in heaven, not on the earth.

"Christians are the family of God and citizens of the saints, not of the world.

"They are the true Christians who do the teachings of Christ with works.

"Flesh and blood display worldly honor and also the

171

world cannot comprehend the teachings of Christ.

"In short, Christ and Belial have nothing in common."

"You hold, then, that as a citizen of heaven you can't partake of earthly orders?" Capito asked. "What about marriage?"

Michael smiled, "An order of creation, my brother, but the sword is a necessity of sin. As citizens of heaven, Christians obey the authority of the state under God, but the state is ordained of God; when its way is counter to God's way, 'We ought to obey God rather than men.'"

The three men discussed these points with a good attitude of love and peace. It remained evident, however, that they were not reaching agreement. This called for a wholly different kind of church from what they now knew. At the close of the discussion Michael was sure that the situation would now become more difficult. On the one hand, to continue working with these friends and learned theologians would mean subjecting his own faith to the possibility of compromise. In his mind this would be a denial of the Word of God as he understood it. On the other hand, if he continued to argue with them, he would destroy their friendship and eventually fall into the hands of the magistrates.

Of late, Bucer was working more openly with the magisterial persecution. In short he had become more intolerant of Anabaptists. His last words to Michael had been pointed enough. "Make up your mind, Sattler; we can't shelter you forever. The pressure is too great." But he had made up his mind—this was the whole point of his life—he would be a disciple whatever came. And so Michael and Margareta decided that they should leave.

In late November they bade farewell to their friends

in Anabaptist gatherings around Strasbourg. The last Sunday they were present Michael explained their reasons for leaving, and called them to fidelity in the faith. "My going," he said, "will symbolize the complete otherness of our movement."

In a final sermon in Strasbourg Michael was quite clear about the differences that existed between himself and the other reformers. He encouraged the brethren to steadfastness in the face of persecution on the one hand and to stand against heresy on the other. Hans Denk had secured a sizable following. Some of his earlier converts had been deceived into thinking his position was that of the Swiss Brethren. Michael now sought to clarify their relation to two fronts. Against the Lutheran voices he emphasized the spirit of the Scripture as more important than the mere letter, and against Denk he emphasized the need of the letter of Scripture as a guide to discern whether one was led by the spirit of the Scripture or by his own spirit. Michael, admitting this to be a difficult distinction, said, "The Holy Spirit alone can help you understand what spirit ye are of."

His sermon was from Philippians 3:3, a message in which he called for faithfulness to Christ and His Word.

"Paul says, 'Beware of dogs, beware of evil workers, beware of the concision,' etc. (Philippians 3.)"

Everywhere it is said that one may indeed escape the persecution of false prophets and avoid the cross, that the prohibition of love does not forbid a bodily following of the state, but forbids only the attachment and consent of the heart. But it is written, "Prove all things; hold fast that which is good" (I Thessalonians 5).

What man would wantonly and knowingly imbibe poison,

imagining that his skill would prevent his being harmed, and would perish by his sportive act—surely everyone would say that he perished by his wanton behavior.

What man would see openly before his eyes the fruit of an evil tree, or would see that many people died by eating of a certain food, and then would wish first of all to test the tree or the food as to whether they were evil or good, and would thereby poison himself—surely everyone would say that such a person had perished justly.

Or would it be good, if a shepherd should, after a wolf had come among his sheep on two successive days and done great damage, on the third day make the wolf the keeper of the sheep in the hope that this time he would behave himself properly? He who, being sufficiently informed of evil, wantonly runs after it, wishing to make his own investigation, let him see to it that he does not plunge his neck into the pit which has been prepared, and perish wantonly in the prepared net!

Everywhere the apostles of the angel of darkness are now speaking, presenting themselves as the apostles of Christ (II Corinthians 11), to all those who wish sincerely to walk in the way. The sincere believers ought to flee as birds to their mountain, for they bend their bow and lay their arrow upon it, so that in the darkness they may shoot the souls of the living and put them to death (Psalm 11).

Indeed it does stand written, "He shall give his angels charge over thee, to bear thee up in their hands, lest thou dash thy foot against a stone" (Psalm 91), but it also stands written, "Thou shalt not tempt the Lord thy God" (Deuteronomy 6). Had Dinah, Jacob's daughter, remained at home and not strolled out to see the daughters of the land, she would not have become a courtesan (Genesis 34).

If anyone has such a great desire to listen to prophets who are known and demonstrated to be false, he is holding the very worst in his bosom. Even if he does not believe him, he will be terrified by his ceaseless prattle so that he will not know how to escape. It is said, one dare not set the louse on the fur; it will soon be inside!

174

For this reason, it is Christian and prudent in these most evil days to do as Christ says, "If any man shall say unto you, Lo, here is Christ, or there; believe it not. For there shall arise false Christs and false prophets, and shall do great signs and wonders, insomuch that if it were possible they should deceive even the elect" (Matthew 24).

The abomination is now becoming evident in the holy place (Daniel 9, 11), and those who have posed for a long time as brethren are beginning to show openly their fury against the miserable, attacked flock of the Lord, so that by their own fruit, yea before all the world, they may be recognized and may make evident in deed that for a long time they have concealed themselves under the conceited sheep's clothing of Scripture (Matthew 7).

Yea, do thou as the Lord through Isaiah commands, saying, "Go thou, O my people, into thy chamber and shut thy door after thee, and remain hidden there for a little while until the wrath be passed over" (Isaiah 26). For yet a little while and he that shall come will come and will not tarry.

Now the just man shall live by his faith, but if any man draw back, my soul shall have no pleasure in him (Hebrews 10). Yes, He saith, If the righteous man turn away from his piety, and live unjustly so that he practices all the abominations of the godless, shall that man live? (Ezekiel 18.)

But the God of peace and the Father of mercy shall graciously deliver both you and us from the present power of darkness and of the antichrist through the revelation of His Son, our Lord Jesus Christ. Amen.

Accompanied by Wilhelm Reublin and Matthias Hiller, Michael and Margareta left the city for the long journey to the Hohenberg region of South Germany. Their journey was to the east, but crossing the Rhine they traveled south along the Kinzig River to Offenburg as their first day's trek. En route they made plans to divide the area between them. The Reublins would work further east and south while the Settlers would stay around Horb in the north. Matthias lived in the area and would assist as a lay worker. The headquarters for Michael's work would be Horb, where he had once ministered briefly.

They went south along the Rhine some distance before turning east toward Horb. The terraced fields sloped upward from the river bank. Although it was fall and the growing season was over, the well-tended fields were picturesque and varied. Margareta and Michael walked arm in arm here, talking of their hopes and dreams for the work in Horb. Margareta was eager for a home of their own again, a place where they could be alone together.

Pausing to rest as they turned their backs on the Rhine to make their way inland, they looked down at the water shimmering beneath them.

"Perhaps," Margareta said, "we can find a home on the Neckar. I like the peace in the eternal flow of the waters."

Michael smiled, "That shouldn't be too difficult; at least we'll try."

Their quarters were small but private. The tailor shop at the edge of Horb had a few small rooms at the back which were converted into living quarters. The rooms projected out over the Neckar River, adding to the beauty and peace of the setting. With people coming and going from the tailor's, they would not be as conspicuous to authorities who might be searching for Anabaptists. The tailor, Johann Kniss, had himself joined their movement, and they would not be betrayed. It appeared that God had opened a door for them here.

Soon after getting settled in Horb, Michael wrote a lengthy letter to Capito and Bucer. This he sent as an official and courteous farewell, in which he asked for their understanding. He listed for their study the twenty confessional differences between them. He requested prayer and mercy for the imprisoned Anabaptists, asking for greater tolerance on points of difference. He wrote several paragraphs introducing his theses.

"The main issues that divide us center in the nature of the church. On the authority of the New Testament I must insist on a believers' church and upon a clear separation between the world and the church.

"The New Testament," he wrote, "teaches that a Christian church is not a promiscuous multitude such as constitutes the membership of the state churches. The church in the New Testament is a union of believers in Christ who have resolved to render obedience to Christ as their Lord. The true church is not an organization to which every inhabitant is compelled by civil law to consider himself a member regardless of his personal religious attitude."

The truth burned in his soul as he wrote. To him this was not a light matter. To Margareta he commented, "It is Christ's church that the Spirit is creating. I must make them understand our faith!"

"True Christians," he wrote, "are those who carry out Christ's doctrine in their lives. They are fellow citizens with the saints and of the household of God, and they are not of the world. They are chosen out of the world; therefore the world hateth them. The kingdom of Christ is not of this world; believers are members of the kingdom of heaven. Those who err should be reproved in love, not persecuted as the state church is persecuting the Anabaptists. The true church does not use the sword;

177

that is only for the magistrates. Within the church those who err are to be disciplined but by a discipline of love.

"In addition to the nature of the church," Michael added, "there are also points of Christian practice taught in the Scripture which are disregarded by the Strasbourg church." He listed such points as church discipline, the observance of ordinances, loving one's enemies in the spirit of nonresistance, and the New Testament teaching that we refrain from using the oath. Anticipating their answers to this list he added a further comment.

"I cannot agree that any divine commandments are of minor importance, or that love makes obedience unnecessary. This question involves the authority of Christ, the very authority of the Scriptures. Having left the authority of Rome, do we now accept another authority which substitutes charity or forbearance as the final authority instead of the authority of the Scriptures themselves?"

Michael signed the letter, "A brother in God, the heavenly Father." He knew that he was closing the door for further fellowship on their terms. He sent the letter to his former host and associate with a satisfied but heavy heart. With the message on its way to Strasbourg, Michael said, "Margareta, this closes another chapter in our lives. They have been great friends and brothers in Christ. If only they could see the truth of the believers' church. From here on, Strasbourg is in the background."

Resolutely she answered, "We cannot stop at this level. Our call is to build His church. The road still stretches on. His will becomes more clear."

Michael reached for her hand. "We may yet pay the highest price for this! But if it be a martyr road, it is lighted by His truth."

Chapter XIX

The little town of Horb in Württemberg, Germany, had been involved in struggles of the Reformation for nearly four years. As early as 1522 Johann Murer had acted as a lay preacher for the Lutheran faith. The Protestant schoolteacher, Herr Krautwasser, was also an ardent exponent of the gospel. In this same area a local businessman by the name of Sebastian Lotzer was a zealous preacher and writer. An especially eloquent man, he called persons to faith in Christ as the sufficient Savior. He made a sharp distinction between church faith and justifying faith. Boldly, he emphasized the priority of the Scriptures over the actions of any local council.

"Waiting for a decision of the council," he said, "is superfluous for him who hears the Word of God and buys a New Testament. That is sufficient counsel."

As a result of the Protestant stirrings, local authorities reported to Archduke Ferdinand that the Protestant movement was making rapid strides in Horb. Ferdinand, brother to Holy Roman Emperor Charles V, had been given Austria by the emperor, and had just this year been made king of Hungary and Bohemia as well. Of the house of Hapsburg, he was a militant Catholic, and news of the progress of Protestant influence around Horb and Rottenburg displeased him immensely.

Thus, before the Sattlers' return to Horb, Protestantism had increased in its spread and impact in the community. Especially had the Anabaptist church grown since Michael's former witness there. The ministry of Wilhelm Reublin had added to its progress, setting off almost a chain reaction, the spread of which converted many to justifying faith.

Michael and Margareta were warmly welcomed by Ludwig Scheurer, who had been of Reutlingen to the east. Scheurer had been baptized by Reublin on his previous trip. He related the event to them. "Upon my confession of faith, Reublin paused at a well in a field near the Neuneckerhelde to baptize me. He dipped up water with his hands and poured it on my head, in the name of the triune God."

Michael found in this man an ardent Christian with a testimony of transforming grace which was fresh and vital. With his assistance and that of Hiller they launched an evangelistic program to cover the territory around Horb.

It was the month before Christmas, 1526, and Michael and Margareta were deeply involved in evangelistic and pastoral work. They sought new converts and visited the homes of committed disciples. This was the nature of the believers' congregation in Horb, assembling in different homes often on Saturdays, but also in afternoons on the Lord's day. Michael instructed them in the Scripture, uniting them together around the Confession of Faith which he had outlined. He and Margareta enjoyed singing, and together they taught songs of praise to the congregation, some of which were his own composition. Above all, he sought to teach them what it meant to have a believers' church.

"The church," he said, "is a voluntary fellowship of the regenerate, who have been saved by faith in Christ, and are living obedient to Christ's principles. We follow neither the Roman church nor a national state church. Christianity must be a voluntary commitment to the Lord Jesus Christ in answer to the call of the Holy Spirit."

Within their group they referred to each other as brethren, rejecting the name Anabaptist which was forced upon them by their enemies. "We are baptizing," he taught, "in the strict sense of the Scripture. Infant baptism is really no baptism. The baptism of believers is the original, valid baptismal experience. Therefore, we aren't actually Anabaptists, or rebaptizers."

But their stand on the issue of baptism became increasingly the crux of the dispute between Michael's group and the other Protestant movements in the area. The church which he was building had to be a free church! He exhorted the members of his brotherhood that, "as Christians we shall deny all interference from the state in matters of religion, and maintain complete freedom for the church and for individual consciences."

This was a bold thrust, but Michael knew it to be the only scriptural position—that of complete separation of church and state. His teaching on separation made discipleship costly.

"The Christian will refuse to hold offices in the political program, to bear arms, or even to take oaths that bind him to an organization which could undermine his allegiance to the authority of the Scripture. We will live by holiness and by love. The true church is called to follow the Prince of Peace, to witness of His transforming grace, and to love our enemies. We are to beat our swords into plowshares."

The congregation at Horb was growing in stability and in size. Michael's influence was known widely among the brethren of South Germany, and he often traveled to meet various groups of believers. Again and again it was his privilege to baptize new converts into the brotherhood. There was deep satisfaction in contributing to the fulfillment of the Great Commission of the Lord. It was on the authority of this commission that he, with the brethren, was building a free church, was calling disciples to Christ! Let others ignore it; the true church would evangelize!

News came of the continuing growth of the church in Switzerland. The persecution was intense, but it seemed to spread the movement all the more rapidly. In St. Gall, Appenzell, and in Grüningen, multitudes had joined the Anabaptists. It now appeared that nothing would stop the movement short of being ground under the heel of the state. On one of his journeys beyond Horb, Michael joined Wilhelm Reublin and shared services with him. At the close of the meetings Wilhelm said, "Michael, I have been told that Zwingli says the conflict with the Roman church was child's play in comparison to the conflict he now has with the Anabaptists."

"This is not bad news, Wilhelm," responded Michael. "This means the believers' church is making a real impact. The world will yet see the church of Christ in its own right—a free church, a voluntary church of persons who have been born again by the Spirit of God.

One of the greatest needs in Christendom today is a fresh moving of the Holy Spirit. How I thrill at every new evidence of His presence! But with this experience, Wilhelm, we must make clear that the norm of the Spirit's work is the Holy Scripture! If this is not made clear, I am afraid that even the strong church that we have seen started will fall apart at the seams. We have perversions from individuals who have the enthusiasm of a new movement but not the content."

Wilhelm nodded in agreement. "It is clear, Michael, that we need the careful teaching of the Scripture in our brotherhood. A great responsibility rests upon your shoulders as a scholar, to help interpret the Bible. What do you think about our calling a conference of the churches in South Germany and Switzerland to arrive at a more unified understanding among the brotherhood?"

Michael looked up eagerly. "Yes, Wilhelm, why don't we call a synod? The church needs a good organization if it is to stand under the persecution of the Romish church. Luther and Zwingli have had the backing of the state. Why can't we call a synod apart from the state? There is nothing to prevent us. An Anabaptist synod in which we would arrive at agreement in a confession of our faith—" he paused a moment in his enthusiastic response, "that would serve both to unite the brotherhood and to give guidance for the generations to come."

"This is a must, Michael. I'm glad for your enthusiasm. It will take a few weeks to develop our plans. The Spirit of God may be leading in this direction."

The morning after Michael returned to his work in Horb, a messenger came from Zürich. He arrived at the tailor shop just as Margareta was leaving for the morning market. He asked to see Michael Sattler, and on learning that she was Michael's wife, he said, "I have some news from Zurich."

She showed him to their apartment and he immediately addressed Michael: "Felix Manz and George Blaurock were surprised at a meeting of the brethren in Grüningen, were arrested, and taken to Zurich. This happened the third of December. They are now in the Wellenberg Prison. We can expect harsh treatment for Felix Manz. At his last imprisonment his sentence was most severe."

Michael said, "We heard a bit of that from Reublin."

The visitor continued, "The prisoners were placed on straw in the new tower, allowed only bread and water until they would die and decay. No one could visit them or change their condition, even if they were sick. And the council decreed that any repetition of the offense of rebaptizing persons would be punished by drowning. Of course, he has been baptizing converts since his escape. We fear the worst for Felix!

"For several weeks he has been in prison, and the brethren felt I should come and tell you and Reublin. We're asking special prayer for him—" the messenger's voice faltered, ". . . that if it be God's will he be released—but should the council carry out the full length of the verdict against him, that he witness as nobly in death as he has in life."

Michael pondered this news with a heavy heart. Conrad Grebel had died of the plague during the summer of 1526. Bolt Eberli had died in the fire of 1525. Now his associate, Felix Manz, was in prison, no doubt to be sentenced to death. He could see Felix now in his mind, his flashing eyes expressing his enthusiasm. He was a man committed to Christ and His cause. Michael remembered his zealous words in prison when he testified to his faith—"The Scriptures alone have led me to my position on baptism, and that no Christian should strike with a sword nor resist evil." He knew Felix Manz to be a devoted Christian, one who spoke out of a personal experience with Jesus Christ, one committed to be His disciple regardless of the cost.

Margareta excused herself, needing to make her trip to the market so that she could prepare lunch for them. Upon her return Michael's spirit betrayed the heaviness of his heart and mind. Quickly she prepared a simple meal, which they shared with their guest. The visitor offered thanks at Michael's request and the conversation was continued over details of the arrest of Felix. Each of them feared that this would be the end of the road for their brother.

At the close of the meal they bowed their heads and Michael prayed—especially remembering Felix Manz, his mother and family. He prayed that God would give Felix grace for this hour, for his trial and for whatever might come. He closed his prayer by asking God to work out that which would bring most glory to Him, whether it be releasing Felix from prison or whether it be in his death.

His voice, choked with emotion, faltered as he closed the prayer. His eyes met Margareta's tear-filled ones and he said, "This is the price men pay for following scriptural convictions. We too will pay a price. It may not be the same as our brother will pay, but we have also given our lives to the service of our Lord Christ."

His last words took in all three of them, but Margareta knew his word was for her.

Their guest thanked them for their hospitality and slipped out the door. He would now seek Reublin and share this concern with him.

The last weeks of December seemed interminable. Winter had opened early and they rarely saw the Reublin family. Margareta longed for a good visit with Frau Reublin. She was a dependable soul, and in Margareta's opinion a more consistent personality than Wilhelm. She sensed that this family found its deeper strength in the lady of the house. She wondered how Wilhelm would hold up if he was in prison as Felix was. They waited for every bit of news from Zurich. Manz remained in the dungeon.

The turn of the year had come and 1527 dawned white and cold. As Michael walked silently through the beauty of the snow-mantled forest, he began to sing softly to himself. It was a song he had written for his congregation with words from Holy Writ—"Unto him that loved us, and washed us from our sins in his own blood, and hath made us kings and priests unto God and his Father." This same passage would be his text for today. He would bring a message on the atonement Christ accomplished on the cross.

Margareta had not come today, since this was a long forest trek. He thought of her now. She would be meeting with the group in Horb at the Scheurer home. Ludwig was a genuine Christian and his family a real asset to the cause.

Arriving at the cottage where a small fellowship of believers was gathered, he was greeted warmly. Drawing off his mittens, he stood by the hearth warming his hands, watching the little group who had gathered to express their faith. The peace in their faces was witness to the joy and security in salvation. What a difference between them and the guilt-ridden people who knew no forgiveness! He was reminded that the cross stands as a symbol of God's self-giving love in redemption, but also as a dividing line between those who receive God's grace and those who continue their rebellion against Christ. Today his message on the cross would not be so much about what God had done in giving man salvation as about who it is that benefits from this salvation. He would make clear that only those who cease their rebellion against God by a commitment to Jesus Christ actually share in His forgiving grace and love.

Beginning his message with the words of John the Baptist, he presented "the Lamb of God, which taketh away the sin of the world." He interpreted the cross as God's provision for a new life, as God's pattern for the disciple's life, and as God's power for a holy life.

When Paul says in Romans 3 that those who are justified through Christ are justified without any merit or without the works of the law, he does not mean that a man can be saved without the works of faith, since Christ and the apostles demand such, but without those works which are done outside of faith and of the love of God. Therefore whenever Paul and Christ apply the term justifying to works, they do not mean that those works are of men, but they are of God and Christ through whose strength the man performs them. Such works are not performed by the man as if he received something as his own, but are performed because God wishes to give the man such works that they are His works.

But when Paul calls Christ the righteousness and wisdom of the believers, does he mean the outward Christ without the inward? Does he not mean the inward with the outward? Namely, since He is the Word of the Father, He makes known to us the true obedience by which alone the Father is satisfied. He says, He who wisheth to follow me, let him deny himself. No one cometh to the Father but by me.

Although Christ is truly a reconciliation with God for the whole world, that does no one any good except those who recognize and accept Him by faith. And those who accept Him keep the commandments of Christ. But he who does not keep the commandments and yet boasts of Christ as being his reconciliation is a liar, inasmuch as he has never known Christ. Do we think that Christ so offered Himself for the sins of men that they are pronounced free whether or not they believe in Him, whether or not they turn from sin, whether or not they have a change of mind, as the works-saints think?

Those are without faith who have not ceased from sin, whose sinning is even worse than before, yea those with just as slavish and ugly a disposition toward God and their neighbor as they had before. How can such people appropriate the promise of Scripture for themselves?

Did then Christ do enough for our sins? The answer is yes; He did enough, not only for ours but also for the sins of the whole world, insofar as they believe in Him and follow Him according to the demands of faith. He has done enough as the Head of His church: He does no less for His members day by day, continuing to do enough for those who are His. Just as He has done from the beginning so will He continue to do until His return.

Just as one speaks of justification through Christ must one speak of this as through faith. Repentance is not apart from works, yes, not apart from love which is itself an unction. Only such an anointed faith as one receives from the resurrection is a Christian faith, and it alone is reckoned for righteousness.

We therefore preach works of faith, that is, a turning away from trust in one's works, possessions, and one's own abilities.

188

Works of faith are only possible through faith in Christ the crucified—confessing that one cannot do this of himself but is able to do so through the strength of faith in Christ. Such is not of man but of God, inasmuch as the will and the ability to turn back to God are not of man but the gift of God through Jesus Christ our Lord.

Chapter XX

The next several days Michael spent visiting several families recently converted to Christ. In the evenings friends gathered for Bible reading and discussion of Christian experience at the home of Hans Schrag. One of the men attending was from Lahr, where a friend of Bucer's, Jacob Ottelinas, was pastor.

In the conversation Michael learned that this man was a catechumen himself, anticipating a switch from the Roman to the Lutheran church. He explained to him the cost of discipleship and the meaning of surrender to Christ. Listening to Michael's interpretation of the Word, he responded by asking to be baptized.

"I've been contemplating a transfer from one church to another where the rites are similar, and I discover in your words that what I really need is a transformed heart."

Michael called the group to prayer and kneeled and prayed with him. He then asked for water and poured it upon his head, baptizing him before the group with the simple expression, "In the name of the Father, and of the Son, and of the Holy Spirit."

He had planned to leave early the next morning for Horb, but in the night a fierce blizzard broke. The wind moaned through the firs and drove the snow against the shutters. Inside the house the glow from the fireplace sent out its feeble warmth against the cold. Early in the morning Michael was up helping Hans and at work tending the cattle. The wind had stilled, and in the cold the snow crunched underfoot. Between the buildings the snow was piled in deep drifts. It hung over the edge of the roofs where it was piled several feet thick. Michael carried wood out and tended the fire under the water trough while his host carried the water. At first the water froze as it spread over the trough, but as the heat penetrated the cold metal, it gave off a bit of vapor into the cold air. It mixed with the breath of the cattle as they crowded to the trough.

"At times like this I envy the farmers who live in the village," said Hans. "There are advantages in a common *Bauernhof*."

"Perhaps so," Michael replied, "but next best may be tying your buildings together. Look at all this animal warmth you would share."

"You can remind my wife of that at breakfast, Herr Sattler; she's from the Tirol and doesn't especially love our German combinations."

Their work awakened their appetites and they made quick work of the breakfast prepared by Frau Schrag.

But it was late forenoon when Michael exchanged "*Auf Wiedersehen*" with his friends and started for Horb. It would be dark before he would arrive, but the desire to be with Margareta spurred him on through the heavy snow.

Scarcely a week later a messenger arrived from Zürich. Michael sensed immediately that he carried grave news. And grave it was, for he bore the dreaded news that Felix Manz was dead! Two days before, on January 5, Felix had been sentenced to die. His execution had been immediate; he had been drowned in the Limmat River for his faith. The messenger told it in graphic detail: "They led him from the city hall to the fish market on the river. But on the way he sang! He actually sang the *Te Deum* on the way to his death! By the bank of the river in those last moments while they tied his hands, he saw his mother and brother and, perhaps for their sake, asserted again his joy in Christ. His mother, with tears running down her face, called out a parting word, "Felix, my son, just don't deny your Jesus." Having bound his hands, they pulled his knees up between his arms, and put a stick through under his knees. He couldn't even struggle. Then they took him into the river in a boat, and held him under the water until he was dead."

The messenger ceased, and the little room was as quiet as death. Michael bowed his head in his hands and unashamedly wept. Margareta sat with her fists closed tightly, tears trickling down her cheeks, splashing on her clenched hands in her lap. Her face was pale as she looked at her husband and knew this could have happened to him. Michael looked up and catching her expression smiled through his tears and said, "His triumph only precedes ours."

It was a bold word, but each knew that a bit of fear had touched the other's heart.

The visitor pulled from his pocket a folded piece of paper and handed it to Michael. "This is the sentence which the council pronounced against him."

Michael took the paper and began to read:

Because contrary to Christian order and custom he had
become involved in Anabaptism, and accepted it, taught others,
and become a leader and beginner of these things, because
he confessed having said that he wanted to gather those
who wanted to accept Christ and follow Him, and unite
himself with them through baptism, and leave the rest, living
according to their faith, so that he and his followers separated themselves from the Christian church and were about
to raise up and prepare a sect of their own under the guise
of a Christian meeting and church; because he had condemned capital punishment, and in order to increase his
following had boasted of certain revelations from the Pauline
epistles. But since such doctrine is harmful to the unified
usage of all Christendom, and leads to offense, insurrection,
and sedition against the government, to the shattering of
the common peace, brotherly love, and civil cooperation and
to all evil, Manz shall be delivered to the executioner, who
shall tie his hands, put him into a boat, take him to the
lower hut, there strip his bound hands down over his knees,
place a stick between his knees and arms, and push him
into the water and let him perish in the water; thereby he
shall have atoned to the law and justice. . . . His property
shall also be confiscated by my lords.

When Michael finished, he asked, "Would you tell
me more about his death?"

The visitor answered, "How could I ever forget it?
The scene is etched in my mind forever. And not only
in mine—his drowning has made quite a stir in Zürich.
Believe me, he left a tremendous testimony upon those
who watched him die. You see, he was led from Wellenberg Prison to the fish market and to the boat. Crowds
of people lined the streets as he passed. But there was

an unusual hush over the crowd. Walking between the shops, you could hear his voice clearly as he praised God and testified cheerfully to the people. Several times he called out that his death was the price of freedom, that he was about to die for the truth!

"The crowd increased as they followed him to the place of execution. It was three o'clock in the afternoon. He stood there, as though framed in a picture, the river at his feet, Lake Zurich below him, the blue sky above, and the mountains covered with glistening snow high beyond him. It seemed that his soul in the face of death looked out above all of this, looked away to God.

"A Zwinglian minister standing by his side spoke some words of sympathy and encouragement to him, asking him to be converted to the state church. Manz acted as though he didn't even hear him. But hearing his own mother's voice from the other bank of the river, together with that of his brother, admonishing him to be stead-fast, he responded with a gesture of recognition. Then he sang with a clear voice in Latin, 'Father, into Thy hands I commit my spirit.'

"What a contrast between his spirit and the attitude of the men who dragged him into the boat! The crowd stood in awed silence and watched the waves close over his head. He was gone! You could hear a gasp run through the crowd. When they finally brought his body up, even the executioners were shaking. They sat in the boat a while and looked at his body as though they could scarce-ly believe he was gone. But he was. Gone to be with his Lord."

For some time the little circle sat in silence. Michael had placed his arm around Margareta. Finally he said,

"The cross is laid upon the flock of God as it was upon the shoulder of our Lord. Whatever the cost, there is only one way, and in that way we go forward."

Margareta looked at Michael as though some new strength had come to her. There was an added note of resoluteness in her voice as she spoke softly: "God's Word alone is the authority in our lives and for such a testimony some men must needs die."

During the next few days the news of Felix' death spread through the group. The following Sunday, when Michael stood before the little congregation at Horb, it was with a new sense of destiny. He had thought and prayed much about the message for today. He had conversed with the brethren about the martyrdom of Manz, and knew that this persecution could do one of several things to the brotherhood. It could strike fear into the hearts of many and weaken the church. On the other hand, the noble death of one who would die rather than compromise his convictions could challenge the brotherhood to a new strength.

It was the latter reaction that Michael wanted to see, that the entire brotherhood of believers might become so convinced of the authority of God's Word and so deeply assured of their own salvation that they would die for a cause greater than themselves. To strengthen them to meet this challenge he would call them to a deeper understanding of the meaning of discipleship. He would speak to them this morning on the subject of Christian obedience.

He began with a brief interpretation of the martyrdom of Felix Manz, with special mention of his victorious testimony, even in death. He announced his theme and with deep conviction began his discourse on the nature of true devotion. Reminding his congregation of how the state church voices charged them with being legalistic, he called attention to the victorious spirit of Felix Manz in contrast with the legalistic action that sentenced him to die. His message presented the contrast between an inadequate obedience of the letter and a true obedience in the spirit of love.

Obedience is of two kinds, servile and filial. The filial has its source in the love of the Father, even though no other reward should follow, yea even if the Father should wish to damn His child; the servile has its source in a love of reward or of oneself. The filial ever does as much as possible, apart from any command; the servile does as little as possible, yea nothing except by command. The filial is never able to do enough for Him; but he who renders servile obedience thinks he is constantly doing too much for Him.

The filial rejoices in the chastisement of the Father although he may not have transgressed in anything; the servile wishes to be without chastisement although he may do nothing right. The filial has its treasure and righteousness; the servile person's treasure and piety are the works which he does in order to be pious. The filial remains in the house and inherits all the Father has; the servile wishes to reject this and receive his lawful reward.

The servile looks to the external and to the prescribed command of his Lord; the filial is concerned about the inner witness and the Spirit. The servile is imperfect and therefore his Lord finds no pleasure in him; the filial strives for and attains perfection, and for that reason the Father cannot reject him.

The filial is not contrary to the servile, as it might appear, but is better and higher. And therefore let him who is servile seek for the better, the filial; he dare not be servile at all.

The servile is Moses and produces Pharisees and scribes;

196

the filial is Christ and makes children of God. The servile is either occupied with the ceremonies which Moses commanded or with those which people themselves have invented; the filial is active in the love of God and one's neighbor; yet he also submits himself to the ceremonies for the sake of the servants that he may instruct them in that which is better and lead them to sonship.

The servile produces self-willed and vindictive people; the filial creates peaceable and mild-natured persons. The servile is severe and gladly arrives quickly at the end of the work; the filial is light and directs its gaze to that which endures. The servile is malevolent and wishes no one well but himself; the filial would gladly have all men to be as himself.

The servile is the old covenant, and had the promise of temporal happiness; the filial is the new covenant, and has the promise of eternal happiness, namely, the Creator Himself. The servile is a beginning and preparation for happiness; the filial is the end and completion itself. The servile endured for a time; the filial will last forever. The servile was a figure and shadow; the filial is the body and truth.

The servile was established to reveal and increase sin; the filial follows to do away with and extirpate the revealed and increased sin. For if a man wish to escape from sin, he must first hate it, and if he would hate it, he must first know it, and if he would know it, there must be something to stir up and make known his hidden sin. Now it is law or Scripture which does this: for as much as the law demands, that much more the man turns from God to that which he has done, justifies himself therein, by his accomplishments, clings thereto as to his treasure and the greater such love becomes, the more and the greater will grow his hatred for God and for his neighbor. For the more and the closer a man clings to the creature, the farther he is from God. The more he desires the creature, the less he will have of the Creator.

Moreover the law gives occasion to people to depart farther from God, not because of itself (for it is good) but because of the sin which is in man. This is also the reason why Paul says that the law was given that it might increase sin, that sin might thereby become known. Yea, the law is the strength of sin and therefore it is just like the servile obedience, that is, obedience to law, which leads people into the most intense hatred of God and of one's neighbor. Therefore filial obedience is a certain way through which man escapes from such hatred and receives the love of God and of one's neighbor. Therefore, as one administers death, the other administers life. The one is the Old Testament; the other, the New.

According to the Old Testament only he who murdered was guilty of judgment; but in the New, he also who is angry with his brother. The Old gave permission for a man to separate from his wife for every reason; but not at all in the New, except for adultery. The Old permitted swearing if one swore truly, but the New will know of no swearing. The Old has its stipulated punishment, but the New does not resist the evil.

The Old permitted hatred for the enemy; the New loves him who hates, blesses him who curses, prays for those who wish one evil; gives alms in this manner that the left hand does not know what the right has done; says his prayer secretly without evident and excessive babbling of mouth; judges and condemns no one; takes the mote out of the eye of one's brother after having first cast the beam out of one's own eye; fasts without any outward pomp and show; is like a light which is set on a candlestick and lightens everyone in the house; is like a city built on a hill, being everywhere visible; is like good salt that does not become tasteless, being pleasing not to man but to God alone; is like a good eye which illuminates the whole body; takes no anxious thought about clothing or food, but performs his daily and upright tasks; does not cast pearls before swine, nor that which is holy before dogs; seeks, asks and knocks; finding, receiving and having the door opened for him; enters through the narrow way and the small gate; guards himself from the

Pharisees and scribes as from false prophets; is a good tree and brings forth good fruit; does the will of his Father, hearing what he should do, and then doing it.

The church of true believers is built upon Christ the chief cornerstone; stands against all the gates of hell, that is, against the wrathful judgment of the Pharisees, of the mighty ones of earth, and of the scribes; is a house and temple of God, against which no wind and no water may do anything, standing secure, so that everything else which withstands the teaching which proceeds from it, denying its truth, may itself finally give evidence that it is a dwelling of God.

The believers' church is now maligned by the Pharisees and scribes as a habitation of the devil: yea, finally they shall hear, Behold, the tabernacle of God is with men, and He will dwell with them, and they shall be His people, and God Himself shall be with them, and be their God, etc. But of the house of the Pharisees and scribes, it shall be said, Babylon the great is fallen, is fallen, and is become the habitation of devils, and the hold of every foul spirit, and a cage of every unclean and hateful bird, etc.

But to God (through whom everything which boasts that is not, may be manifested that it is) be all honor, praise and glory through His beloved Son, our Lord and Brother Jesus Christ. Amen.

Chapter XXI

The death of Felix Manz was the act in which the state church threw down the gauntlet before the Swiss Brethren. But it was taken up in a different way than they expected. The brethren were men of peace who rejected the sword, but also men of courage who believed that all men had a right to freedom of faith. They set out to evangelize Europe, and the movement spread with a new intensity. The death of Manz had occurred less than two years after the break with Zwingli, but the supporters of Manz were more in number than they of Zwingli. The sword was in the hand of Zwingli, but this was a struggle not of might or of power but of spirit.

Zwingli was busy. He wrote a refutation of Grebel's booklet on baptism. He urged the council to carry out its sentence to punish by death any persons found rebaptizing. They drowned a number in Lake Zurich in a further attempt to crush out the movement. They succeeded best at Zollikon. There the brethren had almost ceased their witness for the believers' church. Thirty brethren had been imprisoned and most had agreed to attend the state church again and to cease propagating their doctrine. Jacob Hottinger, the elder, was resolute and one of the few who kept alive the vision of a free church even though silenced for the present.

But in St. Gall and Appenzell some fifteen hundred more persons had been baptized! Under the leadership of Uolimann, an early convert of Grebel, the brotherhood was expanding, and gatherings were held in scores of homes. The genius of this success was the ardent spirit of the converts in witness and evangelistic activity. Men and women alike were active in Bible studies and witness gatherings. The message of the gospel was being taken to the populace, and religious services were being conducted on street corners, in forests, and in open fields. While this was a radical innovation, the involvement of the populace was the strength of the movement.

The same expansion was taking place in South Germany and in Austria. Michael and Wilhelm Reublin both marveled at the new enthusiasm for the free church. They were on the move constantly, preaching to gatherings in homes, and baptizing new converts. A growing fellowship had developed in Augsburg. But of this Michael was deeply concerned, for Hans Denk had come back into this area with his doctrine of the "inner light." His emphasis would minimize the authority of the Scripture even though encouraging the spirit of freedom.

News came from Augsburg that one of Denk's converts, Hans Hut, was a very eloquent man, and was having great success as an evangelist. He saw the difficulties of the day as signs of the end of the age and spoke much about the return of Christ. His extreme eschatological convictions created more problems. Teaching that the return of Christ was very near, Hut's followers somehow lacked the serious ethical concern of the brethren. The brethren called believers to full discipleship in the affairs of normal life. Now a difference developed between those who emphasized a total discipleship, and Hut's more emotional and shallow emphasis that seemed to minimize obedience.

From a small beginning in Zurich two years earlier to a membership of thousands across Switzerland, Alsace, South Germany, and Austria, there was much divergence of thought. Michael was concerned lest the movement fail for lack of unity. Various excesses had already appeared in the group. There had been the unfortunate incident of the Zollikon group running through the Zurich streets, crying their "woe" upon the inhabitants. In St. Gall a man of eccentric character had recently sought to join the movement. Under the claim of an inner spiritual impulse the man had beheaded his own brother. Members of the small group with which he associated ran through the city naked in a demonstration of judgment upon the people. But Michael feared the danger of heresy now as much as the fanaticism. Haetzer was in Augsburg with his interpretation of grace permitting licentious living.

But these perversions not only stirred up the community in antagonism against the Anabaptists; they stirred up the Anabaptists themselves. They would not be associated with this kind of behavior! Using every possible opportunity, they explained their conviction for true biblical discipleship and renounced these perversions.

In early February Wilhelm Reublin called at Michael's home in Horb. He brought with him more shocking news. George Wagner, a missionary to Bavaria, had been arrested in Munich and burned at the stake. This barbarous death was a more severe step designed to intimidate those who deviated from the accepted way of faith. Wilhelm was obviously shaken. "We're in for real trouble now, Michael; what shall we do?"

"What can we do, Wilhelm, but abide by the truth?"

"Yes, but we are men, Michael, just men—how could one stand in fire?"

"How well I know our weaknesses, but we are not alone. Tell me, how did Wagner die?"

"He left a wonderful testimony for the truth. His wife and child were brought to the prison to move him to recant, but he replied, 'My wife and child are so dear to me that the prince could not buy them with all his dominion; yet I will not forsake Christ on their account.'"

Michael's response was firm, determined. "The struggle is on—others have suffered as well. Blaurock's colleague, Melchior Vet, was burned recently as well. George himself is in prison. The state means to stop us all right. How long 'til they learn that truth cannot be crushed; it will rise again!"

He paused a moment, then continued, "To make matters worse, within the brotherhood we have need for spiritual discipline. Some have fallen prey to the false doctrine that interprets freedom as license. We will be sapped of our strength from within as well."

Reublin burst out, "We must do something to safeguard the brotherhood. You are right. Persecution besets on the one hand; perversions divide us on the other. Perhaps I've been more concerned over the persecutions than the perversions! Persecution can sift and strengthen, but divisions and excesses will destroy us—I see what you mean."

Michael nodded. "Wilhelm, I've been thinking about our idea of calling a synod of the brethren. The time has come for us to hold such a meeting. Here at Horb we have seen the Spirit of God at work in converting souls and in building a strong congregation. It is my conviction that one of the things that has strengthened our fellowship is our having a clear confession of faith by which we weigh our teachings. This has been something of a balance. Wouldn't it be helpful if we could hold a general assembly and agree on a confession that would unite and strengthen our witness?"

"I've thought more about it," Reublin replied, "and have been talking to others as well. Earlier when I met Blaurock in Schaffhausen we spoke of the need for such a synod. If only he could come. He suggested then that you should be the leader of the assembly. Your scholarship fits you for the work, and your experience in Zürich, Strasbourg, and now here, has won for you the respect of the people."

Michael's spirit responded to the challenge. He had thought and planned for such a gathering and now it appeared urgent.

"Wilhelm, if you will spread the news of the synod, and arrange the meeting, I'll work on a confessional statement to crystallize our discussion. We cannot wait longer. We'll answer persecution with a plan of action."

Reublin nodded, his enthusiasm evident. "Hubmaier teaches with us on believer's baptism, but he does not take the New Testament position against military service. Perhaps we can convince him to come all the way."

"Whether he does or not, if we want a truly separate church, a holy and peaceful church, we must be clear on bearing the cross in love! And another danger is found among those who make the authority of the Scripture subservient to an inner prompting said to be of the Spirit. This results in excesses and fleshly living. Those who live only by the 'inner light' have no clear standard to obey. Our people must see that a man is not more spiritual than he is scriptural."

"Having already talked with others about holding such a synod, Michael, many feel the best place to meet is at Schleitheim on the border. Give me several weeks to get the invitation spread over the country. Let's announce the meeting for St. Matthias Day, February 24."

And so it was agreed to call the synod, the first such gathering in a thousand years, where Christian leaders would gather under no authority save that of the Lord of the church. This time the brethren would throw down the gauntlet, a gauntlet of freedom!

After Reublin left, Michael considered the responsibility of preparation. He well knew that far more difficult than drawing up a confessional statement would be the work of arriving at unity through mutual conversation. If the synod was a success, it would solidify the Anabaptist movement into a strong believers' church, holy and biblical. If the assembly failed, the divisions that had come into the movement would fragment the brotherhood through attention being given to minor issues at the cost of losing the major principles. Such division would mean the doom of their cause. But he was confident that a consensus would be their strength.

With the gravity of the situation weighing upon his soul, Michael went to prayer. He asked God to give him the wisdom to guide this assembly truly in the way of Christ. During the next several weeks he read and studied much. He reread Grebel's booklet on baptism, Hubmaier's writings, and of course Zwingli's refutations. He incorporated the articles in his letter to Capito and Bucer, and documented his Confession of Faith both by the Scripture and by theological writings.

Wilhelm reported enthusiastic interest in the synod. This would be their answer to their opponents—a stronger program. But Michael was sure the differences of thought and the various excesses meant that the meeting would not be an easy one.

With the increased persecution Michael knew it was impossible to extend the meeting. If news of such a gathering became known, they could anticipate being interrupted. The assembly would need to be brief, perhaps for only one day. It would be necessary to deal with a minimum number of points. He attempted to select the distinctive points on which there was difference with the other reformers, and on which there was need for unity among the brotherhood.

Michael outlined these issues in advance, preparing a brief statement on each to focus the discussion. The central issues which he planned to raise were baptism, excommunication, the Lord's Supper, separation from evil, the role of pastors in the church, the sword, and the oath. With unity on these seven points, they would be strengthening the movement for the trying days that were upon them.

The week before the scheduled meeting, the Reublins arrived from the East where they had been staying with Wilhelm's sister at Reutlingen. Frau Reublin and their little daughter planned to stay with Margareta while the men were gone. They were welcome guests to Margareta, for she was not happy about being alone for this period. Michael and Wilhelm left Horb early in the morning, with a three-day trek before them. They hoped to arrive early enough to converse with Uolimann and Blaurock over the Seven Articles before the meeting. They at least hoped Blaurock could come, but having heard that George had been arrested by authorities in Chur, they could only pray that he was free again. Michael anticipated some additions to his outline through conversations with them, as well as support in a statement more representative of the total brotherhood.

They planned to travel as far as Oberndorf today. Tomorrow they would travel down the Neckar, meeting other representatives as they went.

It was a bright day and the sun glistened on the snow. They walked along narrow trails cut by a horse or another foot traveler, sometimes along a double path cut by oxcarts. The air was bitter cold and loose snow swirled about them. They were grateful for the forest regions where they were more sheltered from the driving wind.

As they neared Rottweil, they talked of the meeting at Schleitheim and the importance of the coming synod. Michael was optimistic. "This is a most important occasion. I feel that we may be making history in this assembly."

Wilhelm was also in good spirits and responded enthusiastically. "The world will bear witness in years to come that freedom is not to be surrendered to power and that faith is to remain a trust."

They found friends in Rottweil and were offered lodging

for the night. Tired from the long walk through the snow, they retired early. As Michael kneeled to pray for success in their mission, he prayed for Margareta waiting in Horb. He thought now of her words as he bade her "*Auf Wiedersehen*." She had clung to him briefly and whispered, "I'll be praying for you, dearest. I'm glad God has called you—the assembly will succeed, for His Spirit is guiding, I'm sure,"

Chapter XXII

Schleitheim on the border was a small village in the western territory of Schaffhausen. The region was a buffer zone between the canton of Zurich where Zwingli resisted the church of Rome, the area of the Hapsburgs' Catholic rule, and areas of Germany where Luther's voice had defied the pope. This made it a somewhat more neutral spot for an Anabaptist assembly, and its central location made it readily accessible for many. And they came, from Alsace, from Strasbourg, from South Germany, from the cantons of Switzerland, and from Austria. Most of them walked, many alone, but others in twos and threes.

Had men been searching for Anabaptists, they could have spotted some of these. None of them carried a sword, since they had a strong conviction for peace. Many of them dressed in common garb, carrying only a walking stick. But it was St. Matthias Day and people were engaged in their own festivities. No one was aware of an unusual number of Anabaptist leaders converging on Schleitheim.

In late evening of February 23, Michael and Wilhelm

arrived in Schleitheim. The trip had been a difficult one, through the heavy snow that had fallen during the past several days. They trudged wearily up the slope of a high hill overlooking the village. Upon achieving the summit, they inquired for the home of Jan Hertzer, a member of the brotherhood. They were thrilled to find Blaurock and Uolimann there awaiting them, with Jacob Hottinger from Zollikon. There were misty eyes as they greeted each other.

George's booming voice spoke for all as he said, "Praise God for answered prayer. Many times in the last weeks I questioned whether this would come to pass for me."

"But we prayed, George," Wilhelm added, "and God has honored our prayers."

For the next hours into the late evening they talked and shared both experiences and concerns. Jacob Hottinger was deeply perturbed over the failure of the Zollikon church. "Since the drowning of Felix Manz most of our group is hesitant to say much. We have been ordered by the magistracy to refrain from meeting in groups. We are asked to attend the state church for instruction in the Word. I still long for a believers' church, but every attempt to develop such a brotherhood in Zollikon has been crushed."

Blaurock's voice was sympathetic. "I can't be too harsh in judgment, Jacob, when I too have suffered in your area, and have been banished from Zurich. As you know, the last time I was arrested there they demanded that I swear never to return. I wouldn't commit myself until I saw it was back to the dungeon; so I assured them I wouldn't return!"

Michael added, "Jacob, we understand your position,

and in one sense we all share your problem. Most of us have been imprisoned and banished from the canton of Zurich. However, we can't continue to run. The day has come when the believers' church must pay a price in martyrdom before it convinces the world of the validity of the free church. Our meeting here must strengthen the brotherhood to withstand compromise."

Then turning to Uolimann, he said, "Tell us something of St. Gall. We've heard reports of the continued growth of the brotherhood there, but we've also heard pathetic reports of some evil behavior."

Uolimann drew a deep breath. "I hardly know where to begin. We have seen the Spirit of God at work. Hundreds have been baptized into the brotherhood in St. Gall and Appenzell. But there are stirrings among us similar to what I hear from Augsburg and this area. Haetzer's teaching has affected our group through some brethren exiled from Augsburg. They seem to give room for license under the guise of liberty. There is also a strain of mysticism which has resulted in making men a law unto themselves. We have had a few very unfortunate events among a fringe group who tried to join us, but wouldn't accept our discipline. You may have heard of the man who beheaded his brother, and of the group that ran through the streets naked to emphasize their message of judgment. We have spoken out against this, and it is fairly well understood that this action was not with our approval. Our most serious problems arise among those whose emphasis on the inner word of the Spirit minimizes the authority of the Scripture. We can hardly expect to build a disciplined church without a clear standard."

Reublin took up the conversation. "Michael and I have been talking about this very matter. One of our urgent needs is for unity of thought in our interpretation of the Scripture. We do not have one major voice in our group, a Luther or a Zwingli. We have simply the Word. This synod can be important as we all share in outlining a Confession of Faith. From this synod there can follow a unity that will strengthen the entire brotherhood."

They concluded the evening with general discussion of procedure for the assembly. The men knelt together, and each led in prayer before retiring. Michael was pleased with the attitude of the group. There was general agreement on the goals for the meeting on the morrow. He had an inner assurance that this synod would be a monumental assembly.

By nine o'clock on the morning of February 24, scores of Anabaptists had slipped into the little tailor shop on the north edge of the village. The shop was kept by Ray Sauder, one of the Swiss Brethren. When Michael and his group stepped into the room, it was already well filled. This was a momentous meeting, and the weight of it rested heavily on Michael's soul. This day, February 24, 1527, was the gathering of the first Free-Church Synod. There were no government officials present, as had been the case for all ecclesiastical councils for the twelve hundred years since Constantine.

Inside there was a holy hush of expectancy. Outside at various spots a few men were posted as lookouts. George Blaurock led the group in singing, a practice which had become quite universal in their meetings. All participated even though there was no professional choirmaster as in the state church.

212

Reublin took the floor next. "Brethren, let us pray for the Spirit's direction in our assembly."

As a ripple of "amens" was heard across the room, the men began to kneel by the improvised benches to join in prayer. The period of prayer was informal, with numerous persons leading out, asking God for the illumination of the Spirit as they thought on His Word.

After the prayer period, Reublin presented Michael to the brethren as leader of the conference. There was little need of introduction as he was well known. With a brief word he presented him and explained that he had prepared a confession of faith to guide them in their discussion.

Michael stepped before the group with a sense of destiny in his soul. These were his brethren—men who shared the grace of God with him, who were committed to be disciples of Christ. These men held to the supreme authority of the Scripture. They stood for a believers' church. They would die for their faith. This was God's work, and this meeting was by the direction of His Spirit.

"Beloved brethren, we have met here today because we are committed to follow Christ above all else. We who have gathered here are men who have experienced the joy of the new birth and the power of the Holy Spirit. We are committed to one authority alone, the authority of Christ through His Word. We claim Him as Lord and profess to be citizens of heaven here in the world. Ours is a dangerous position in the world, a position beset by persecution from both the Roman church and the Protestant church. Ours is a confession that is unpopular because it calls men to the way of the cross, yet it is a position of power, for it has led many from a mere formalism to fellowship in the Spirit.

"Today we have met to seek a greater unity of faith and life. That there are differences among us is known to all, but that there are basic agreements is equally true. Many of the differences may be due to our varied backgrounds, our differences in temperament, or in our approach to the Scriptures. If we are to stand, if we are to build a strong brotherhood, if we are to see again a church after the pattern of the apostles, we must pay the price the New Testament outlines for unity. There is 'one Lord, one faith, one baptism . . . ,' and in this oneness of Christ we too shall be one."

He paused, and there were audible "amens" heard over the room. "The articles of faith which I shall present today are only a brief attempt to suggest what it means for us to be disciples of Christ. These articles do not deal with the major areas of the gospel in which we agree with the reformers, but with what seem to be the more significant differences between us. I want you to join in discussing these articles, and together we shall arrive at our Confession of Faith. It seems to be necessary that we express ourselves on the following issues: baptism, the ban, the Lord's Supper, separation from evil, pastors in the church, the sword, and the oath."

In addition to the audible "amens" to Michael's introduction, others nodded in assent.

Michael opened the meeting for response, and in the next few hours there was a free and concentrated discussion on each of the points he had raised.

On baptism the discussion centered around Grebel's booklet. There was general agreement on the importance of adult baptism. The role of baptism as an ordinance was discussed, distinguishing believer's baptism as a "testimony of a good conscience" rather than a sacramental rite to free the conscience.

Much time was spent on the subject of excommunication. At first some held that the stringent use of the ban was militating against the freedom of the Spirit. Others held that it was impossible to create a disciplined church without excommunication. It was finally agreed that those who deviated from the scriptural standard of holiness should be excommunicated from the fellowship after following the admonition of Matthew 18.

There were divergent views on the meaning of separation from evil, and from the abomination of those who were not following the true gospel of Christ. The discussion was lengthy, and Michael attempted to summarize the unifying elements of thought by turning their attention to the principle rather than to attempt a blanket answer for all of the problems.

The article receiving most discussion was the sixth, pertaining to the sword. Some had accepted the ideas of Hubmaier, who agreed with the Anabaptists on adult baptism, but not on their stand against the use of the sword. Here Michael emphasized the importance of interpreting the Scripture through Christ. Elevating the New Testament, or the perfection of Christ, above the Old Testament, he emphasized the way of love and nonresistance for the regenerate. Turning to Romans 13, he pointed out that the authority of the state is given it by God; therefore, the state is under God. There was general agreement on this principle, followed by a discussion of the Christian calling. They agreed that the New Testament forbids the regenerate to serve in the magistracy or to use force.

This method of interpretation was followed as well in discussing the oath. The Sermon on the Mount was quoted as teaching the believer's prohibition from swearing. In all honesty one under the lordship of Christ could not pledge binding allegiance to a lesser power. Avoidance of oaths results from the simple acceptance of Christ's prohibition and is testimony to one's acceptance of his creaturehood. Further, the acceptance of Christ's prohibition testifies to the believer's acceptance of his creaturehood and humility before divine Providence.

It was agreed that Michael should add the benefits of the discussion to his notes, and prepare a letter that would include these seven articles. He was asked to entreat those who had turned from scriptural discipleship to return. The letter was then to be distributed in the various congregations as the action of this synod. Special reference was to be made of the difference between the views of the brethren and the views of Denk and Haetzer.

Absenting himself from the fellowship, Michael prepared a letter, explaining and reporting the Schleitheim synod and the articles agreed upon. Late that same evening the group met again so that they might hear and ratify the final form of the Confession.

Michael sat at a little table at the head of the room. The free spirit in the conversation preceding the meeting gave evidence of a good spirit of understanding. He was thrilled by the singing and by the spirit of the opening prayer. Bowing his head over his script, in the flickering light of the candles, he began to read:

BROTHERLY UNION OF A NUMBER OF CHILDREN OF GOD CONCERNING SEVEN ARTICLES

May joy, peace and mercy from our Father through the atonement of the blood of Christ Jesus, together with the gifts of the Spirit—who is sent from the Father to all believers for their strength and comfort and for their perseverance in all tribulation until the end . . . be to all those who love God, who are the children of light, and who are scattered everywhere as it has been ordained of God our Father, where they are with one mind assembled together in one God and Father of us all: Grace and peace of heart be with you all. . . .

As he paused, the group uttered an "amen" of approval and then listened as he read on:

Beloved brethren and sisters in the Lord. First and supremely we are always concerned for your consolation and the assurance of your conscience (which was previously misled) so that you may not always remain foreigners to us and by right almost completely excluded, but that you may turn again to the true implanted members of Christ, who have been armed through patience and knowledge of themselves, and have therefore again been united with us in the strength of a godly Christian spirit and zeal for God.

As he finished reading this paragraph, Michael looked up into the faces of the group for response, and there was a fervent "amen" from them all. He turned again to his reading:

It is also apparent with what cunning the devil has turned us aside, so that he might destroy and bring to an end the work of God which in mercy and grace has been partly begun in us. But Christ, the true Shepherd of our souls,

218

who has begun this in us, will certainly direct the same and teach us to His honor and our salvation.

As Michael paused and received an "amen" from the assembly, he made a notation in the margin of the script of the endorsement by the group. He was hoping that they would all agree to his addressing this report directly to the issues which had been dividing them. The success of the synod hinged on the unity of the group, both in resisting excesses and in agreeing on specific articles of faith. He read on:

Dear brethren and sisters, we who have been assembled in the Lord at Schleitheim on the Border, make known in points and articles to all who love God that as concerns us we are of one mind to abide in the Lord as God's obedient children, His sons and daughters, we who have been and shall be separated from the world in everything, and completely at peace. To God alone be praise and glory without the contradiction of any brethren. In this we have perceived the oneness of the Spirit of our Father and of our common Christ with us. For the Lord is the Lord of peace and not of quarreling, as Paul points out. That you may understand in what articles this has been formulated you should observe and note the following:

A very great offense has been introduced by certain false brethren among us, so that some have turned aside from the faith, in the way they intend to practice and observe the freedom of the Spirit and of Christ. But such have missed the truth and to their condemnation are given over to the lasciviousness and self-indulgence of the flesh. They think faith and love may do and permit everything, and nothing will harm them nor condemn them, since they are believers. Observe, you who are God's members in Christ Jesus, that faith in the heavenly Father through Jesus Christ does not take such form. It does not produce and result in such things as these false brethren and sisters do and teach.

Guard yourselves and be warned of such people, for they do not serve our Father, but their father, the devil.

But you are not that way. For they that are Christ's have crucified the flesh with its passions and lusts. You understand me well and know the brethren whom we mean. Separate yourselves from them, for they are perverted. Petition the Lord that they may have the knowledge which leads to repentance, and pray for us that we may have constancy to persevere in the way which we have espoused, for the honor of God and of Christ, His Son. Amen.

As Michael completed reading this pointed statement, the assembly responded with enthusiastic endorsement. There was no question now about their unity of purpose and faith. He picked up the script to read the discussion of the seven articles.

The articles which we discussed and on which we were of one mind are these: (1) Baptism; (2) The Ban [or Excommunication] ; (3) Breaking of Bread; (4) Separation from the Abomination; (5) Pastors in the Church; (6) The Sword; and (7) The Oath.

First. Observe concerning baptism: Baptism shall be given to all those who have learned repentance and amendment of life, and who believe truly that their sins are taken away by Christ, and to all those who walk in the resurrection of Jesus Christ, and wish to be buried with Him in death, so that they may be resurrected with Him, and to all those who with this significance request baptism of us and demand it for themselves. This excludes all infant baptism, the highest and chief abomination of the pope. In this you have the foundation and testimony of the apostles. Matthew 28; Mark 16; Acts 2, 8, 16, 19. This we wish to hold simply, yet firmly and with assurance.

Second. We are agreed as follows on the ban: The ban shall be employed with all those who have given themselves to the Lord, to walk in His commandments, and with all those who are baptized into the one body of Christ and who are called brethren or sisters, and yet who slip sometimes and fall into error and sin, being inadvertently overtaken. The same shall be admonished twice in secret and the third time openly disciplined or banned according to the command of Christ. Matthew 18. But this shall be done according to the regulation of the Spirit (Matthew 5) before the breaking of bread, so that we may break and eat one bread, with one mind and in one love, and may drink of one cup.

Third. In the breaking of bread we are of one mind and are agreed as follows: All those who wish to break one bread in remembrance of the broken body of Christ, and all who wish to drink of one drink as a remembrance of the shed blood of Christ, shall be united beforehand by baptism in one body of Christ which is the church of God and whose Head is Christ. For as Paul points out, we cannot at the same time be partakers of the Lord's table and the table of devils; we cannot at the same time drink the cup of the Lord and the cup of the devil. That is, all those who have fellowship with the dead works of darkness have no part in the light. Therefore, all who follow the devil and the world have no part with those who are called unto God out of the world. All who lie in evil have no part in the good. . . .

Fourth. We are agreed as follows on separation: A separation shall be made from the evil and from the wickedness which the devil planted in the world; in this manner, simply that we shall not have fellowship with the wicked and not run with them in the multitude of their abominations. This is the way it is: Since all who do not walk in the obedience of faith, and have not united themselves with God so that they wish to do His will, are a great abomination before God, it is not possible for anything to grow or issue from them except abominable things. For truly all creatures are in but two classes, good and bad, believing and unbelieving, darkness and light, the world and those who have come out of the world, God's temple and idols, Christ and Belial; and none can have part with the other. . . .

Therefore there will also unquestionably fall from us the unchristian, devilish weapons of force—such as sword, armor and the like, and all their use either for friends or against one's enemies—by virtue of the word of Christ, Resist not him that is evil.

Fifth. We are agreed as follows on pastors in the church of God: The pastor in the church of God shall, as Paul has prescribed, be one who out-and-out has a good report of those who are outside the faith. This office shall be to read, to admonish and teach, to warn, to discipline, to ban in the church, to lead out in prayer for the advancement of all the brethren and sisters, to begin to break the bread, and in all things to see to the care of the body of Christ, in order that it may be built up and developed, and the mouth of the slanderer be stopped.

This one, moreover, shall be supported of the church which has chosen him, wherein he may be in need, so that he who serves the Gospel may live of the Gospel as the Lord has ordained. But if a pastor should do something requiring discipline, he shall not be dealt with except on the testimony of two or three witnesses. And when they sin they shall be disciplined before all in order that the others may fear.

But should it happen that through the cross this pastor should be banished or led to the Lord through martyrdom, another shall be ordained in his place in the same hour so that God's little flock and people may not be destroyed.

Sixth. We are agreed as follows concerning the sword: The sword is ordained of God outside the perfection of Christ. It punishes and puts to death the wicked, and guards and protects the good. In the law the sword was ordained for the punishment of the wicked and for their death, and the same sword is now ordained to be used by the worldly magistrates.

In the perfection of Christ, however, only the ban is used for a warning and for the excommunication of the one who has sinned, without putting the flesh to death—simply the warning and the command to sin no more. . . .

Seventh. We are agreed as follows concerning the oath: The oath is a confirmation among those who are quarreling or making promises. In the law it is commanded to be performed in God's name, but only in truth, not falsely. Christ, who teaches the perfection of the law, prohibits all swearing to His followers, whether true or false—neither by heaven, nor by the earth, nor by Jerusalem, nor by our head—and that for the reason which He shortly thereafter gives, for you are not able to make one hair white or black. So you see, it is for this reason that all swearing is forbidden: we cannot fulfill that which we promise when we swear, for we cannot change even the very least thing on us. . . .

Christ also taught us along the same line when He said, "Let your communication be Yea, yea; Nay, nay; for whatsoever is more than these cometh of evil." He says, Your speech or word shall be yea and nay. However, when one does not wish to understand, he remains closed to the meaning. Christ is simply Yea and Nay, and all those who seek Him simply will understand His Word.

As Michael completed reading the report of their discussion on these articles, there was again a fervent "Amen." Smiles spread across the room and head nodded to head. There was a feeling of noble purpose and of having achieved a new strength in unity.

"If I may presume upon your patience," Michael added, "I have yet a conclusion, which I'm sure will express your spirit."

Dear brethren and sisters in the Lord: These are the articles of certain brethren who had heretofore been in error, and in a new faith had failed to agree in the true understanding, so that many weaker consciences were perplexed, causing the name of God to be greatly slandered. Therefore, there has been a great need for us to become of one mind in the Lord, which has come to pass. To God be praise and glory!

Now since you have so well understood the will of God which has been made known by us, it will be necessary for you to achieve perseveringly, without interruption, the known will of God. For you know well what the servant who sinned knowingly heard as his recompense.

Everything which you have unwittingly done and have confessed as evil doing is forgiven you through the believing prayer which is offered by us in our meeting for all our shortcomings and guilt. This state is yours through the gracious forgiveness of God and through the blood of Jesus Christ. Amen.

Keep watch on all who do not walk according to the simplicity of the divine truth which is stated in this letter from the decisions of our meeting. Everyone among us will be governed by the rule of the ban, and henceforth the entry of false brethren and sisters among us may be prevented. Eliminate from you that which is evil and the Lord will be your God and you will be His sons and daughters.

Dear brethren, keep in mind what Paul admonishes Titus when he says, "The grace of God that bringeth salvation hath appeared to all men, teaching us that, denying ungodliness and worldly lusts, we should live soberly, righteously, and godly, in this present world; looking for that blessed hope, and the glorious appearing of the great God and our Saviour Jesus Christ; who gave himself for us, that he might redeem us from all iniquity, and purify unto himself a people of his own, zealous of good works." Think on this and exercise yourselves therein and the God of peace will be with you.

May the name of God be hallowed eternally and highly praised. Amen. May the Lord give you His peace. Amen.

The Acts of Schleitheim on the Border, Canton Schaffhausen, Switzerland, on Matthias' Day, Anno MDXXVII.

The work was done. They had answered persecution by clarifying their position and achieving greater unity. The free church had asserted its freedom in a responsible manner. When the voice of the group was taken, they ratified the Confession unanimously. No other vote had been taken in the whole assembly, but there was consensus of opinion, an obvious spirit of agreement. The Holy Spirit had been honored among them and through the sense of His leading they had achieved a remarkable unity. All were humbled by the sense of divine blessing.

Some of the men engaged in a discussion on the role of the local congregation. Ray Sauder, owner of the shop, asked Michael for his convictions on congregational procedures.

"Each congregation," he said, "is a church in its own right, responsible to provide local leadership and to make the necessary decisions pertaining to Christian behavior in its locality. Above all, each congregation must be prepared to appoint a new leader if and when the pastor is arrested. In addition, the Great Commission must be carried out. Ours is the responsibility of evangelism, be it city or country, cathedral or forest."

Jan Hertzer asked for the floor and proposed that they outline plans for their evangelistic work before separating. Together they worked out plans for evangelistic activity across Austria, Upper Germany, and into the Netherlands. Michael closed the synod with the ringing statement, "The kingdom of Christ exists in its own right, free and active, and we share His cause. God's program shall never fail—let us not fail to remain on His side!"

The meeting was over, and one by one the Anabaptist leaders took their leave. They bade farewell with deep emotion, knowing that never again would they meet in this manner in this world. Their expressions to one another evidenced that this meeting was of deep significance. Many said it had served to strengthen them in

225

the faith. Since it was late, some slept through the night and left at the first flush of dawn.

Michael and Reublin left early in the morning on their return to Horb, to their wives and their work. The temperature had dropped during the night and a bitter wind blew the snow into their faces. As they trudged along, their feet spraying the soft snow before them, the wind would pick it up and send it swirling to the next drift. Michael pondered to himself the trail their movement might be cutting in history. Pausing to get his breath, he looked back to see that their tracks were already nearly blown shut. Of one thing he was certain—footprints made by meetings like the synod of Schleitheim would not disappear like footprints in drifting snow.

True, there was diversity in their program. There were expressions of the Spirit which could not be systematized. But God was acting among them. He thought of Jesus' words, that the Spirit moves like the wind which "bloweth where it will." He was convinced that history would know that the Spirit had operated in their midst.

Chapter XXIII

Michael Sattler and Wilhelm Reublin returned to Horb in high spirits. The Schleitheim synod had been a momentous meeting.

Wilhelm was enthusiastic. "A genuine basis for unity has been established in our brotherhood. The leaders will go back to their areas with new vision and a new sense of purpose."

"Yes," Michael answered, "and the plans for more evangelistic outreach will show further that we have done something concrete."

Deep in his heart Michael knew the time would come when the Anabaptist movement would face more severe persecution in South Germany just as it had in Zurich. But the two returned with the enthusiasm that comes from a mission accomplished.

Margareta and Frau Reublin welcomed them warmly. They listened eagerly to the news and rejoiced with them over the success. But they had more somber news to report.

Margareta introduced it. "It was time such an assembly should meet. We will soon be in real trouble here. The authorities are stirring up opposition to our missions from here to Rottenburg!"

"I've been expecting this," responded Michael. "The winning of converts cannot long be kept secret, nor should it be."

The following morning the Reublins left for Rottenburg. Michael and Margareta saw them off by walking with them to the beginning of the trail through the forest. Here they said "*Auf Wiedersehen*" and watched their friends disappear down the trail. As they returned, Michael related further details of the Schleitheim synod recounting the discussion of the seven articles. She caught the thrill of unity that prevailed in the assembly.

Arriving at home, Michael spread out his copy of the letter containing the seven articles. Leaving her to read the report in detail, he left to call on some of the lay leaders of the congregation. From them he learned that the danger of persecution was no secret.

This threat hung over them like Damocles' sword as they gathered for worship on Sunday morning. Their warm spirit of love and their evident commitment to Christ were a triumph in the face of danger. Michael led in prayer for the Spirit to dispel fear and anxiety about the future. Following prayer, Michael used the greater portion of his sermon hour to review the content of the Schleitheim Confession. Together they discussed the content and value of the declarations from the synod. There was a note of strength in the assembly as the group felt their association with the larger brotherhood.

At the close of this message the congregation joined heartily in singing. The hymn was one of Michael's own, written as a prayer and most fitting for the occasion.

O Christ, our Lord with teaching true,
Walk with Your faithful few;
And grant that each with patient care,
His cross shall daily bear.

O Christ, we would disciples be,
With peace and joy from Thee,
Thy truth obey forevermore,
And only Thee adore.

O Christ, Thy people truly keep,
Who follow as Thy sheep;
And if through bitter death we pass,
We'll be with Thee at last.

O Christ, our God, upon the throne,
Praise Father with the Son;
Praise to the Holy Ghost the same,
Come now Thy kingdom claim.°

Several days later Michael and Margareta were returning from a forest meeting where they had reported on the synod. Having spent the night with friends, it was late morning until they got away. A clock was already striking the hour of twelve as they reached Horb. Their feet dropped heavily as they turned into the familiar street, weary from their long walk.

Margareta saw them first—a small crowd gathered before the little tailor shop, the local bailiff and some soldiers. For a panic-stricken moment she wanted to run back to

---

°This is the author's translation of four stanzas of a song written by Michael Sattler, and found in the German *Ausbund*. The entire song has thirteen stanzas.

the safety of the forest. She caught Michael's arm as her courage faltered. But flight was futile. This was the appointment she had known must come. It was clear now, the dark forebodings she had so often tried to erase from her mind when she waited alone for Michael's return.

The words, "Fear not . . . I am with thee," came to her now. She looked at her husband, but he had not spoken. The words were within her, the words of the Lord. He was there, she knew, right there with them in the sunlit street. They were not alone as they faced the terrible danger barring the way to their home, the home they had shared so briefly. But suddenly one thought crossed her mind for which she was glad—she and Michael were at least together. Her chin lifted bravely, and her fingers relaxed their fierce grip on his arm.

"Margareta, we were expecting this." His hand closed over hers. "We are His witnesses," he whispered, "and His grace will be sufficient."

Together they walked the remaining distance to where the bailiff stood. Apparently he had not expected them to try to escape.

"Michael Sattler, we know you are a leader of the Anabaptists. You and your wife are under arrest."

"Under arrest, sir, for being good citizens? We have done nothing that violates law and order. You are making a mistake, my lord. And these—my brethren, what have they done?"

"I am not asking for your defense, Sattler; others will care for that, but I must ask that you come along. I am under orders."

The Sattlers stepped into the circle of Anabaptist prisoners who had already been apprehended, nodding to each in a gesture of silent support. The soldiers marched them along the street through the village of Horb. Local citizens stepped out of their houses to watch. A few called out some word of abuse, but most derided the officers for their violation of freedom in the arrest of good citizens.

They were herded before the little prison in the heart of the village. Here they discovered other of their friends already compounded. Reublin's wife and youngest child were in the group. Wilhelm was missing. Margareta made her way to Frau Reublin as the groups milled about. She was a bit taken aback by her resentment.

"If I had only gone with Wilhelm today, we could have gotten away."

"But at least he's free."

"Yes, he's free, and I must not begrudge him, for if he could, I reckon he'd trade places with me."

Margareta looked about for Michael, to see him talking with Matthias. Several more soldiers came in, bringing other prisoners from the congregation in Horb. There were now over a dozen prisoners. The bailiff called them by name and each of them was searched for evidence that could be used against them.

Michael knew that he carried dangerous proof of "guilt." In an inside pocket they would find the copy of the Schleitheim Articles with his notes. He had outlined an itinerary for spreading the doctrine of the brotherhood. Just last night he had reviewed this with the forest church in quite a different atmosphere! The soldiers gleefully confiscated the document and passed it to the bailiff.

"There's no doubt about this one—we've captured a prize!"

"This is the one Duke Frederick wants silenced," the

bailiff smiled. "He may be due another baptism—only he'll stay under longer."

The prisoners looked at Michael, but he seemed not to have heard. He was gazing at Margareta, and their eyes were locked in mutual understanding.

The bailiff stood beside the open prison door and motioned the prisoners to enter. The soldiers shouted orders but the Anabaptists were already walking toward the prison. At the door they turned one by one and scanned the crowd—several nodding to a loved one as though it were a last word of farewell.

The little prison was scarcely large enough for all who were pressed into it. Margareta sat with Frau Reublin, trying to comfort her little girl. The child's dark eyes held an almost adult awareness of what might come, and a bewildered question as to why this must be. Margareta took her into her arms, holding the frail little form close, and whispered words of courage and love, "God will take care of us."

Michael and the men were trying to piece together the events leading to their arrest. Outside a crowd was gathering. Above the murmur of voices and scuffling of many feet, the prisoners heard shouting. Angry citizens had gathered and were asking the bailiff to explain his action.

"I'm obeying my orders," he snapped.

"Whose orders?" retorted the crowd.

The prisoners knew whose orders—the real testing time had come. Rome had decreed that this Anabaptist movement must be crushed! A free church was too great a threat to their system. Duke Frederick was a Hapsburg, a loyal member of the Roman Catholic Church, and an aspirant for political power. He meant to make good at ruling the territory assigned to him by his brother Phillip. If he couldn't crush the Turks on his eastern border, he'd crush the Anabaptists within his boundaries.

The day wore on with many local citizens coming to protest the arrests. The citizens of Horb wanted the prisoners released at once. At first the bailiff threatened those who came with arrest as Anabaptist sympathizers. But now the number was too great, and a real clamor had spread throughout the village. The bailiff was accosted so repeatedly with the demand, that he feared an uprising.

The prison was neither strong nor large. The prisoners watched as the bailiff examined the walls. They understood when he said, "Don't hope for an escape. If the townspeople try to set you free, they'll find I've posted extra guards for the night."

The prisoners were forbidden to speak and therefore sat in silent prayer. Adjusting themselves to each other, they spent the first of many nights to follow in cramped, filthy confinement. The night seemed long, so long that for Michael a whole life seemed to pass. He reviewed each step and each decision until the step that placed him where he was. As he looked about at the sleeping forms in the darkness and then at Margareta's figure as she sat slumped at his side, he said to himself, "If I had it to do over, I'd not do it any differently. I'm still free, free within—more free than the bailiff. Iron bars do not imprison the soul . . . " and he was off to sleep.

Early next morning Count Joachim von Zollern joined the officials of Horb. After some deliberation they decided to move the prisoners to safer quarters. Coming to the prison with an escort of fourteen horsemen, they gave the prisoners a little warm broth and ordered them on the way. In the early morning cold they filed out of the village, traveling to the secluded little town of Binsdorf.

The long walk in the bitter cold of February was almost too much for some. Having been seized suddenly, not all were dressed to face the weather. They stumbled along through the snow, men trying to help women, soldiers shouting orders and abuse. Margareta walked in front of Frau Reublin to shield her from the wind. Michael carried the child until it cried again for its mother. After several hours the soldiers themselves grew quiet, barely enduring the bitter cold. The group moved in silence, except for the sound of the horses, of many feet dragging through the snow, and of labored breathing. Binsdorf was a welcome sight as they climbed the last hill. Regardless of what lay ahead, the promise of shelter lifted their spirits after this numbing journey.

The prisoners' quarters were somewhat larger here. They were fed a meager ration of black bread and warm water. Each day as the guards brought their meager rations, they threatened them with execution. They must recant or die! Nodding down the corridor, one of the soldiers said, "You ought to see in yon dungeon; we're all fixed to handle you there."

"A few hours on the rack," remarked another, "and you'll be ready to confess anything. Wait until old Master Tibald gets to you; he's a real artist!"

After several days of threats the master of punishment himself came to their cell. Tibald looked the part. He

wore a sleeveless leather jerkin, open on the chest and spattered from much use. His head had been shaven, and the hair had grown, standing up stiff and sparse. Looking them over contemptuously, he spoke in a flat voice. "Sattler, you will follow me."

Michael arose and stepped out of the cell after him. The gate clanked shut and he looked back through the bars into Margareta's eyes. The guards shoved him down the corridor toward a heavy door, at the bottom of a brief flight of steps.

He stepped into a vaulted area filled with odd implements. The heavy door swung shut with a deep boom. His eyes grew accustomed to the dim light which came from a fire in a glowing brazier. From this blaze the room was quite warm, obviously by design. Tibald stood watching Michael's reaction as his eyes took in the implements of torture—the rack, the wheel, the estrapade, while all about were overhead ropes and pulleys, a neat array of iron, leather, and copper instruments—forceps, ewers, tongs, and dippers of lead.

With a sneer Tibald ordered, "Tie his hands, fellows—behind him."

Michael was seized roughly and his hands were tied with a leather thong behind his back. Then he was placed under a pulley and the rope was tied to his bound wrists. Slowly the guard tightened the rope, turning the crank until Michael's body hung suspended. The pain of his weight pulling on his arms was so intense it made him dizzy, but he refused to cry out. Tibald watched with satisfaction. "A few hours of that and he'll sing a different tune."

They left him there for several hours, but mercifully

he fainted. Later they let him down where he lay for several more hours until they returned to take him back to his cell. His only answer was complete silence. Upon returning to the cell, he said very little. All knew he had suffered, but only Margareta really shared.

Each day the hanging lasted longer and Michael's resistance was wearing thin. "What is it you want of me?" he asked Tibald.

"A confession of your alliance with the Turks, traitor!"

"But I'm innocent, I tell you. I am not a Turk. My sole offense is that I hold to different religious convictions. Is there no freedom for a man's soul?"

Stretched by the rope, his body revolted. He heaved until his stomach was empty and there was no more relief. Mercifully, after a half hour of this he would faint, to regain consciousness after they had let him down.

"It looks hopeless," one of the soldiers ventured to Tibald. "He doesn't crack."

"We shall see—perhaps fire can change your mind on confessing, or the sword!"

But the fire was not applied—only as a threat. They took him to the room and held him before the brazier. He was held as Tibald took tongs and heated them until glowing, threatening him until he could feel the hint of searing flesh. Perhaps it was the impending trial that kept them from disfiguring him. But with the sword they were not as reserved. He returned to his cell with blood dripping from wounds on his sides and back where they had threatened to run him through!

But through all this excruciating treatment he maintained an incredible composure, continuing to encourage his fellow prisoners. Twice Margareta was forced to sit and watch while Michael was tortured with the sword. All that she could do was pray for strength of spirit for him. The soldiers seemed to delight in tormenting them with threats. They joked about Michael's leaving the monastery, and asked who would care for his wife.

"Ferdinand will answer that," chuckled one. "He says the only antidote to Anabaptism is a third baptism of drowning."

Another soldier replied, "That may suffice for the women, but it's too good for the men."

The days and weeks dragged slowly by, and yet there was no trial. Unknown to the prisoners, the authorities were having difficulty arranging a trial. After several months' delay, the prisoners feared they'd be executed without a trial. Michael was certain now that martyrdom awaited him. His deep concern was for the church, and he prayed much for his own congregations.

By now the prisoners were permitted more freedom for conversation. The soldiers even seemed less interested in inventing ways to harass them.

Michael was quite broken in health, but not at all weakened in spirit. After they relaxed the rigors of torment, he regained some strength. A week later he even secured script and pen and wrote a letter to his little congregation in Horb. He kept the letter hidden, hoping to be able to send it some way. Divine Providence intervened through a visitor admitted to the prison, and the letter was on its way:

My beloved companions in the Lord!
    Grace and mercy from God our heavenly Father, through Jesus Christ our Lord, and the power of their Spirit, be with you, beloved of God, brethren and sisters.

I cannot forget you; though I am not present with the body (Colossians 2:5), yet I continually care for and watch over you, as my fellow members, lest the body be taken away, and the whole body [the church], with all its members, be overwhelmed with sorrow. Especially at this time the ferocity of the ravening wolf has risen to such a pitch, and increases in power, so that he has aroused also me to fight against him. But eternal praise be to God, its head is completely broken, and I hope that his whole body shall soon be no more, as is written.

Dear brethren and sisters, you well know with what ardent love I admonished you the last time I was with you, that you should be upright and godly in all patience and in the love of God, by which you may be known among this adulterous and ungodly generation, as shining lights (Matthew 5:14) whom God the heavenly Father has illuminated with His knowledge and the light of the Spirit. With like fervency I now beseech and admonish you; that you walk surely and prudently towards those that are without as unbelievers, that our office, which God has imposed upon us, may in no wise be profaned and justly reproached.

Remember the Lord, who has given you the talent, for He shall require it again with usury. That the one talent may not be taken from you, put it to usury, according to the command of the Lord, who has given you the talent. Matthew 25:19.

I say to you through the grace of God, that ye be valiant, and walk as become the saints of God. Consider what the Lord metes out to idle servants, namely, to utterly lukewarm and slothful hearts, unfit and cold for all love to God and the brethren. You have experienced what I now write. . . .

Furthermore, dear fellow members in Christ, be admonished that you forget not charity, without which it is not possible for you to be a Christian flock. You know what charity is, from the testimony of Paul our fellow brother, who says: "Charity suffereth long, and is kind; charity envieth not; charity vaunteth not itself, is not puffed up, doth not behave

239

itself unseemly, seeketh not her own, is not easily provoked, thinketh no evil; rejoiceth not in iniquity, but rejoiceth in the truth; beareth all things" (I Corinthians 13:4-7). Understand this passage and you will find the love of God and the love of your neighbor; and if you love God, you will rejoice in the truth, and believe, hope, and endure all that comes from God. In this way the aforesaid failing will be removed and avoided. But if you love your neighbor, you will not punish or excommunicate with fire, you will not seek your own, think no evil, not vaunt yourselves, and finally, not be puffed up; but will be kind, just, liberal in all giving, humble and compassionate with the weak and imperfect. Romans 13:8. . . .

And let no man remove you from the foundation which is laid through the letter of the holy Scriptures, and is sealed with the blood of Christ and of many witnesses of Jesus. Hear not what they say of their father, for he is a liar; and do not believe their spirit, for he is entirely swallowed up in the flesh. Judge what I write to you; take these matters to heart, that this abomination may be separated far from you, and that you be found humble, fruitful, and obedient children of God. Beloved brethren, marvel not that I treat this matter with such earnestness; for I do so not without reason. The brethren have doubtless informed you that some of us are in prison; and afterwards when the brethren at Horb had also been apprehended, they brought us to Binsdorf. At this time we met with various designs of our adversaries. They threatened us with bonds; then with fire, and afterwards with the sword. In this peril I completely surrendered myself into the will of the Lord, and together with all my fellow brethren and my wife, prepared myself even for death for His testimony. Then I thought of the great number of false brethren, and of you, who are but few, namely, a little flock; and also, that there are but few faithful laborers in the Lord's vineyard (Matthew 9:37); hence, I deemed it necessary to stir you up by this admonition, to follow after us in the divine warfare, in order that you may comfort yourselves with it, that you may not become weary of the chastening of the Lord.

In short, beloved brethren and sisters, this letter shall be a farewell to all of you who truly love and follow God (others I do not know); and also a testimony of my love which God has given into my heart towards you, for the sake of your salvation. I did indeed desire, and it would have been profitable, I trust, if I had labored a little while longer in the work of the Lord; but it is better for me to be released, and to await with Christ the hope of the blessed. The Lord is able to raise up another laborer to finish this work. . . .

Remember our assembly, and strictly follow that which was resolved on therein; and if anything has been forgotten, pray the Lord for understanding. Be liberal towards all that are in want among you (Hebrews 13:5), but especially towards those who labor among you in the Word, and are driven about, and cannot eat their bread in peace and quietness. Forget not to assemble yourselves together, but give diligence that you constantly meet together, and be united in prayer for all men, and in breaking of bread; and this with the more diligence, because the day of the Lord is approaching. Hebrews 10:25. In this assembling you will make manifest the hearts of the false brethren, and will speedily rid yourselves of them. . . .

Bear in mind, most beloved members of the body of Christ, what I indicate by this Scripture, and live according to it, and if I be offered up to the Lord, do for my wife what you would do for me. The peace of Jesus Christ, and the love of the heavenly Father, and the grace of their Spirit, preserve you unspotted from sin, and present you glad and pure for the beholding of their glory, at the coming of our Lord Jesus Christ, that you may be found in the number of those called to the feast (Luke 14:15) of the one essential, true God and Saviour Jesus Christ, to whom be eternal praise and glory. Amen.

Written in the tower at Binsdorf. Brother Michael Sattler of Staufen, together with my fellow prisoners in the Lord.

Chapter XXIV

The imprisonment stretched out like a long nightmare. The prisoners in the tower at Binsdorf had given up any hope of release. March had dragged by, and April had passed. The sounds of spring, the songs of birds, and the showers of rain made them aware of life outside. Easter had been celebrated in the cell. On the occasion of Good Friday they shared communion together with bread and water as emblems of the body and blood of Christ. The hope of the resurrection was never more meaningful to a group of mortal men than to those prisoners living in the shadow of death.

Most of them were staunch in their faith. But occasionally several mentioned the possibility of recanting. Very patiently Michael explained to them what this would mean. Instead of wavering in his faith his convictions became even stronger through this experience.

"Take heart, brethren. We are called upon, as Paul says, 'to fill up in our bodies the afflictions of the Lord Jesus.' The church is not the continuation of the cradle of our Lord, but of His cross. He builds His kingdom through the suffering church. By His grace our cause will triumph. We may not live to see it, but the day will come when the free church, the true church, will be numbered by thousands and the kingdom of our Christ will be known in all the earth."

Michael put his thoughts into verse, and they sang it with new fervor and hope.

> God, who called us to this hour,
> Will make us triumph by His power,
>   And through His grace alone,
> Our eternal joy procure,
> That beyond this life' tis sure
>   Emptiness we'll never know.

All was not well in the world, and bits of news filtered in to the prisoners of struggles between the Roman church and the reformers. Perhaps, they dared to hope, even now the bondage was being broken down and the free church could move ahead.

Far beyond them Rome lay under the crushing hand of war. On May 5 the constable Bourbon had appeared before the walls of Rome. As servant of the emperor Charles V, and as a member of the church of Rome, he offered to parley with Pope Clement. The offer rejected, he found himself excommunicated and so identified with his Lutheran captains. Bourbon died taking Rome, leading the Imperialists to their victory as Spaniards, French, and Germans took the city.

The pope was a prisoner; the city was ravished by the sack. Brave men shuddered; they had dragged down the world and watched as men died in the chaos. The emperor Charles V had rashly slipped the noose over Rome and was choking out the very life. In unleashing

243

war against the Holy Mother Church the nations of the earth were threatened. Take from these infants, who had yet to learn the freedom of faith, the very life they found in Rome as their wet nurse, and a clamor would continue to swell until it would shake all Europe.

The territory of South Germany was under the jurisdiction of Innsbruck, Austria. The officials had decided to hold court in Rottenburg. Shocked by the clash in Rome, they were anxious to get this over. On March 18 they had sent to the towns of Ueberlingen, Radolfszell, Stockach, and Villingen, asking each to send two doctors of imperial law. They feared that if the court were composed of laymen, they might pass less than maximum verdict. While designing to get the verdict they wanted, their plan was to protect themselves against public opinion. To do so, they announced that the government could not deal lightly with so serious a matter as a religious trial. This could not be committed solely to the laity!

The trial had first been set for April 12. The prisoners had been relieved that the time had finally arrived. But April 12 had come and gone with no trial! They were left in suspense. Almost a week later they learned a few details of postponement.

The citizens of Horb petitioned the officials against delivering the prisoners to the court. They refused to give up a dozen more prisoners confined at Horb. This spirit of the citizens of Horb encouraged the prisoners. But the government ignored them. They had taken the Anabaptist leaders to Binsdorf, and they meant to go ahead with the trial! The persons they were most desirous to sentence were in their custody, and no citizens' appeal was going to stop them.

But weeks had elapsed in securing a court for the trial. The Catholic University of Tübingen had sent a flat refusal to the request for two lawyers. They well knew that the outcome was to be a death sentence. They were not willing to involve themselves in such a trial, for their standards regarded any who served in this capacity as disqualified for the priesthood. Their men who had already taken the first steps toward entering the office as well as others who planned to do so soon could not be consecrated if they took part in a criminal court. Further, the university objected that Rottenburg belonged to another district, and Tubingen had work enough accruing from the courts in its own principality. And a final reason for abstaining was that the Rottenburg parish belonged to the University of Freiburg, which should be interested in an ecclesiastical trial in its own district. But the basic objection was the university's horror of the capital punishment its representatives would be expected to approve!

If Freiburg responded, Michael would be tried before men he had known as prior of St. Peter's. That would be a trial in several ways!

The populace began submitting a large number of appeals, asking mercy for the prisoners. The authorities were perturbed at the deep sympathy for the Anabaptists and worked hard to promote sentiment against them as heretics. But it became evident that they may have waited too long. There was something contagious in the conviction of freedom the prisoners held. A new dynamic threatened to undermine the power structures of religious and political security. If this caught fire among the populace, the favored elite could find their status threatened.

The prisoners would have to go!

Count Joachim was a man of indolent calm, but the nature of this case disturbed him and was most inconvenient. He sought for a way to avoid holding court. The imperial provost Aichele could be called to hang the Anabaptists quietly on the nearest tree. The Swabian League had recently done just that! Making this proposal to the higher officials of government, they sent him a contemptuous reply. "The honor of the house of Austria does not permit execution without trial and sentence."

Ferdinand was consulted for advice, and in his hasty manner he declared, "The third baptism, drowning, is the best antidote to Anabaptism. I would wish especially that Sattler be drowned without delay by Aichele. As for the others, there is no need to hurry."

But being of the house of Hapsburg, he listened to his advisers. Persuaded to wait, he agreed to a postponement until the court session, May 15.

A court was finally assembling. The officials had gotten the town of Ehingen to send representatives to Rottenburg. Freiburg responded by sending two men, but out of respect to Michael, they were not members of the university. In desperation the Innsbruck authorities appealed to Stuttgart to use its influence on the University of Tubingen to send two jurists. They now adjusted their requirement. "Send two, if not doctors of spiritual law, then of imperial law—though they be laymen!" But once more the university protested that it had no jurists but those who were either priests or were about to take orders. To avoid involvement, they claimed papal and imperial law, and on May 6 they even sent two members of the university to Stuttgart to present their refusal to send delegates. But the officials of Stuttgart rejected the appeal, wanting to please the authorities at Innsbruck, and suggested a clever evasion. And so, by May 15 two doctors were sent to Rottenburg for the first court session. But they were not doctors of law, but of the arts! They were Georg Farner of Kirchheim and Balthasar Stumpp of Waiblingen—both doctors lacking both legal and theological training, hirelings who came because of their offer of extra pay.

The Innsbruck authorities asked for two men from Ensisheim because of their wealth of experience in religious trials. No other government had so violent a reputation as that of Ensisheim. Theirs was an ambitious attitude, full of sycophancy toward their superiors and bloodthirstiness toward their inferiors. The choices of Ensisheim were men who had no lack of experience, nor inclination for "*Blutgericht!*" They sent the city secretary, Eberhard Hoffmann, and Jodokus Gundersheim, the city secretary of Neuenburg, men who had persecuted many Anabaptists. The court was prepared for a verdict.

By now, Michael and Margareta, with their fellow prisoners, had spent eleven weeks and three days in jail. The awaited news, that a court had finally been secured, that the trial was imminent, was almost a relief.

The mayor of Binsdorf, Peter Putz, brought a guard of twenty-four horsemen and took the prisoners from Binsdorf to Rottenburg. He was vocal in expressing his anxiety to get them off his hands.

The weather was warm in contrast to that of the former trip, but the prisoners were much weaker. Nearly three months in prison had drained the strength from each of them. They stumbled along the road, past familiar sights and homes, scarcely noting them. They were prisoners of the state church on the way to be tried. Mayor Putz was in a hurry, and they were hard pressed to keep up with the walking gait of the horses.

Arriving at the familiar streets of Rottenburg, they were greeted by the strange sight of soldiers stationed at regular intervals. Count Joachim, fearing a revolt in the town, had secured fifty-six additional foot soldiers from the villages of the lower district and brought them to Rottenburg. Things were clearly well in hand!

The Anabaptists were packed into the prison cells at Rottenburg; Michael led the others in prayer. Tired and weak, bravely they uttered their solemn "amens" to Michael's words. Their fortitude and courage irritated the soldiers who had them in charge. Their treatment as they brought them their meager rations was extremely rough.

The prisoners sought to encourage one another in the spirit of Christ. Michael placed his arm around Margareta and told her of his love, of how he wished he could save her from what she needed to face. She responded bravely, her ready smile expressing her own strength and encouraging him in turn. It was evident to the group that the Sattlers faced this trial as one.

The evening before the trial Michael sought to encourage the group. "I wish there were words which could free us from this problem, but as it is, I can only quote words that will show us the strength to endure. Peter wrote to those in trial as persons who are kept by God. Think with me on his words:

" 'Kept by the power of God through faith unto salvation ready to be revealed in the last time. Wherein ye greatly rejoice, though now for a season, if need be,

248

ye are in heaviness through manifold temptations: that the trial of your faith, being much more precious than of gold that perisheth, though it be tried with fire, might be found unto praise and honour and glory at the appearing of Jesus Christ: whom having not seen, ye love; in whom, though now ye see him not, yet believing, ye rejoice with joy unspeakable and full of glory: receiving the end of your faith, even the salvation of your souls.' "

Michael looked around upon the little group with a sympathetic gaze. They were nodding their heads in assent.

"This is our assurance and our support. We have committed ourselves to follow Christ, knowing full well that His way is the way of the cross."

Chapter XXV

There was an air of expectancy around the prison on Wednesday morning. It was May 15, 1527, and the prisoners were told that the judges had arrived. The bailiff informed them that the men were in preliminary session and the court would soon open. Consisting of twenty-four judges, the court would be in charge of the *Landes-hauptmann* (local governor), Count Joachim of Zollern. The attorney for the defense was the mayor of Rotten-burg, Jacob Halbmeyer. He was to be assisted by Eberhard Hoffmann, a man Michael had earlier known in Alsace. It was evident to the prisoners that the defense would not be inclined to really understand them. Hoffmann had a vindictive spirit and a reputation of severity with Anabaptists in the trials held under the Austrian government in Alsace. Having passed on this information, the bailiff looked over the group with a smirk—"You'll be off our hands and well taken care of."

The prisoners feared the worst for Michael and were expressive of this. He was a marked man, and in view of Ferdinand's earlier expression that his mouth be stopped by immediate drowning, they all knew the trial would focus on him. Margareta was a pillar of strength at his side. He only hoped that she might be spared. Repeatedly, Michael had admonished her that if opportunity was given for her release, she was to accept it. As he voiced this again, she calmly replied, "My place is with my husband whether it be in life or in death. I'll not compromise the faith to save my life."

Her noble stand increased his pride in her. As they looked into each other's eyes, there was a depth of mutual understanding back of the sparkle of love. Again, as often during their trying imprisonment, they drew strength from each other.

They expected to be called into court anytime during Wednesday, but the day passed and nothing happened. It appeared that they were being tried without appearing. When the bailiff came to their cells in the evening, they expected a sentence! But he informed them that the trial was delayed and would not open until Friday. This was as difficult as a sentence. The suspense was hard to bear.

Thursday they waited, prayed, discussed the Word, and waited. Their discussion was not in preparing arguments for the trial, but in strengthening one another. Obviously the pressure was having its effect. Several were finding it difficult to maintain emotional strength. But on Thursday evening the prisoners experienced a deep sense of God's presence as they shared together in prayer. Their cramped cell seemed aglow with the presence of the Lord. Before they slept that night they assured each other that they would stand together for freedom in Christ no matter what the cost.

Michael and Margareta found themselves especially close

to one another in spirit during this time. The brief years of their married life had been full, rich years. They had shared together the joys and the depths of two hearts bound in love. The thrill of their love in belonging to each other had not waned but rather increased. Never once had either regretted the day that they left their respective roles in the Roman church and joined together in holy matrimony. Above all was the satisfaction of being joined in the pursuit of Christ. The two years of their sharing had led them through many experiences. They had seen the beginning of the Anabaptist movement and witnessed the growth of a church that was spreading across much of central Europe. They were equally convinced of the validity of their cause. God was creating a believers' church, a church of committed disciples, a fellowship that was bringing new life, a new freedom, and a new character to masses of people now involved in personal faith.

They were now on trial together for their lives. In spite of Michael's hopes and prayers for Margareta's release, both of them personally anticipated martyrdom. In conversation they agreed that the death of a few soldiers was necessary in the cause of spiritual warfare to which they were committed. And soldiers they were, as brave as any who ever entered a battle. They were in the avant-garde, expendable workers who would die to bring in a new freedom!

The morning of the trial finally arrived! The court assembled in full regalia, to the blowing of horns and the cries of heralds. The trial opened on Friday, May 17, and would continue on Saturday before it closed. The entire group of prisoners was taken to the courtroom.

They filed in, nineteen in all, silent and composed. The bailiff motioned them to the bench of the accused. Michael, Margareta, Matthias Hiller, and Veit Veringer of Rottenburg sat on the front bench. Behind them sat the seven other men and the eight other women. There was an immediate sound of whispered conversation over the courtroom as the group was inspected.

The gavel sounded and Count Joachim called the court into session: "In the name of the House of Austria we convene this court, the 17th day of May, the year of our Lord, fifteen hundred and twenty-seven. Let justice be done without favor to any personage."

A smile passed over the court as the count continued: "Under the mercy of the House of Austria the accused are hereby offered the privilege of choosing an attorney to represent their case. You may now speak."

Sattler spoke for the group. "We appreciate your offer, most noble lords and servants of God, but we must decline, since this is not a legal matter but a religious matter. In matters of faith such as this, the way of law is forbidden us by God's Word. If you can show us the contrary from the Word of God, we will follow the Scripture. We only appeal to you to fulfill your responsibility as servants of God in a fair and just trial."

"Do you mean," the count asked, "that you refuse to accept an attorney?"

Michael's manner was courteous, modest, but definite. "Servants of God, if we accepted your attorney, we would be entrusting the defense of our faith to him. This we cannot do. As believers we must give answer for our own faith."

He had called the judges the servants of God, respecting their authority as to position, if not in religious matters. He meant to appeal to their consciences in calling attention to their responsibility. Now looking at the judges seated in two rows of twelve each, he needed to say one thing more. "Since this is a matter of faith, of our understanding of the Holy Scripture, I must ask whether this court is prepared to deal competently with the issues to be faced."

The men smirked at his statement and exchanged amused glances. They had been appointed by the Austrian government, a supreme testimony to their qualifications. Their derisive smiles revealed their assumption that with such authority they were most competent.

Count Joachim rendered a decision. "Court will proceed without a legal defense. The prisoners may speak for themselves."

Michael nodded, "If it please my lords, we should like to have the articles read so that we may speak to them."

One of the court retorted, "He claims to have the Holy Spirit; let the Spirit reveal the articles to him."

Michael ignored the taunt and addressed the count. "Your honor, may I hear the charges?"

The objection was overruled, and Count Joachim ordered the reading. The charge comprised nine articles, seven of which pertained to all the defendants, and two to Sattler alone. The charge was skillfully written, but it was immediately apparent that there was no understanding of the Anabaptist case. The authors did not have even the pertinent facts about Anabaptist faith and practice!

The first article was read, accusing the Anabaptists of trespassing against the imperial mandates.

Michael knew this charge was deadly and deliberate. Anabaptism, contrary to its true nature, was being presented to this court not as a religious crime, but as a civil one. The charge ignored the reformation of the church and suggested insurrection in general Christian society. This implied an unchristian attack against the faith. It placed the Anabaptists on the same level with the Turks, and condemned them for secret revolt. The imperial mandate had been posted in all the churches and town halls. So identified, they were condemned before being tried. This being the case, the court of course would be competent!

The emperor was the protector of the church—this was the premise and conclusion of medieval history—and the church was none but the Roman Catholic Church. This church, its doctrine, its organization, and its law were alone recognized as valid on Austrian soil. The Reformation which had been going on for ten years, to prove the untenability of this medieval view, did not exist for Austria. Where it showed itself, be it Lutheran, Reformed, or Anabaptist, it was to be extinguished like a dangerous fire.

This first article was thus treated as violating the law of the church as acknowledged by the empire. They read the other articles in turn. They were concerned with the life of the church, its means of grace and miracles, especially its sacraments. The second article condemned the Anabaptist denial of the Roman doctrine of transubstantiation, of the presence of Christ in the emblems, as a crime. The third condemned their rejection of infant baptism. The fourth denounced their rejection of extreme unction. The fifth article accused the Anabaptists of despising the "Mother of God" and the saints. The sixth dealt with their refusal to swear an oath to the government. The seventh article reproached the Anabaptists for having an unheard-of practice in the communion, that they broke bread into a dish of wine and took them together.

The defendants smiled a bit at this latter charge. This was clear evidence that the court was completely misinformed regarding the Protestant method of observing the Lord's Table. Their Schleitheim Confession spoke of communion in the New Testament pattern of breaking bread. Michael suspected a false rumor played a part here, connected with their practice of passing the broken bread on a tray, a practice which was foreign to the court. He knew that for the Roman Catholics the bread was broken and handled only by the priest. To pass it and let each communicant help himself was unthinkable. The bread was regarded by them as the body of Christ, and to be guarded with reverent care, handled by the priest alone.

These charges were made against all the Anabaptists and involved the entire defense. Two more charges were read which applied to Sattler alone.

The eighth article accused him of abandoning the monastic order and marrying. Nothing was said of his appointment as an Anabaptist preacher. But the ninth article, a statement of Sattler's taken from one of his writings, was cleverly placed at the conclusion. This statement, taken from its context of Christian love for one's enemies, was used to make him appear especially dangerous in the eyes of any Austrian. He was accused of having taught that if the Turks came into the country, no resistance should be offered; indeed, if war could be morally justified, he would rather fight against the Christians than against the Turks!

This charge could not fail to make the deepest impression on the court. The Turks for years had been considered the worst foes of the empire and the Christian faith. Vast sums of money had been sacrificed by the faithful and paid as a Turkish war tax to make war on this archfoe of Christendom. The Turks had caused Ferdinand inexpressible distress. At great pains he had aroused the German estates and raised an army to fight them. And now the Turk was to be considered less dangerous than he and the representatives of the old faith! This charge against Sattler was sufficient to make him an archtraitor to the empire.

Michael had a few moments to consider the nine articles. He knew at once that the center of gravity rested in the first article, and besides it the sixth and ninth were most important. But the accusations concerning erroneous views on the sacraments and disregard for the saints were concerns for an ecclesiastical court, such as at Constance, not of this secular court at Rottenburg. A secular court could not condemn him as a criminal on the basis of a question of the communion, or of baptism, nor even for marrying, if no other crime could be proved against him. If each of these articles were to be discussed, Michael knew the hearing could not be just. These were theological matters, and in most of these areas the court could not speak.

The gravity of the situation was clear. The accusation was based on the law of the empire. The faith of the Catholic Church was the only legitimate one in the empire. The imperial mandates had confirmed this since the Diet of Worms in 1521. These mandates were alone valid in Rottenburg. The view of the law here was still that of the Middle Ages.

Michael stood opposed to this, promoting a new and free world. Individual freedom was a central part of the principles and vision of the Anabaptists. His was the principle of faith, of freedom of conscience, and of adherence to the Word of God. But this vision was held only by a minority, and was far from becoming the law of the empire. To his judges, representatives of medieval mentality, this position appeared as sedition.

Halbmeyer, the attorney for the defense, was glowering at the prisoners. "Are you going to answer, or must I speak for you?"

Count Joachim said, "Sattler, you say you wish no attorney; it is up to you to defend yourself if you can. We offer you this opportunity to explain your heretical activities."

Michael rose to his feet to speak. As he looked at the faces before him, their overt hostility could be felt.

The charges were difficult enough. But even more serious was the atmosphere of the courtroom. The hostility and bitter remarks exchanged between the judges made the procedure of the trial a horrifying experience. Responsibility for this state of affairs in the court could be attributed to the indolence and bungling of the presiding judge and the venom of the secretary of Ensisheim. The latter did not hesitate to speak slanderously and threateningly to Michael and his fellow prisoners.

Michael glanced briefly at each of the other defendants as if to include them in his defense. Then he began, unafraid, skillfully, but modestly, to discuss each article in its turn. His first answer was to refute the charge that the Anabaptists were disobedient to the imperial mandates.

"The imperial mandates," he argued, "require that the Lutheran doctrine and error should not be followed, but alone the gospel and the Word of Christ. As Anabaptists we have not violated this, for we are not Lutheran, and we seek to follow the authority of Scripture alone."

But his distinction between the Lutheran movement and the "believers' church" movement was lost on the court. They only realized that the mandate condemned Lutheran doctrine, and of course all deviation from the gospel as Rome understood it. To the Catholic court, the Anabaptists were merely a Lutheran sect. They knew little of Zurich and the movement there.

On the second article Michael said, "We admit that the Anabaptists reject the teaching of the presence of the body and blood of Christ in the communion. We hold that the bread and wine are signs or holy symbols of the body and blood of our Lord." He attempted to prove his point from the Scripture, but to no avail.

"You deny Christ's presence in the sacrament?" asked Hoffmann.

"Christ has gone to heaven and is seated at God's right hand. If He is in heaven, He is not in the bread and cannot be eaten."

There was silence after his answer, and he went on to the third article. Michael admitted the charge, sincerely and openly expressing their understanding of believer's baptism. He made no attempt to conceal the Anabaptists' repudiation of infant baptism. "According to the New Testament Scriptures," he said, "the command to baptize sees faith preceding baptism. Baptism is the symbol of one's covenant with Christ. The Scripture says it is the answer of a good conscience before God. This cannot apply to an infant."

The "amens" of his fellow prisoners let it be known that they supported Michael in this point, but the significance of the argument was clearly rejected by the judges. They did not understand what he meant by faith, or by a covenant with Christ, nor by a good conscience.

"You have charged me with rejecting extreme unction. We must make a distinction between oil as a creation of God, which is good, and the pope's oil. The pope has never created anything good. The oil mentioned by Mark and James was not the pope's oil. We reject any idea that there is saving power in his oil."

Michael very emphatically but graciously denied the charge that the Anabaptists despised Mary and the saints. "But we do not believe Mary was elevated, but like all men is awaiting the judgment. We do not accept her as a mediatress and intercessor."

The hostile expressions from the court were intense. Hoffmann broke in again, "That's blasphemy enough to end this matter!"

"According to the Scripture," Michael continued, "those who live and believe are to be thought of as saints now. Saintliness is a quality of spiritual life. Those believers who have died and await the resurrection we think of as the blessed ones.

"That we refuse to render an oath is true, but not from lack of honesty and loyalty to my lords. We follow the words of Jesus: 'But I say unto you, Swear not at

260

all; neither by heaven; for it is God's throne: nor by the earth; for it is his footstool: neither by Jerusalem; for it is the city of the great King. Neither shalt thou swear by thy head, because thou canst not make one hair white or black. But let your communication be, Yea, yea; Nay, nay: for whatsoever is more than these cometh of evil' " (Matthew 5:34-37).

Feeling it unnecessary to refute the charge that the Anabaptists ate bread mingled with wine as the Lord's Supper, Michael passed over this charge. He had earlier spoken of the symbolic nature of the emblems.

"Those are the charges, most noble lords, which you have placed against us as a group of prisoners, and you have heard our answer. I entreat you to be merciful with these my associates. I have yet to answer the court on the accusations specifically made against myself. First, I would answer your charge against me for leaving the monastery.

"From my past experience I know the monastic position to be an unchristian, deceptive, and dangerous one. From my own experience as a former prior, I know that the life and conduct of the monks and priests is a show, a deception, and a usury. They are also guilty of great fornication, seducing this man's wife, that one's daughter, and the third man's maid. Paul prophesied this in his first letter to Timothy, speaking of seducing spirits and doctrines of devils, forbidding to marry and demanding abstinence from meats which God has created to be received with thanksgiving from them which believe and know the truth. I was convinced it was more noble, more Christian to leave the order and to marry than to be a partner with men in such sin."

After waiting for the comments of the court to cease, Michael said, "There is some truth in the last charge. I have taught that if the Turk should come, no armed resistance should be made, for it is written, 'Thou shalt not kill.' We should not resist any of our persecutors with the sword but with prayer, clinging to God that He may resist and defend."

Count Joachim muttered, "Impossible, impossible."

Michael went on. "I have said that if war were right, I would rather march against supposed Christians who persecute, capture, and kill the God-fearing. The Turk knows nothing about the Christian faith; he is a Turk according to the flesh. But you want to be considered Christians, boast of being Christ's, and still persecute His pious witnesses. You are Turks according to the spirit!" He paused and let this declaration find its mark, then added: "You as a magistracy, as servants of God, are called to punish the wicked and to protect the good. I can bear witness that the Anabaptists have done nothing contrary to God and the gospel. If you will take time to discover the truth, the closest examination will substantiate my statement that neither I nor my brethren have ever opposed the government by any act or word, either in revolt or sedition or in any other way."

As he looked over the court, he made one last appeal. "Let experts be called and the Bible used in whatever language they choose and permit that I might debate with them. We so-called Anabaptists are ready to be taught from the Bible. If we are proved to be in error, we will gladly bear the punishment. But if we are not shown to be in error, I hope to God that you will accept teaching and be converted."

At the idea that they might be taught and converted by Sattler, some of the judges put their heads together and burst out laughing.

The secretary at Ensisheim snapped at Michael, "Why, you rascal of a monk, should we dispute with you? Ah, the hangman shall and will dispute with you."

The chairman was silent. Halbmeyer offered not a single word in defense of the accused. Michael, with a prayer for composure, replied, "What God wills, will happen."

His unshakable calm irritated the city secretary who cried out, "Indeed! It would be good if you had never been born, you archheretic. You have seduced pious people. If they would only acknowledge their error and commit themselves to mercy!"

Michael replied, "Mercy is with God."

Matthias Hiller, one of the other defendants, responded, "It is wrong to deviate from the truth."

The secretary was overcome with his wrath. He glared at Michael, incensed at his composure. His face flushed with rage and he pounded the desk. "Oh, you desperate rascal! You archheretic! I say, if there were no hangman here, I would hang you myself and be doing God a good service thereby."

He leaped to his feet, partially unsheathed his sword, adding, "If you do not desist, I will execute you myself with this sword."

The secretary, sensing that his attitude was making an unfavorable impression on the court, began to speak in Latin with Sattler. Many in the court could not under-stand his verbal attack, but at its close it was clear that Michael had understood. He replied in Latin as well, ending with the simple appeal, "*Judica.*"

The city secretary suddenly became aware that he was playing a role that was not his. He turned to Count Joachim in an attempt to cover. "He will not cease this chatter today anyway. You may as well proceed with the sentence. I call for the decision of the court."

Joachim turned to Michael. "Are you ready now to ask for the verdict?"

Michael replied, "You servants of God, I am not sent to judge the Word of God! We are sent to testify; but we are not for that reason removed from being judged, and we are ready to suffer and to await what God is planning to do with us. We will continue in our faith in Christ as long as we have breath, until we are shown from the Scripture to be wrong."

The city secretary broke in again with his threats. "The hangman will instruct you, he will debate with you, you archheretic!"

Michael ignored the threat and said to Count Joachim, "I will appeal to the Scriptures."

Count Joachim broke off the discussion with a wave of his hand. "The judges will retire."

They filed out of the room to consult on the verdict. Their discussion evidently did not proceed as smoothly as the city secretary had imagined, for it lasted one and one-half hours. The prisoners were retained in the courtroom under the supervision of the soldiers. The suspense was enough but the soldiers added indignities and slander. Michael especially was subjected to buffeting and mockery. One burly soldier swaggered before him. "Sattler, when I see you get away, I will believe in you!"

Another seized his sword from the table, drew it, and said, "See with this we will dispute with you." He placed the point on Michael's chest and flipped it expertly across Michael's coat laying it open. "We'll soon know if your heart is so calm."

Klaus von Graveneck, while against the Anabaptists, was horrified by the acts of contempt. Expressing to those about him that such behavior was not at all fitting to the gravity of the situation, he called to the soldiers, "In such a situation men should have pity on the worst murderer, but in this court innocent people are tormented cruelly with no defense."

The soldiers looked at him with quizzical expressions, but his words did little to alter the situation. Michael's silence toward all personal insults seemed to annoy the soldiers. They sought to break his spirit.

The prisoner, Matthias Hiller, answered the rough soldier's insult with the words, "Pearls should not be cast before the swine," to be promptly struck for his remark.

One then asked Michael, "Why did you not remain a lord in the monastery? You would not have come to this." The question was asked this time as though it was incomprehensible that anyone would, for the sake of his faith, sacrifice the high rank of a priest and the comfortable life of a prior in a monastery.

"According to the flesh I would have been a lord," Michael replied, "but it is better so. This is the price of freedom. In Jesus' words, 'Whosoever forsaketh not all that he hath cannot be my disciple.' "

The period of painful waiting came to an end. The twenty-four judges reappeared, filing into the room, some troubled and some with malicious expressions on their faces. The prisoners expected the worst and listened calmly as the verdict was read.

Count Joachim read the verdict: "The prisoners are condemned by the court as guilty of violating the imperial mandate. Michael Sattler, their leader, shall be committed to the executioner. The latter shall take him to the square and there first cut out his tongue, then forge him fast to a wagon and there with glowing iron tongs twice tear pieces from his body, on the way to the site of the execution five times more as above, and then he shall burn his body to powder as an archheretic. The other men shall be beheaded. The women shall be drowned."

Michael listened without flinching, then bowed his head and shook it slowly from side to side as though the barbarity was unbelievable. Margareta moved to his side, placing her arm across his shoulder. There was a resoluteness about her spirit and a spark in her eye that for the moment silenced the courtroom. She spoke firmly and clearly: "Michael, my husband, God's grace will be sufficient. To die for truth is better than to live in error. The death of Christ shall be our example. The pillar of fire will only end in glory."

Michael looked into her eyes for a long moment. The room was hushed. His face expressed his appreciation. "*Liebchen,* you are so brave." Then he turned to the court.

"I should like a few words with the mayor of Rottenburg."

The two walked from the room into the private chamber. Michael's face appeared calm in contrast to the mayor's troubled countenance.

Michael addressed him pointedly. "Most honorable lord, you are responsible to God for the final verdict. Although

I can safely assume that the city secretary of Ensisheim bears most of the guilt for the barbarity of the sentence, this does not excuse you."

Looking into the agitated face of the mayor, he added, "You know that you with your fellow judges have sentenced me contrary to law; therefore take care and repent. If you do not, you will with them be condemned to eternal fire in God's judgment."

Returning to the courtroom, Count Joachim gestured the bailiff and the soldiers and ordered the prisoners out. As they walked back to the prison, Michael held Margareta's hand in his. Out of sympathy the soldiers did not interrupt them.

"God bless you, Margareta, for those words and your victorious spirit before that crowd. I was still praying that you might be spared," and his voice choked with his emotion, "but I'm proud to have a companion who shares the cost of discipleship so nobly as you."

Margareta looked at him through tear-filled eyes. "Michael, we did not blunder into this. We chose His cross deliberately, and together. It is His cause. As He died for us, so we must be prepared to die for Him. His grace is our only strength and His promise our hope. The fire will bring your death and the water mine, but we will be united in His glory." And then she added, "I've never been afraid of the water, you know."

On that Saturday evening, May 18, 1527, Michael and Margareta knew that their fate was sealed. Michael had hoped that Margareta might be granted a release. Yet he knew that her bold stand and evident conviction for the faith could only cause the authorities to desire her death as well.

When they arrived at the prison, the bailiff announced that the group would be divided into several cells. Michael was to be held in solitary confinement. He reached his arm around Margareta and drew her to himself. He pressed a kiss to her lips and whispered, "We'll trust Him together, darling, for grace to bear this cross."

As he was roughly jerked away and shoved down the corridor, she stood gazing after him. Great tears welled up and filled her eyes. In her heart she was crying, "Farewell, my husband, my love. It has been only a few short years that we've shared, but full years, full of love and joy, of peace and satisfaction. We do not part in spirit—an eternity lies before us, an eternity to share His grace."

She bowed her head and followed the other women into their cell. As was Michael so was she, a prisoner of men but a pilgrim of faith.

Chapter XXVI

When Michael Sattler was shoved into his cell and heard the gate locked behind him, it seemed that the very demons of hell gathered to torment him. He had been placed in the dungeon on the lower floor. It was damp and stank from the offal of other prisoners who had been there before. At least they had not chained him to the block. As he sat on the stone bench, slumped over under the weight of his doom, the stark horror of death suddenly gripped him. From down the corridor and outside the prison came sounds of soldiers, jesting and laughing about the affairs of the day, mocking the foolish Anabaptists.

Something in Michael's spirit stirred in indignation. What did they know of the meaning of life, of its value and purpose? Yet they can live and we must die. His thoughts were of Margareta in the cell with the women down the hall on the opposite side of the prison. To think of her being drowned, he shuddered and broke into tears. Their life together had been so short, so wonderful and full, but so short! Never again would they be free to share life together, to enjoy the embrace of love, to sit in conversation, or to walk the forest trails together. Life was closing here for both of them. His heart beat with heavy thuds. But they had thought of this; it was not unexpected. They had agreed to pay the price!

His thoughts moved to the cause to which they were committed and to the little gatherings in the surroundings of Horb. Tomorrow the believers would meet over the Word and share in prayer. The specter of martyrdom would drive them to their knees. A warm glow stirred around his heart as he thought of their faith. There were others among them who would die before they would surrender.

He thought of the local work in Rottenburg in contrast with the state church which had sentenced him to death. He groaned in his spirit; tomorrow was Sunday, and many would gather in the cathedral to profess worship who only today had perpetrated this crime on his group of believers. He wondered what was happening in Rome, what the political changes might mean, how soon this picture would change. Not soon enough to be of help to him, of that he was sure.

But in the hours that followed Michael was tempted with the weight of despair. The pressures of the day's trial, all its tensions, seemed to converge on him in one moment of strain. Alone now he was not supported by the challenge of bravery before others. The horror of the sentence and the anguish of anticipated pain caused him to break out in a cold sweat. In his mind he could hear the words of his tormentors. "Why didn't you remain a lord in the monastery?" And again, "The hangman shall dispute with you." It seemed the devil himself was mocking him. It echoed in his mind, "Was it worth it? Where has it gotten you? What have you gained?"

Suddenly, into this darkness of despair he heard the words, "Lo, I am with you alway, even unto the end of the world." Like a light in the darkness he sensed the presence of the Spirit of God. He was not alone in this cell! The Lord he had come to serve would grant him grace for this trial.

His shoulders shook with emotion as he prayed, "Not my will, but Thine, be done." Through tear-dimmed eyes he looked up toward the dark ceiling and continued to pray.

"Lord, I'm just a weak man, called upon in this hour to give my life for Thy cause. In myself there is no strength to bear this cross, but Thou canst give me strength. By Thy authority I have walked this path, and now in Thy grace I face its end. Help me to play the man for Thee. Be gracious to Margareta." His voice broke. "Keep her from undue suffering, grant her strength for this ordeal, and then accept us each with Thee."

Scarcely had he uttered these words when in the distance he heard the soft but vibrant tone of singing, women's voices. It carried down the corridor and floated into his cell:

> O Christ, our Lord, with teaching true
> Walk with Your faithful few;
> And grant that each with patient care
> His cross shall daily bear.

> O Christ, we would disciples be,
> With peace and joy from Thee;

Thy truth obey forevermore
And only Thee adore.

O Christ, Thy people truly keep,
Who follow as Thy sheep,
And if through bitter death we pass,
We'll be with Thee at last.

O Christ, our God upon the throne,
Praise Father with the Son,
Praise to the Holy Ghost the same,
Come now, Thy kingdom claim.

The music was broken off suddenly by the rough sound of soldiers' voices ordering them to cease. But it had been enough. The song had brought to Michael a word of comfort and courage. It was a song of his own earlier composition, an expression of faith. He had caught the voice of Margareta leading the others. He knew she was sharing with him in this hour. This trial seemed to bring out a hidden strength in her which he knew was of God. The final words of the last stanza continued to run through his mind, words that strengthened his faith and gave courage to his heart:

Praise to the Holy Ghost the same,
Come now, Thy kingdom claim.

He looked up toward heaven and said, "Thank You, Lord. Thou hast said, 'When thou passest through the waters, I will be with thee,' and surely this promise includes fire as well."

Michael leaned back against the stone wall and repeated these words to himself, "I will be with thee." And suddenly he was asleep.

Sunday morning dawned warm and clear. Michael awoke from his sleep refreshed. But his early morning prayer brought him face to face with reality. Again he petitioned God for His grace through the day. Outside the narrow skylight in the stone wall a little bird was warbling its song of praise. Michael looked out at the little creature and said softly, "Sing on, little fellow. Life is too short to waste it in despair."

A guard brought him a cup of water and a piece of black bread. He handed the water carelessly to Michael, spilling most of it on the stone floor, and backed out of the cell, locking the gate. As Michael thanked him, he spat out the word, "Heretic!" and hurried down the hall. Bowing his head, Michael thanked the Lord for even this small bit, asking for physical strength to support his spirit in the trials just ahead.

Later Michael heard the cathedral bell toll out the call to worship. He could hear people on the way to the service. He suspected that more were going to see what might be said about the condemned Anabaptists than to worship the Lord.

Sitting in his cell he prayed that his martyrdom might be used of God as a testimony to those blinded to the truth of saving faith. His greatest concern in prayer was for strength that each could endure the ordeal of death with a calm spirit, concerned both for his own need of inner strength, for Margareta, and for his fellow prisoners. He prayed for the little congregation at Horb, that God would use this persecution to strengthen them in the faith.

Thoughts of the little "forest churches" to which he had ministered crossed his mind. He was confident they would go on. The continued growth of the movement and the conversion of men of talent and potential leadership gave him assurance of this.

He thought of the last three men he had baptized. Instructing them in the New Testament, he now recalled their discussion of believer's baptism, of the spiritual meaning of the Lord's Supper, and of the New Testament teaching on fasting. He smiled a bit as he recalled the enthusiasm of one of the three, Wolfgang of Mos, as he said to a second, Martin von Neck, "Martin, join me in the sign. I believe that salvation is in one Mediator, and that one is neither the Virgin Mary nor the pope, but our Lord Christ."

Recalling the testimony of all three and the baptism of each brought an inner satisfaction to him even now. The work would go on; of that he was sure. God's Spirit was at work. His program would succeed though a thousand men die at the stake!

Repeatedly through the day there were sounds of conversation from the other walls in the prison. Michael was removed far enough that he could catch only a few words. He discerned that an attempt was being made to get the prisoners to recant. He was concerned for several who had evidenced an emotional weakening under the pressures of the past weeks. They could hardly be responsible to make intelligent decisions at this point—having been broken in body and spirit! Toward evening a crowd gathered outside the prison. Michael tried to interpret snatches of the conversation to discover what was happening. Some minutes later he heard harsh voices in the corridor and the sound of gates being opened. Evidently several of the prisoners had broken under the strain. He was embarrassed for their sake. To live as outcasts would not be an easier lot than martyrdom.

Unable to see the proceedings, he bowed his head and prayed for those who were compromising the faith. He was sure Margareta was not in the group. He asked God to strengthen the faithful to be true. Outside, the officers presented four of the prisoners to the crowd as persons who had decided to recant from their heretical position. One was the furrier's apprentice of St. Gall, another the wife of Stoffel Schumacher, another was Veit Veringer, and the fourth was Salome Kapler of Rottenburg itself.

It was as well for Michael that he could not view the shame of this occasion, the mockery of his comrades in the faith, and then to hear their public recantation. After they had renounced Anabaptist doctrines, they were banished from Rottenburg and expelled forever from Austrian territory. The crowd took burning torches and prodded the four down the street, their cry of mockery like that of a pack of wild animals as they roughly expelled them from the city.

As Michael was to learn later, that same evening the Countess of Hechingen, the wife of Joachim von Zollern, came to the prison and asked to talk to Frau Sattler. She was admitted to meet Margareta in her cell and to converse with her. The countess was gracious and compassionate and sought to persuade Margareta to desist from her faith and to recant. "If you will recant, you can escape death. I can arrange that you need not make a public statement or appearance. I will gladly share with

275

you the protection of my own home. I have talked with the count, and in our position we are able to grant you life and freedom."

Margareta interrupted her. "Thank you for your good intentions and your gracious offer. I know you mean it well—from the depth of your heart. Your expression of pity and of love is most deeply appreciated. And I would like to live more than any other earthly consideration. We do not seek death. Our goal is not martyrdom but life in the freedom of Christ."

Pausing a moment she continued. "I cannot, however, accept your offer. I have committed myself to the way of Christ, and I intend to be true to my Lord and to my Christian husband. Together we have committed ourselves to be disciples of Christ, and if this discipleship means that we die, we will die for Him together. This is a cause greater than our lives! This is the cause of Christ. It will ultimately triumph, and the world will learn what it means for men to be free in Christ. My preference would be to die in the same fire with my husband, but be it as the Lord permits. But our cause will win, Frau Joachim, for it is God's cause—you shall see."

The countess shook her head sadly and rose to leave. "Is there any last favor or comfort I can grant?"

"Yes, my lady. If you could arrange it, I'd like to be with my beloved once more before we die."

The countess looked a bit taken aback by the request. "That may be impossible, you know; he's in the dungeon. But I shall see."

As she walked down the hall, Margareta watched her go, knowing full well that she had just turned down her only chance of escape.

The other women watched her in silence, admiration showing on their faces. They shared in prayer and slumped into fitful sleep, exhausted in body and spirit.

But Margareta's thoughts were with Michael as she prayed for one more opportunity to assure him of her love and faith. In the darkness she wept silently. Great scalding tears splashed on her bodice unnoticed. The vision of the tortures assigned to him became a crushing weight upon her own soul.

Monday morning, doubtless through arrangements made by the countess, Margareta was permitted a last visit with Michael. She fell into his arms in the coldest surroundings in which two lovers ever met. For some time they did nothing but hold each other close. Then he led her to the stone bench where they sat together. She told him of the conversation between her and the Countess of Hechingen. He gazed fondly into her face, his own spirit rising to the challenge as his strength was matched by her strength.

"Margareta, it would be most wonderful to live out a full life with a wife like you. What a life it could be—home, a family, love, and joy." A far-off, wistful look filled his eyes. Then he came back to the present to add, "But it's also wonderful to come to the end of our pilgrimage and stand together as persons committed to live or die for our Lord. Today's experience of death will be much easier in knowing that we have already died to ourselves in committing our lives to the way of Christ."

The two spent nearly an hour together. They prayed and exchanged promises from the Word. They assured each other of their joy in the faith and exchanged their last expressions of love.

"Margareta," Michael said with a husky voice, "I'll be gone when they take you out to die. . . . I can scarcely bear the thought . . . but you'll remember that He'll make up for my absence from you."

She nodded through her tears, "My Michael, my brave one, I think more of you! In a few hours you'll be gone; it will be over. I'll live through a hell here in this cell, thinking of you burning. . . ."

"Don't, my *Liebchen*; think rather of Him, as I must in the flames."

In midmorning the officers came to the prison door to take Michael away. They ordered Margareta out and stepped back for her to leave the cell. Michael drew her into his arms and kissed her good-bye. They looked long into each other's eyes. "Margareta, this is the end in this world . . . but only the beginning for the world to come. By His grace I'll triumph in my hour, and by the same grace you will triumph in yours."

She bit her lip and nodded bravely. Michael continued. "I want to testify that Christ is faithful even in death. In my last moments I'll raise my hand in a signal of His victory. Some of our group will doubtless be standing in the crowd. You'll get the details of the end in some manner."

The soldiers were impatient. "Enough," one said roughly and pulled Margareta from the cell. Michael called after her softly, "Good-bye, my dearest, until we meet in glory."

The soldiers bound his hands behind his back. Throwing a rope around his neck, they led him out of the prison.

278

Roughly they pulled him after them through the street to the marketplace. He hurried to keep the rope from cutting his throat. A crowd had gathered now to observe his execution. Some were boisterous, a bloodthirsty lot. But among the crowd were sympathetic faces, persons who longed to see him freed. Others were there merely out of curiosity. A few followed behind them and supported the order with shouts of derision. The soldiers in back of him prodded him with their swords, while others made a show of dissuading hecklers who kept coming near enough to spit at him.

They were at the marketplace now. Michael was held while the blacksmith forged heavy chains to his ankles and wrists. The heat of the hot irons seared his flesh, and the smell of burned flesh permeated the air. His body strained under the pain as he kept from crying out. He was picked up by several attendants and his body thrown roughly onto a platform laid across a cart. His chains were now forged fast to this frame.

The executioner stepped up with tongs and a knife. Roughly forcing Michael's mouth open and searing his tongue with the tongs, he pulled it out far enough to cut half of it off with a sweep of the knife. As he held it into the air with the tongs, he shouted, "That will stop the heretic's mouth."

A shudder ran through the crowd. Several voices in the crowd cried, "To the stake, to the stake!"

Michael lay on the cart, blood running from his mouth. He was softly praying with his muted voice, "Lord, be merciful, be merciful."

But the torture was not over. The sentence called for burning tongs to be applied to his body. Suddenly there was a cry. "Make way, make way." A man came rushing through the crowd with glowing, red-hot tongs. He handed them to the executioner with exaggerated care. He stepped up to the cart with a leer on his face and thrust the burning tongs into Michael's stomach. His body contorted in pain as the smell of burned flesh rose from the wagon. The executioner then tore a strip of flesh from his right leg by twisting the tongs and burning away the muscle. The crowd pressed forward in their curiosity. Michael's body lay trembling with the agony, the muscles jerking in spasms. At first it appeared that he had fainted. Then words of prayer were audible to those near the cart. There was no crying out, no uttering of sound.

One of the soldiers broke into a hard, brittle laugh. "What do you appeal to now, Sattler, the Scripture?" The crowd failed to respond to his jest. For the moment they were impressed by Michael's fortitude.

The executioner gave the order, and the cart started on its journey out of town and along the highway that led to Tübingen. The cart creaked and bounced over the cobblestone street. Michael's body was jostled along, racked with intense pain. It made him less aware of the soldiers' slander and mockery. But there was no respite. He writhed in anguish as the burning tongs were applied again and again. Five times on this journey, at about three-minute intervals, the tongs were heated and the executioner would lay them on another part of Michael's body. He would let the tongs burn through the cloth to the flesh; then he roughly tore flesh from his bones.

These tortures had Michael completely exhausted by the immeasurable agony before he ever arrived at the site of execution! But at the site he seemed to receive supernatural strength. Michael's acceptance of the torture and his calmness in this monstrous heightening of the execution were a remarkable witness to his unshaken faith and character.

As he had prayed at the marketplace when his tongue was cut off, now at the site he prayed for his executioners. Final arrangements were being made for his death. He watched without fear, praying audibly for his persecutors. He especially mentioned Klaus von Graveneck, who he felt had some conviction against this.

Pulling the pins from his manacles, they pulled him from the cart and bound him to a ladder with ropes. The ladder was held by several attendants as they bound him to it. Now they were ready to push him into the fire, already burning. As he hung bound upon the ladder, he was given a last chance to speak. In great pain and with a muted voice he admonished the people to be converted. An awed hush settled over the crowd. His strained voice could be heard, and they listened to catch his words.

"You are called of God to repent, to fear God, to be converted to the Lord Christ. My greatest concern is that you might come to saving faith in Christ, and that you might pray for my judges that they may be converted as well."

Michael turned his head slowly and addressed his remarks to the judges themselves, calling on them to repent. He asked for the mayor of Rottenburg to give ear and reminded him of the earlier admonition he had given to him. "You have sentenced me contrary to the law, and thereby you have condemned yourself before the judgment of a just God."

The mayor stepped forward from the circle. His face livid with anger at being so publicly admonished, addressing Michael defiantly he said, "You should concern yourself now only with God!"

But Michael only responded by beginning to pray. "Almighty God, Thou art the way and the truth. Because I have not been shown to be in error, I will with Thy help on this day testify to the truth and seal it with my blood."

The executioner summoned one of the soldiers, and a small sack of powder was tied around Michael's neck as a token of mercy to hasten his death. The officers picked up the ladder and, swinging it between them, threw his body into the fire. From the fire his voice could be heard in prayer and praise.

Suddenly there was a moving of his body. The ropes had burned through, releasing his hands. He raised his arm, and the two forefingers of his hand pointed toward heaven. It was his signal that his faith in Christ was adequate in death. This was a signal he wanted passed on to his group, a signal he wanted Margareta to hear about.

A moment later, with a clear voice, there came ringing from the fiery pyre his last prayer: "Father, into Thy hands I commend my spirit."

The fire suddenly flared up as the little bag of powder caught. Michael's body twitched and his hand dropped across it. He was still—still and silent. Death had separated him forever from their torture.

The crowd melted slowly away. Some few were jesting with brutal laughter, but most of them were almost over-

come with horror. Klaus von Graveneck muttered to someone near him, "A miserable affair when men need to die
for their convictions. I'm beginning to think he is more
free even in death than we are."

The mayor of Rottenburg wiped his brow and beckoned
to his comrades in execution. They walked from the scene
without a word.

Back at the prison the bailiff talked continually about
the execution. It weighed heavily on his conscience.
Through him Margareta heard the news of her husband's
noble death. She smiled through her tears at his triumph.
She was deeply torn by sharing in his suffering even
though she wasn't present. Now she sighed in relief that
his ordeal was over. At least her own would be without
torture. She prayed that God would give her grace to
die as nobly. Although her death would be less painful,
it would be just as final!

The next day the soldiers came for the other men.
They were to be executed by beheading. The ax would
be less torturous than the stake, yet it held the deepest
of terror for the men. Their faces were pale and drawn
as they were led down the corridor. The women wept
as they watched them go.

Later, when the bailiff returned with the soldiers, they
drank heavily. The women heard him mutter, "A bloody
affair, I'll be glad when it's all over." A new solemnity
had settled over the officers.

On Wednesday, May 22, Margareta was called from
her prison cell. They were almost tender in their handling
of her. She held her hands before her as the officers
bound them. They led her toward the river where she
was to die. Walking calmly between them, she thought

of a stanza of a farewell song written by Michael in the early days of their imprisonment here in Rottenburg. She hummed it even now as an assertion of her unshaken faith.

> The time has come for us to part
> And God is now our one escort,
>   Each one to his own place will go
> In fiercest trial there to die
> With our lone lives to certify,
>   That men God's Word may know.

They had come now to the bank of the Neckar. As she looked at its surface now, the beauty had all fled. Looking over the small group, she sought to testify to those who had gathered to see her execution. But the executioner interrupted and called for the job to be done. Quickly a large bag was stripped over her head and tied around her ankles, rendering her completely helpless. As her enshrouded body was carried to the river, her voice could be heard in prayer. The soldiers threw her from the pier and waves closed over her. She was gone. The group stood in silence, watching the bubbles burst on the surface. Only a few ripples on the water gave evidence that she had been there. Her spirit had gone to join her husband's. They had sealed their faith with their lives. They chose to die rather than to surrender the freedom they had found in Christ—the freedom to be responsible disciples. Having heard the call of the Master to have done other than obey would have been to sin. They paid the ultimate price. Both were pilgrims aflame.

EPILOGUE

While Michael Sattler was not the first Anabaptist, his work, and the significance of the Schleitheim Confession, may be seen as the beginning of the group's self-consciousness of being a third and viable church in Christendem. Although Michael Sattler's leadership among the Swiss Brethren was brief, those few years were full of spiritual activity in creating and strengthening congregations. Sattler, a committed Anabaptist, with his wife lived and died for the believers' church. He was respected, not only in his own brotherhood, but by the reformers Capito and Bucer.

On May 31, 1527, Capito wrote to the council of Horb:

> "This Michael is known to us here in Strasbourg and he was somewhat in error, which we showed him through the Scriptures; since he saw lack in our preachers and other preachers of the true doctrine, especially in the outer life of the congregation, he perhaps paid less attention to our admonition. But at the same time he showed such great zeal for the honor of God and the church of Christ, which he would have pure and blameless and without reproach to those who are outside. We never censured this, but praised it highly, but his method and the articles of his faith we always kindly rejected, and that after mature reflection before God. Now we did not agree with him herein. He wanted to make pious Christians through a fixed creed and outward compulsion which we considered the beginning of a new monkery. But we desire to correct the life of the believers through consideration of God's good deeds, which He has shown us in body and soul, that it might be a fruit of love and gratitude, for this is the way and the order of salvation."

> Bucer also wrote: "We do not doubt that Michael Sattler, who was burned at Rottenburg, was a dear friend of God, although he was a leader of the Anabaptists, but much more skilled and honorable than some."

The Anabaptist movement, which Michael Sattler had

championed, did not die with his death, but was spurred to ever greater activity. The movement spread across Germany and Holland until both Protestants and Catholics were afraid that everybody would become Anabaptist.

On August 20, 1527, another synod was held in Augsburg, Germany. Here was outlined evangelistic strategy to continue this movement throughout Europe. Within two years practically all who met at this senate had died for their faith. In 1529 at the Diet of Speyer both Catholics and Protestants agreed together that Anabaptists should die for their faith. The report of the Diet read:

> Although the common law forbids upon penalty of death to baptize again an already baptized person, and the emperor at the beginning of 1528 has given a new warning against the transgressors of this prohibition, this sect is still increasing. Therefore, the regulation is ordered again, that each and every rebaptizer and rebaptized person, man or woman, of an accountable age, shall be brought from natural life to death with fire, sword, or the like, according to the circumstances of the persons without previous inquisition of spiritual judges. Against the preachers and leaders of the sect as well as those who persisted in the same or fell back into it, no mercy shall be exercised but the threatened penalty shall be ruthlessly performed. Those who confess their error, recant, and beg for mercy may be pardoned. Whoever does not have his children baptized shall be considered an Anabaptist. No pardoned person shall be permitted to immigrate, so that the authorities can see to it that he does not backslide. No prince shall receive the subjects of another who have escaped. This mandate shall in all points be most strictly performed by all, in order to perform the duties imposed to the emperor and empire and to avoid the serious displeasure in punishment of the emperor.

During the first seventy-five years of the Anabaptist movement, some five thousand believers died for their faith. In this persecution the blood of the martyrs became the seed of the church. The intolerance did not crush the convictions of these committed Christians. The vision of the free church lived on. Today Protestants who share in free church privileges are indebted to these noble saints.

Nearly four and a half centuries have passed since that burning pyre in 1527, but the cause of freedom lives on. The Sattlers were some of the first of thousands of Anabaptists who died as martyrs for Christ in the years immediately following the Rottenburg Horror. History discloses that the successors of the Anabaptists, known as Mennonites, still experience persecution from persons who either do not know or do not understand the freedom of being "new creatures in Christ." By the twentieth century many of the convictions which the Sattlers died for have become recognized as vital facets of evangelical Christian faith.

From this Anabaptist rootage come various denominations in the world of our day. The Anabaptist-Mennonite brotherhood with over 600,000 members throughout the world carries on the heritage of theology of Michael Sattler and his colleagues. Research into sixteenth-century Anabaptist history and thought points to Michael Sattler as one of the leading formative theologians and pastors in the movement. The larger worldwide Baptist brotherhood is also indebted to this background for its origin and its theology.

Today many of the convictions of these early Anabaptists have come to the fore again in the study of leading theologians in various theological schools.

Truly Michael Sattler, a martyr for his faith, was as deserving of a monument at the site of his execution as John Huss in Constance. On August 16, 1957, the sixth Mennonite World Conference dedicated a memorial plaque to Michael Sattler in the Lutheran Parish Church in Rottenburg, at which time a memorial service was held.